SPARROWS

Book 2

Laura Mae

Sparrows is sequel to the first book *Fliers*.

You can find this book on Amazon, Barnes & Noble and other sources listed on her website.

www.lauramaeauthor.com

Sparrows by Laura Mae

Edited by Sarah Jane Day

Cover art by Christian Covers

www.lauramaeauthor.com

This is a work of fiction. Names, characters, businesses, places, events, locales, and incidents are either the products of the author's imagination or used in a fictitious manner. Any resemblance to actual persons, living or dead, or actual events is purely coincidental.

First Edition

ISBN: 9781645701637

I am dedicating this book to anyone who has ever felt
discriminated against because of a choice they
never made.

To anyone who has struggled in life simply because of
who you are. Do not let anyone tear you down. Know
there are people out there who love you and will
support you. Be proud of who you are, and remember:

Fight and love without fear.

Chapter One

Sydona found herself in complete darkness and silence. Her heart pounded with every passing second. Through padded earmuffs, she heard a faint beeping noise coming from her wrist. She ripped off the thick blindfold and earmuffs and threw them to the ground. The blinding sun caused her to squint her icy blue eyes but not enough to prevent her from investigating the new surroundings. She stood in a sparse stand of spruce and could easily see into the distance. Many of the trees had broad trunks large enough for objects to hide behind. The forest stood eerily quiet with only an occasional bird chirp and flutter of wings. She touched the ground and scattered the leaves in search of clues. Several lines of leaves laid flattened; she presumed by a car. The tire tracks led north, into the unknown.

She removed a pistol from her hip and held it out steadily in front of her. Moving quickly and silently through the trees in her rugged black boots, she watched her back with every step. Eagle Lake came back into her mind. So many loved ones--gone. The image of Evelyn, her mother, and the look in her eyes as she passed away burrowed its way to the front of her mind. She then thought of Maverick's last moments in battle. All he wanted was to see his daughter one last time.

Just then, a man popped out from behind a tree with a gun pointed at her. Her haunting thoughts tried to distract her, but she squeezed her eyes shut and focused on the blackness. As she breathed in and out, Sydona's eyes flew open, and she steadied her hand. Staring down the sight of her pistol, her index finger jerked the trigger, and he went down. She confirmed the shot and kept moving.

Leaves crunched and she pivoted quickly to shoot. Sydona pulled the trigger each time another appeared. With every gunshot that echoed through the forest, her focus intensified until she moved off pure instinct.

Taking another quick glance around her surroundings, she confirmed she found everyone and moved on. She glided along the ground, following the tire marks. They eventually led her out of the forest and into a small abandoned town. Her senses heightened as she noticed several buildings tall enough for snipers and possible lookouts. Many of the buildings had broken windows, some with cardboard and dated graffiti. Only one car resided on the side of the road, but it was gutted out and stripped for parts. It wasn't the same car from the tracks, judging by three missing tires and one flat. The small town had just one main street straight and short enough to see through to the other side. Sydona thought finding the vehicle wouldn't be difficult. A couple alleyways stretched between buildings on the other side of the road, but she was unsure if they were large enough for a car. With no carports or garages around, she had to investigate.

Sydona glanced down at her wrist watch. She was at the eight-minute mark. She clenched her fists and bit her lip, unhappy with the readout. Sydona ran over to the side of the road and pressed herself up against the buildings with her weapon ready. Spotting a quick movement inside a window on the south side of the street, she aimed her gun and pulled the trigger. She made her way down the wall to an alley she assumed could fit a small car and searched again for tracks. The dirt road looked undisturbed. She dashed down the alley toward a large dumpster. She should have been more cautious. A woman jumped out from behind it and disarmed her.

The woman tried to punch her, but Sydona took her down with a sweeping kick. Before she could make another move, her opponent drove her boot into Sydona's stomach to push her back. All the air in her lungs escaped instantly, and she hurled over in pain. This gave the woman a chance to stand back up and face her. They swung at each other a few more times before Sydona made contact with her jaw and slammed her back to the ground. She pinned the woman down with a fist ready to keep punching, but she tapped Sydona on the leg. They nodded at each other respectfully. Sydona stood back up and ran back to her gun. She continued to look for the missing vehicle. Along the way she took out a couple more people hiding in doors and windows.

As she turned the corner of a brick building, she saw the one thing that stuck out from the rest of the town: a shiny red van. Just to be sure, she approached it and peeked inside the windows. It was empty but still in good condition. It had to be the same one from the woods. She placed her sweaty hands on the hood of the van. It was still warm, and parts rattled from the engine settling. The only other unusual part of the area was a metal door on a nearby building with a mechanism on the side. It reminded her of the numbers on a payphone but with a digital green screen above it.

She picked the most obvious code she could think of and entered it in. 'NFA'.

The indicator light flashed red.

Her hands shook, and she glanced at her watch again. Twenty-two minutes. Gritting her teeth at the time and drawing a blank as she stared at the keypad, she tried a few more codes.

'FLIER', 'MALIK', 'SPARROW'. Nothing happened.

Sydona's hands vibrated even more as each attempt failed to open the door.

"Don't worry, Gia. I'm getting you out," she said to herself.

Glancing down at her wrist, she wasted an entire minute thinking of the code. Then, a light bulb went off in her head. What does the NFA strive to have the ability to do? Of course.

She entered in 'FLY'. The light flashed green, and the door clicked open.

Turning the rusty handle of the abandoned building, she crept into the darkness waiting inside. It reminded her of an old office building. A circular reception desk stuck out proudly in the lobby, while a long hallway on the right side housed several offices. Sydona thought back to what Willow told her about where the NFA kept their laboratories. To keep citizens from stumbling onto them, they normally set up in basements where they could work in secret. She searched for stairs leading down. As she made her way down the hallway, a few more people showed up with guns, but Sydona took them all out.

Time was running out, and she needed to find Giovanna before it was too late. She ran to the back of the building where she hoped to find an emergency stairwell leading to a basement. Another man ran into her on the stairs, and she took him out with no issues. At the bottom, the place opened up into a large hollowed out parking garage. It had remnants of an old camp Willow mentioned the NFA did experiments in: broken glass, cots with holes, a couple white tents that looked halfway broken down. They were in a hurry to leave. A brick wall created a makeshift office in the corner of the lot. It was clear it wasn't made when the original building was constructed, just like the garage. The only place that seemed logical to hold a prisoner was in that room, and Sydona bolted straight for it.

Two guards stood in the doorway. They both seemed surprised at her presence, and she used that to her advantage. As they fumbled with their weapons, she took both out with ease. Sitting on the back counter of the office, Giovonna greeted her with a big smile. Sydona ran past her and slammed down a big black button on the wall to sound the alarm. A clock with big red numbers on the wall synced up with her watch, and it stopped at twenty-nine minutes and four seconds.

"You did it!" Giovonna jumped up and hugged her.

"Yeah, just barely," Sydona panted.

Just then, the two people who were guarding Giovonna walked into the room, unharmed. They held their hands out to shake Sydona's, and she gladly took them.

"Congratulations, Syd. We knew you would pass," said the large man with long brown hair.

"Thanks guys." She paused to catch her breath. "You changed the code on me."

The other man teased. "We couldn't make it too easy for you."

"Yeah, whatever, dude. I know it was you who changed it, wasn't it?" she teased.

"It wasn't me, I swear! It was Willow," he said with his hands up in surrender.

"I heard my name! Y'all talkin' smack behind my back?" Willow burst into the room and gave Sydona a sturdy handshake. Silas and Raoul followed behind.

"Congrats!" Silas grinned and gave her a quick hug.

"What, you couldn't do it any faster than that?" Raoul exclaimed, making himself known to everyone in the room.

"Oh, shut up, Raoul." Sydona laughed.

She glanced around the room of smiling faces and friendly gestures, and she really felt like she belonged. She didn't have to hide her true self from them. More people joined them in the room; almost all of them were the folks she shot on her way down. One of them was Jet who she'd seen a few times from training. He was a young Asian man with silky black hair that covered one of his eyes. He shook Sydona's hand then met up with Lacey from the alley. Lacey had a few scrapes and bruises from the brawl but was still in good spirits. Jet touched Lacey's lip that had a little blood and kissed her cheek. She was young, like Jet, with short ash-brown hair and a vibrant pink strand near her face. She soon made her way over to Sydona and hugged her. It felt strange to fight someone and then hug them minutes later.

Willow spoke up. "Attention everyone." When no one listened, she spoke louder. "Hey! Shut the hell up!"

The room silenced and everyone gave their attention to the big red-haired woman in the middle.

"I would like ta formally announce our newest member of the Sparrows: Sydona!"

The room cheered and applauded. The attention made her face turn slightly pink.

Willow continued as she wrapped her arm around Sydona's shoulders. "I met this snarky minx jus' three months ago, and let me tell ya, she was a damn handful! If it wasn't for her fairy, Raoul, who knows how things would've turned out for us. I know I ain't her favorite person ever, but she got that burnin' fire in her that don't stop, an' I admire her for it. She single handedly took down Dr. Malik at Eagle Lake, and now she wants more! Treat this woman like the princess she is, and help her with anythin' she asks for."

Willow's words resonated deep within her. The feelings she first encountered with Willow were way in the past now. She truly helped Sydona build her trust in humans. The mention of the doctor, however, made her stomach twist. It was still unclear if he was alive or not. But by joining the Sparrows, she would have a better chance of getting the job done in case he was still around.

After a few minutes of cheering for the new member, the crowd dispersed and left the office room. Her friends and family gathered around her.

"Can't believe you're a Sparrow now!" Giovonna exclaimed.

"Are you excited for the tattoo?" asked Silas.

"No," Sydona scoffed, forgetting all about the tattoo part.

"It's not that bad. Trust me… I wouldn't have done it this many times if it was bad."

"Yeah, Silas, you were thinking of joining too, right? Where are they going to put yours?" Raoul asked.

Willow spoke up. "He's right. We haven't had anyone with the amount of tat's you got, Sil. Might have'ta just put it on your forehead!"

Sydona laughed. "Oh, I would pay to see that."

"I'll find a place. Don't you worry," Silas said confidently.

"Where? Like your butt?" Giovonna asked playfully.

The group roared with laughter once more, making Silas grin and bear it. As the rest of the group teased and talked amongst themselves, Sydona joined Silas at the front and had a more serious conversation.

Butterflies filled her stomach as the words she thought about came out. "Where *are* all of your tattoos?"

Silas grinned over at her, and Sydona swore he could see her cheeks turning pink.

"You wanna see all of them?"

"Yeah. I mean, you're the one claiming you have room, but I'm thinking I need proof."

"Okay," he smiled and gently touched her fingers with his. "Does that mean you want to go out tonight then?"

She hesitated. "I don't know, Silas."

The thought of going out in public was nerve racking enough without knowing it would also be a date. With a man. She could tell he wanted to hold her hand, but she swiftly moved farther away so he wouldn't touch her. Silas gave her a look as if he understood but kept trying.

"It's been months since Eagle Lake, Syd. There's nothing to worry about anymore. There still may be camps in hiding, but there's no looming threats anymore. You can finally relax, babe."

Babe.

The pet name made her feel sick. "It's not... that..."

"Oh," Silas said with defeat. "Well, I know it can't be me. I mean, look. I even shaved -- that one time. Yeah, it grew back, but that's biology. No stopping it."

Sydona chuckled involuntary. "Right..."

His comment played like a broken record in her head. *Biology*. It never failed. Except when it did. The conversation fell flat, and the two walked silently side by side the rest of the way.

Her boots loudly crunched through multi-colored leaves and twigs on the way to the fleet of vehicles hidden in the forest. On the way, she kept thinking of Silas. Her feelings for him were growing a little every day, and now he wanted a date? Though she appreciated the gesture, it just didn't make sense right now. They had a peculiar life and nowhere to fit a romantic relationship. More than that, she had too much on her mind to worry about petty things.

As she approached the truck, she took the front seat. She expected Silas to get in the back, but he continued to another car. She watched him with narrowed eyes. It had never dawned on her before that they normally sat together when they went out. She guessed they wouldn't be going on a date, and she felt horrible. It wasn't the first time her walls went up around him.

Sydona didn't say a word to anyone as they took off down the road. She couldn't help but think of the day it happened. The day biology failed her.

A gentle breeze kissed her face as she gripped a backpack full of supplies. It was her group's turn to fly off to the new safe zone on Sparrow Island. The large cabin stood behind them, and they used the several acre field as their take off area. The dense forest stood ahead, and soon Eagle Lake would be behind her forever. Raoul stood ready on her shoulder, Giovonna was on her right, Silas and Ian were on her left. Willow gave the okay, and the group took off running. As usual, her dominate foot pushed off the ground, but all that happened was a jump, and she landed back on the grass.

She shook her head with confusion as she watched her friends flying high above. Willow rushed over to Sydona and lowered herself.

"You okay? What happened?"

Sydona felt like her entire world flipped upside down. Why was she unable to fly? This never happened to her before. When she tried to take off, her body didn't feel light. Something went wrong. Embarrassed by her failed ability, she didn't answer Willow but tried to fly again.

She quickly brushed herself off and took off running again. Her foot pushed off the ground harder, but she fell back down again. Eventually, the group circled back to see what was going on. Raoul was the first to reach her.

"Syd? What's going on?" he asked.

Sydona brushed the dirt off her knees and clothes without a word. She felt like curling up into a ball and shriveling away. Her inability to fly made her feel like a fish drowning underwater, and she gasped for oxygen. The earth around her spun so quickly that she became dizzy and unstable. In the confusion, everyone's voices blurred together. Raoul suggested he try to use his dust to help her, but she refused. If she couldn't fly on her own, she didn't want him helping her the rest of her life. It wouldn't be fair to herself or him. She couldn't deny the blunt truth before her. The feeling hid in the back of her mind since she was electrocuted by the doctor. She was a full human. A blue eyed, grounded, human.

As they headed back home, the rest of the Sparrows went their separate ways. Sydona wouldn't call a cabin near Willow home, though. But it did the job for the time being. She was afraid to return to her real home. Afraid he might still be out there. Watching. Waiting.

"Syd," Raoul said, making her twitch back to reality.

She directed her attention to him and realized they were there already. Willow, Giovonna and Silas walked up to the house while she was still buckled in.

"What were you thinking about?" Raoul asked.

"Home."

Raoul responded with a sympathetic look. He knew how she felt. But it wasn't like it would change anything.

"So, I've been thinking…" he started. "When *are* we going back?"

Sydona unbuckled herself. "I'm not talking about this again, Raoul." She grabbed her green tote and slammed the car door shut.

"But my family…"

"They're my family, too. But we can't go back... Not yet."

"Okay. Not yet. So *when*?" Raoul pried, hovering close to Sydona like a gnat.

"I'm just not ready. I don't even know when I will be…" She walked faster and ran up the stairs to join the others.

The cabin reminded her of Willow's, but it was slightly larger. Willow said it had been empty for years and didn't think anyone knew it was there. There were never any sale signs or people stopping by to lease it. Just four walls and a toilet. She walked through the door and into a living room with one dusty couch and a couple chairs. A large burgundy rug laid in the middle, and the walls were barren except for two windows letting the light flicker in. Sydona nailed a bed sheet covered in cartoon characters over the windows for privacy and security. Although hideous, it helped her feel better.

After everyone put their belongings away, they snatched food from the pantry and put a meal together. They had all been out training since five in the morning. No one was more vocal about being hungry than Raoul.

"I'm glad you're a Sparrow and all, but could you bring those little cheese balls next time?" he complained as he ate an entire loaf of bread. Fairies were opposed to most foods other than fruit, but of course, Raoul had to be dramatic about it.

"I agree, lil' man. I thank some of the members should have jerky in their pockets as a spare, just in case. One time, it took them hours to finish. I thought I was gonna see my pops up in heaven," Willow said.

Sydona rolled her eyes. "Yeah, that's what we need to focus on next time. Sure."

Raoul's mood shifted in the last few months. His normal wit and sarcasm had been replaced with bitterness and short replies. Anytime the doctor's name was spoken, he made an audible sigh. Sydona thought traveling with

Giovonna was enough to deal with, but he acted more like a teenage girl. She wondered if it would ever end.

"Oh, don't forget 'bout the nation-wide meeting in a couple days. You'll need to be there, princess," Willow said as she took a huge bite of sandwich with deer meat.

"What about us?" Silas asked.

"Yeah, are we allowed to go if we aren't members?" Giovonna added.

Willow looked uncertain. "Ta be honest, I have no clue. I can make a call to see. I don't know if Knox will be alright with y'all."

"Who's Knox?" Giovonna asked as she took a seat at the table.

"Just the most important fella to know. He's the big guy on campus. The head honcho. The leader."

"What's the meeting for again?" Sydona asked.

"Not sure. He called it after Eagle Lake. Prolly just a plan on exterminatin' the rest of the hideouts."

"Have you met him before?" Sydona asked.

"No, only heard o' him in passin'. Knox is a great man but not one to cross. Been the leader for a while now."

"Can't wait," Sydona said. She wanted to sound interested, but she received a skewed look from Willow. She didn't bother to correct herself.

Sydona changed the subject. "Who's making a fruit run tomorrow? Any more bread in Raoul's stomach and I think he'll explode."

No one volunteered.

"I'm fine, Syd. You're not my mother. I can take care of myself," Raoul retorted.

Silas snatched the keys sitting on the countertop. "I'll go."

Sydona smirked.

"Bananas and mango, right?" asked Silas.

"Right!" Raoul answered. "And kiwi. I miss kiwi. And strawberries, papaya, grapes, oh and oranges! Or, whatever you can find. Thanks..."

Silas nodded his head and caught Sydona's eye. She couldn't help but smile at his generosity. After everyone finished eating, Sydona and Silas were left alone in the kitchen.

Silas cleared his throat. "About earlier..."

Sydona didn't need him to finish to know what he was referencing. The thought of bringing up the painful subject made her want to shut down. The chair legs reverberated on the tile floor as she sat down and waited for him to finish.

"I'm sorry if I made you uncomfortable about the date thing. I mean, where would we even go, right?" He chuckled and joined her at the table. His hands stayed on top of the table, close to hers.

Sydona knew he meant well, and the look he gave her made it hard to be upset. She noticed his hands fidgeting and all the dirt under his nails. His grungy hands and nails never appealed to her at first, but now it was somewhat familiar and comforting. Those hands taught her sign language that helped find her best friend. Who was she to judge the cleanliness if it meant warmth in her heart? Her feelings for Silas began to feel the same way she felt when she was at home with the fairies.

"No, it wasn't that, actually. I just can't stop thinking of the day I couldn't fly... You said you can't stop biology, but here we are--stopped."

She stared at a knot in the floorboard until she felt her hands being squeezed by the man across the table. Silas curled up a sideways grin and winked.

"I have an idea. Raoul!"

Raoul flew into the room at attention. "Yeah?"

"Come with us."

Silas stood up with Sydona's hand in his and ran outside. Curiosity and nervousness nuzzled together in the depths of her stomach. Deep into the woods, he scanned the area for a clearing to run.

"Where are you taking me?" she asked.

"You'll see!" he said in a witty, high-pitched voice.

Once they found an open area, Silas nodded at Raoul who then covered Sydona with fairy dust. Silas gripped her hand tighter and took off running. Sydona ran alongside him, feeling light as the breeze and carefree. Treetops swayed from side to side below her; it was a sight she was unsure she'd ever see again. Her senses tingled and goosebumps rose on her skin. Fairy dust had that effect, but it wasn't the dust this time. As the two sped up, her hand climbed up Silas's arm and squeezed. Adrenaline soared through her body like a falcon. The amount of happiness she felt in that moment made everything bad disappear. Soon, though, her excitement drained. She was a stone and no longer wanted their help.

"Hey," she yelled at Silas. "Can we get down now?"

Silas's bright smiling face dwindled at her hardened expression. "We just got started."

"Please." Sydona blinked away tears forming in the corners of her eyes. They rolled behind her ears and into her blonde hair, whipping into the cold air.

"What happened?" he asked as he turned them back around.

Sydona stayed quiet. She just wanted to land and bolt.

An awkward silence fell over the pair as they headed back down. Sydona's hand slipped back down to his, but she barely held on. Once she was able to judge the height from the ground, she let go and landed on the dirt with a thud. Raoul's orange dust made the landing softer, and Sydona walked away before they could catch up to her. She needed to fly on her own again if it was the last thing she did.

Chapter Two

As the day settled and the crickets came out, Sydona wandered to the room she shared with Silas. While they both agreed to share, she was less enthusiastic. It was better than sleeping in Giovonna's room, though. Silas wouldn't talk to her at all hours of the night.

Stacks of books and piles of clothes were strewn about the room. Sydona didn't mind the mess. She had more important things to focus on.

Sydona shuffled through the books she brought from Willow's house and the Lake. She paused and pulled out a book with a deep blue cover. It looked familiar, but she couldn't place where she knew it from. Then it came to her. As she flipped through the pages, Maverick's face popped into her mind. During the short time she spent with him, he had it glued to his face and mouthed every word. A scrap of paper fell out, and her heart sank down into her stomach. It fluttered onto the shag carpet, and as she bent down to pick it up, she read the words she wrote down before the revolution.

Borba i amore bez strah -- "Fight and love without fear."

A flash of her late mother's face flooded her memories. Those were the last words she ever heard her speak. Words that changed the fate of their species.

A knock on her door made Sydona shove the paper back into the book for safekeeping.

Giovonna poked her head through the crack in the door. "Syd?"

"Yeah, come in," she answered and threw the book under her bed.

"Where did you go with Silas just now?"

"Nowhere. Just messing around."

Giovonna scrunched her face. "Oh... out in the woods?"

Sydona raised an eyebrow. "What? Oh, no. Not... no, he was just trying to make me feel better."

"Okay?" Giovonna said slowly.

"How are the bracelets coming along?" Sydona asked and flopped down on the squeaky bed.

Giovonna joined her. "Um, not good actually. It's hard to know how to fix it when I can't activate them."

"Why would you need to activate it?"

"Well, um, think of it like a car. When it's on and running, you can see all the moving parts and what it all does. Without seeing how it works to begin with, I don't really know where to start."

Sydona furrowed her brow. "You're just now letting me know this? Haven't you been 'working on it' for a couple months now?"

"Yeah, but I've been helping you train for the Sparrows most of the time. By the time we got home, I'd be exhausted," Giovonna argued.

"But why didn't you mention this to me three months ago? I've been waiting on that bracelet to make me fly again," Sydona said with a twinge of sadness in her voice.

"I know. I'm sorry Syd... I hate to say this, but I honestly don't think it will help. The bracelets were specifically designed to stop flying. It's not a switch you can just turn on and off."

Sydona hung her head low, not wanting to accept the truth. Technology was not her strong suit, and she trusted Giovonna. But reality stung like a thousand yellow jackets.

"Thank you, Gia, for trying. I know it's not your fault... "

Giovonna gave her friend a hug. "I'll keep trying though." She closed the door gently behind her.

Sydona lay back on the bed, and a single tear slipped out. As she soaked in the events of the day in silence, she let out a sigh and closed her eyes. Just then, her door opened again, and Silas made a gross hacking sound that made her scrunch her face. She grabbed a pillow, placed it on top of her face and stuck her arms down at her side. There was never a moment of peace anymore.

The bed sunk down on her left side, and she knew Silas lay down next to her.

"You doin' okay?" he asked softly.

Sydona growled in response, the pillow muting most of it.

"That bad, huh?"

She pushed the sides of the pillow down around her ears.

"You wanna talk about it?"

"No."

Silas stayed quiet, but she felt him shifting around in the covers.

"Willow left, by the way. She said to say she was proud of you."

Sydona sighed. She didn't know why those words made her calm, but she liked hearing them. Soon the room went dark, and Silas stopped moving. She removed the pillow and turned her head to the side to stare at the back of his head. Living with three and half other people took its toll on her. The fairy tree didn't count as it was more of a guest house, and they had their own living arrangements. Raoul didn't make the transition any easier. She hoped it would just be the two of them again like the old days.

After a brief and troubling night, she woke the next morning to an empty bed. Her hand circled the sheets, searching for the missing warm body. A whiff of eggs and pancakes found its way into the room. She sat up and heard singing and laughing from the kitchen. A smile crept up on her, and she made her way into the fun.

"...Come on, Raoul. I wanna hear a song from our culture!" Giovonna exclaimed while flinging a spatula around.

Raoul flew around her, laughing. "I don't sing like *every other* fairy in my family. I will make your ears bleed!"

Sydona spoke up. "I know one."

They turned their heads and stared at the third person suddenly standing in the room.

"My mother used to sing it to me when I was sick," Sydona said.

She took a deep breath and shut her blue eyes. A vision of her young mother sitting on the edge of her bed floated into memory. Evelyn's humming slowly brought the words into melody, and Sydona sang the familiar lullaby.

"Rest your head and close your eyes,
Your spirit soars to the skies.
Let my warmth, my song, and soothing voice,
Heal your aches, return your joys.
Dream of happy days and bliss
I'll melt your pain with my loving kiss."

Raoul caught Sydona's glance and gave her a kind smile.

"That's the sweetest thing I've ever heard," Giovonna said with a cracking, sentimental voice.

Sydona blinked a tear. She then looked around the house, which was growing brighter with the morning sun, and realized Silas wasn't there.

"Where's Silas?"

"He went out for food," Raoul said and sat on her shoulder. It had been weeks since he sat on her shoulder, and her face relaxed with satisfaction.

"This early?" Sydona asked.

"Seems like someone is eager to please." Giovonna winked.

Sydona laughed and blushed. "Didn't think he was such an early bird."

"He seems happier lately," Raoul said.

"Does he?"

"Oh yeah," said Giovonna.

"When he's not being shot down for doing something nice," Raoul retorted.

Sydona was taken aback by his words, but she understood what he meant. They were doing well, and she didn't want to argue about her feelings.

"Sorry about that. I know it was well intentioned," she said softly.

Raoul flew off her shoulder. "You didn't have to run off, though."

Sydona clenched her jaw. Luckily, Silas walked through the door only seconds later. He carried several bags of food; three of them were filled with fruit. As he set them down on the kitchen table, she noticed something different about him. His face was free of stubble and looked ten years younger. It amazed her how a simple thing like removing hair made someone more attractive. Sydona had only seen him one other time with baby soft skin. The way the light shone in between the sheets on the window made his skin glow and his black hair glisten. He wore a t-shirt slightly too small, and his large biceps made her swoon as he carried in a television set.

"Wait, is that a T.V.?" Sydona asked, snapping out of a trance.

"Yep," Silas grunted as he set it on the floor in the living room. "Got a super good deal on it. And some other stuff I got in the car."

As if time escaped her, she looked around and saw Giovonna carrying things inside while she stood there in the middle of the room.

"Do you think you could help, or would you rather stand there and stare at me? I'd honestly be alright with the second option," Silas teased.

Sydona covered her face with her hands, hiding a smile. She punched his arm on her way out to help the others.

Along with the television, he had a lamp without a shade, a couple of small rugs, a scale, a crudely painted picture of an orange cat, a broom with several missing bristles, clothes of varying sizes and a couple of VHS tapes with no sleeves. They dumped everything onto the couch.

"Silas!" Giovonna rummaged around. "Did you get a VCR for these tapes?"

"Oh. I guess not," said Silas with a shrug.

"How are we supposed to watch these then?" Giovonna whined.

"Can't. But it did come with an antenna!" Silas said, pulling out a metal contraption.

Silas dusted off the television and hooked up the signal while Sydona looked through the clothes. "Looks like you stopped by Willow's house or something. Where did you get all this crap?"

"I stopped by a yard sale on the way back from the farmers market. Thought we could start making this place look more like a home."

Sydona grinned and began to fold the clothes, even though some were big enough for Willow to wear as a dress. The mentioning of the farmers market made Sydona wonder about Jim, Annie and her son Joseph. It felt like years since she saw them.

"You stopped by a fruit stand at the market in Redford, right? Did you see a woman with a little boy by chance?" Sydona asked.

Silas poked his head out from behind the television with a puzzled look. "Yeah. I think I did. Why do you ask?"

"Just curious. How did they look? Okay?"

"Like people running a food stand. So a little farmy I suppose?"

"Thanks, Silas. That's super helpful," she said with a slight chuckle.

Silas finished setting up the T.V. but was only able to receive five channels. The group helped to clean up and put the new items away. The lamp stayed in the living room as they only had one light source from the kitchen. Sydona placed the painting in Giovonna's room so she wouldn't have to look at it every day. Since Giovonna would be in the living room watching television most of the time, she didn't mind it.

The rest of the afternoon was quiet and pleasant. Sydona kept busy by reading books on the back patio and identifying bird songs from the surrounding forest. Silas went hunting with Giovonna's bow to catch something not fruit or plant based, and Giovonna stayed inside to clean.

Raoul disappeared, and she imagined he slept most of the day like a cat. Soon, he joined her through the open window and sat on the opposite chair.

"It's really peaceful here," Raoul said as he warmed his body in the sun.

Sydona closed her book and looked down at him glowing in the light. "It is."

"I wonder how much longer we should stay."

"I wonder too. I miss home."

Sydona took another look around the quiet woods. It seemed almost like she was trapped in a dream. At any moment she could discover the doctor's death and wake up. As long as she didn't know, she would be teetering on the edge of a cliff. She stared down at Raoul who drifted off to sleep in the lawn chair and her gut began to twist. They had been bonding more lately, and maybe it was the right time to confess what she knew about the doctor. It was never really the right time, but the longer she kept it a secret, the worse it would get.

Her lip shook nervously. "Raoul. I--"

"Oh thank goodness we found you!" A pink-winged fairy barged in between her words.

Sydona stood up in shock. "Lilly?"

"Xander! Over here!" Lilly yelled out with an extremely high-pitched voice.

Raoul flew up at the sound of yelling and the sight of his relatives. Soon, another fairy with green wings buzzed over with a heaving chest.

"Lilly? Xander? What are you doing here?" Raoul asked, still unable to process their presence.

The smaller pink-winged fairy spoke up. "It's so good to see you two!"

"We've been looking for you everywhere!" Xander said with a slightly lower pitched tone.

Everyone quickly hugged before getting back to the rundown of what was happening.

"Is everything alright? How did you find us?" Sydona asked.

"Something's happened," Xander said and flicked his lime green wings. "The NFA came by the house."

"What?" Sydona and Raoul exchanged a terrified look.

"A few days ago. They… they…" Lilly shook her head and burst out crying.

Xander comforted her and whispered as low as he could. "They burned our tree down."

Another wail from Lilly screeched in everyone's ears.

Sydona's heart stopped like a freight train derailing. The worst possible thing had happened, and it was all her fault. Her mouth went dry, and she drew a blank on what to say next. Raoul looked as if a ghost passed through him. Seeing him speechless was like seeing a unicorn.

Xander spoke with a heavy heart. "Jubilee… I know she was like a sister to you, Raoul."

"What about her?" Raoul said on the verge of tears.

"She, uh, she was captured. It happened so fast. None of us could stop them."

Raoul's eyes flooded. He constantly complained about Jubilee and how much of a pest she was. But she admired Raoul like a role model. Sydona knew deep down he really cared about her. His face said it all. What hurt the most about the news was that Jubilee just learned to fly only a few months ago. The last time they saw her was at her Vila Prah Ceremony, and she was so happy.

"We want you to come back home," Lilly choked.

Sydona wondered how much more the NFA would take from her. They took her parents, killed her mom, and now they had ransacked her home and killed innocent fairies. She didn't plan on making it to the Sparrows meeting the next day. It was a time for family, not revenge.

"Let me get the car keys from Silas," Sydona said. Raoul nodded at her as he cleaned off his face.

"Keys?" Lilly asked. "Driving will take too long. We need to fly."

Sydona clenched her jaw. "I--can't." And she wouldn't fly even if she could. It was too dangerous.

"What do you mean you can't?" Xander asked.

"It was stolen from me at Eagle Lake," Sydona whispered, still ashamed to admit it.

"Oh. Well maybe Shaman Faro can help. Like a V.I.P ceremony!" Lilly exclaimed, her high-pitched voice returning.

Sydona shook her head with uncertainty. "I don't think it will work with me. And I couldn't ask him to do that after what just happened..."

"Poppycock!" Xander stood up straight. "What's the harm in trying if you'll be there anyway, right? Come on."

The afternoon sun had dipped behind the trees and fireflies danced beneath the branches.

"Alright. We should go now, though. Let me tell the others," Sydona said and walked back inside.

Could the Shaman really make her fly again? The thought sent tingles through her pale skin. It might be her only chance to feel whole again, and she couldn't pass it up. Sydona grabbed the keys and an empty suitcase. They were finally on their way back home.

Chapter Three

Several emotions spun in her head. Though she wanted to smile to see her old home again, it felt bittersweet given the recent circumstances. She still couldn't process why they would burn homes of innocent fairies who had nothing to do with anything. Picturing what her home might look like, she twisted her hands tightly around the steering wheel. Tears wanted to surface, but she swallowed and shook her head. She had to stay strong even though she wanted to scream.

"Syd, why are your eyes not lilac?" Lilly spoke up only minutes after leaving the cabin.

"Uh… it's a long story," she answered.

"Is that why you can't fly?" Xander added.

"Basically."

"Is everyone else okay?" Raoul asked.

"Um, well, we did lose some others. Erid, Banjo, Quinsley and Vera. Jubilee was the only one captured…"

Lilly muffled her cries with a piece of cloth she found in the back seat.

"Why did they come to the house?" Raoul spoke softly as if he was mostly asking himself.

"We don't know. They kinda just showed up. Most of us think they were looking for you, Syd."

Once Lilly stopped crying, Sydona could feel all three fairies looking up at her. She glanced back and forth between them and the road with a perplexed look.

"Well, I don't know why either," Sydona said.

They stayed quiet.

"I guess maybe it's because I'm half human?"

"You are?!" Xander and Lilly said in unison.

Sydona breathed out of her nose. "It's a long story, too. You guys missed a lot while we were gone."

"If the doctor is dead, why would they still be looking for you?" Raoul asked.

Her fingers tapped the steering wheel nervously. "I wonder if it was Harold."

Lilly immediately asked, "Who's Harold?"

"I thought Willow killed him," Raoul said.

"No. She didn't really say, honestly."

Xander chimed in next. "Who's Willow?"

Raoul continued to press. "But what happened to him? We looked everywhere."

"I don't know. I was in the hospital the whole time."

"You were in the hospital? What happened?!" Lilly shuttered.

"Why didn't Willow kill him? She's always had it out for him," Raoul asked with a raised brow.

"Your guesses are as good as mine. But I guarantee, that's who stopped by," Sydona said loud enough to cease the conversation.

Raoul took a minute to digest the information, but eventually nodded his head in agreement. A wave of relief passed through her, and they didn't speak of it again the rest of the way.

After a couple hours of driving, the edge of the woods faded, and her great blue house stood proudly in the field. From a distance, everything looked just as she left it. The fairy tree, however, was exactly as the fairies described. Its branches were barren, and its trunk was burnt to a crisp. Even with the windows up in the car, smoke enveloped the inside. It was so strong Sydona had to cover her mouth. Blackness rose from the tree, and as she got closer, she saw embers still crackling from the inside. Everything grew quiet as Sydona turned off the car, except for Lilly's sniffling. Bittersweet indeed.

Sydona pulled into the long driveway and walked up to the porch. With the green tote around her body and Raoul on her shoulder, she stared at the tattered front door with a half smile.

Finally, she thought to herself.

But something wasn't right. The locks no longer worked. Her smile faded quickly as she realized the door had been kicked in. She cracked the door open with her dagger and witnessed a peculiar site. She tried to remember the state she left her home in. Sydona had never been known to be tidy or to dust a piece of furniture in her life. But she didn't remember leaving it in its current condition. She dropped the knife to the floor in pure amazement at her living room and dining room. It was spotlessly clean. And hundreds of fairies filled the empty spaces.

Mouth agape, she could barely form words. "What is this?"

Lilly replied, "We hope you don't mind. Our home is gone. We needed somewhere to stay."

Sydona tilted her head back at her modest statement. "Mind? Of course I don't mind…" Her eyes looked over all the tiny faces; some were happy to see her, but most were still recovering and sadder than usual. She wasn't used to seeing so many fairies upset or gloomy. The air gave off an unfamiliar vibe, and it made her depressed as well.

Xander and Lilly said the incident only happened a couple days ago, yet the entire house was already turning into what she could only imagine the inside of the tree looked like. The walls were covered in branches and vines. Countless make-shift holes were fashioned from books, clothes or blankets draped over furniture to make a home. Sydona was touched by their resilience after the loss of their home.

Many of the fairies hugged her and welcomed back Raoul and herself. Their voices were somber and low. It was nice to be back home, but so far nothing about it felt familiar. A part of her wanted to just talk to the Shaman and get out of there. First, she wanted to see the tree and the graves of the fallen ones.

She entered the backyard, and her stomach shriveled at the close up of the fallen oak tree. Where there once lived bright colorful creatures was a log covered in ash and cinders. Her hands touched the blackened bark; it was still warm. Burnt memories crept into her nose and filled her with immense sadness. She tried to remember the sounds of the yard when they put on parties: music, laughter and beautiful singing. All that remained was old crackling embers and birdsongs in the far off distance. The chickadees, blue birds and cardinals were too afraid to come back.

"I should've been here…" she whispered to herself.

As she turned her red face to the right, she noticed five tiny burial spots surrounded with bouquets of flowers. Each one seemed extremely loved and cared for.

"Don't blame yourself, Sydona."

She turned at the sound of the deep voice behind her. "Oh. Shaman Faro."

"You can't blame yourself for something you have no control over."

Sydona sniffed and stood back up. "Can you tell me how this happened?"

Shaman Faro set his large headdress down on the step and sat down. His gold and emerald wings laid flat. "They came in two cars, five people total. We've been keeping a lookout ever since you left, just in case they came looking for you. After so many days and weeks, we stopped, thinking the threat had passed. They came when our backs were turned. First, they broke into the house without so much as a knock, breaking things and searching for something they couldn't find. They then went for our tree. They attempted to catch us to bring back to the lab. But when we all flew away... most of us flew away... that's when they burned it down. Maybe they guessed some of us would come back to the tree to save it and catch us then. No one came back. Except--they did find someone. And took her."

"Jubilee. Yeah, we heard..."

"She was so young..." He sighed heavily. "A woman referred to as Natalia took her. She had a wicked smile. Said 'he' would promote her for sure."

"Was there a man with her? Indian decent, greasy black hair and a suit perhaps?"

Shaman Faro looked to the sky. "Not that I recall. Most of them were in amateurish military wear. No suits."

"*Interesting...*" she whispered under her breath.

As the two of them sat there in thought, Raoul flew over.

"What's going on?"

Sydona didn't look him in the eyes. "Someone named Natalia took Jubilee… I've never heard of her before. Have you?"

"No…" Raoul slowly balled his tiny fists, and his face flushed a rose color. "No more! This--Ugg! This can't continue. Why--Why is this happening all at once?! It's just too much. Too damn much!" He flew off, parting the sea of fairies listening to the drama.

Fairies weren't known for having tempers. The amount of anger Raoul displayed could freeze hell over. She followed him back into the house and up the stairs. Sticks and leaves arched over the banister and covered the walls. She felt like she was walking into a real live fairy tale, and she took her time to admire the craftmanship and beauty. As she approached the top, reality took a quick turn. Raoul buzzed around her room, throwing around any little object he could pick up.

"Hey, hey, hey!" Sydona marched around him, trying to make him stop. His huffing and squalling made him sound like a puff pastry steaming and ready to pop.

"Raoul? It's just me here. Calm down," Sydona said softly.

As he kept buzzing around, Sydona noticed him eyeing the open bedroom door. She reached her hand out and slammed it shut, trapping him inside with her before he could fly off.

"Leave me alone, Syd," he said with gritted teeth.

"No. You need to talk to me." She stood guard in front of the door with her arms crossed.

Raoul looked around for an exit. The window near her bed was shut, but his bed still sat on the sill overlooking the garden. A tainted scene. They could see much farther but only because of the absence of the great oak tree. He fluttered back over to his bed and sat down with his head low.

She allowed Raoul to calm down in silence. Looking around her room, she noticed several things missing. The fairies cleaned up a lot of it, but she remembered having more stuff, especially in the closet. She bent down to the floorboards in the closet, and her stomach sunk. She extended her hand down to an empty space where she kept her savings and money from her parents. Gone. Her knuckles knocked on the wood with annoyance. It didn't surprise her that the NFA robbed her, but she didn't have much left to remember her parents by.

Sydona turned her head to examine Raoul who sat like a statue in the window. Walking toward her bed, she took a seat and a deep breath.

"Do you want to tell me what happened?"

As if Raoul knew exactly what she was referring to, he started. "I wasn't alone in Malik's office..." He shuttered.

Sydona scooted closer to him with worried brows. "What do you mean?"

"...there was another fairy. He kept us both in cages but took us out when--he wanted to know who I was there with. When I refused, he started the torture..."

"Raoul... I'm--I'm so sorry... What'd he do to you?" Sydona hesitated. Hoping her questions wouldn't upset him.

"Not me. Her... He started by using scissors to cut off tiny pieces of her wings. When I still wouldn't fess up, he shook her until she couldn't produce anymore dust... He shocked her with those incessant bracelets over and over. And then... he ripped her wings off, causing her to bleed out..." Raoul stopped to compose himself. "She looked like a helpless, small human who I killed because I wouldn't talk…"

Sydona's hands shook as she covered her mouth. It took all she had to not cry.

"I--I don't know what to say…"

"Once she died, he turned to me," he continued with rage burning in his eyes. "He shook all the dust out of me as he screamed at me. When I ran out, he started burning the edges of my wings… he would have burned more. But someone interrupted him outside, asking about her fairy."

Sydona sat frozen on her bed. If she had known the absolute terror and abuse he went through, maybe she would have tried harder to kill Malik. One thing she knew without a doubt was that Raoul could never find out about her uncertainty of Dr. Malik's whereabouts. After the things he did to him, Raoul wouldn't forgive her for keeping it a secret for so long.

"I didn't think you were ever going to tell me what happened up there."

Raoul scoffed and shook his head. "I wasn't. But… for some reason, I feel lighter."

"Yeah," Sydona whispered and breathed deeply to hold back tears. "Did you know her?"

"No. She was real pretty though. Golden yellow wings and teal eyes… I still think of her every day."

It was no wonder Raoul's attitude changed. Sydona's heart ached. He did so much to protect her. She feared he would never fully return to the happy-go-lucky guy she had always known. She couldn't find any words to make the moment better. She stood up and grabbed some of her own clothes to bring back.

The frame with the photo of her parents laid broken on the floor by her bed. With a heavy heart, she flipped it over to take the picture with her. To her dismay, the photo was tampered with.

A big black 'X' crossed her mother's face out, while over her father's head they wrote "1 to go". Rage pulsed through her, but she held back from squeezing the life out of the photograph and damaging it further.

"Who did that?" Raoul asked over her shoulder.

"I have an idea."

"Harold's gonna pay." Raoul buzzed around angrily.

Sydona's eyes lingered on her young father's face. She wished she could see him and ensure his safety. The fateful day of his departure stung in her memory.

After the news of Sydona's lost abilities and not being able to fly to Sparrow Island, her father approached her in the cabin.

"How you doin', sweetheart?" Ian whispered and clasped a hand on her back.

Sydona shrugged as she folded her clothes, keeping herself busy. Her father sat down next to her on the sleeping bag as close as possible. From the corner of her eye, she could see him watching her pack, waiting on a moment to speak up.

"What's up, dad?" she asked.

"Oh. Nothing…" he faded and rubbed her back more.

"Nothing? Come on. I know you better than that."

Ian stayed quiet and grunted as he switched positions on the floor.

"It's going to be weird living with me again, huh?" She nudged him with a small grin. "'Course, I'm as tall as you now, and I don't care for pink anymore. But otherwise…"

"I'm going to the island," he interrupted.

She stopped folding the jeans and stared at the hem with loose stitching. Her heart beat faster. She couldn't believe what she heard.

"And don't try to stop me. I know you, too."

Sydona shook her head, letting the information sink in. But she still couldn't make sense of it.

"Why?"

"I've caused this family enough trouble. I can't do it anymore. I'll have a fresh start on the island. Willow says they have the most amazing beaches."

"You sound like you're retiring…"

"No. I'm just *so* tired, Sydona." He lifted her trembling chin and made her look him in the eye. "I'm sorry, baby.

"I just found you. Now you're wanting to leave again?" Sydona asked. Tears poured down her rose-colored cheeks.

"I love you. But this might be my only chance to get away from it all and live peacefully. It's got nothing to do with you, sweetie. I promise."

She hated the idea of losing him again. But if the doctor still lingered out there, at least her father would be in a place most people didn't know existed. She longed to spend the rest of her days with her elderly father, but she had to respect his wish. Who was she to stand in the way of someone kept in captivity for fifty years?

Her heart ached, and she wished she didn't have to agree. "I'll miss you."

Ian kissed his daughter on the forehead with shaky lips. "I'll write."

Sydona finished packing and headed back downstairs. The sun disappeared, and the moon shone brightly through the windows. The fairies lit the house with old candles sitting on every flat surface. There were so many, in fact, it seemed brighter than when the lights were on. Heat radiated from the plethora of candles, calming and relaxing her. It gave her confidence to speak with the Shaman.

She found him outside, sending up prayers for the family members of the lost ones.

"Shaman Faro?" she asked as he bowed his head at the last fairy.

"Ah, Sydona. How are you?"

"Um, not good, actually."

"What's wrong?"

She dusted off a spot to sit on the lower, cracked concrete step. "Would it be possible... to make me fly again?"

Shaman Faro flew backward in despair, then came closer to her. "Good heavens, dear. What happened?"

She shook her head, dreading the inevitable question. "Is it possible?"

"Oh, well, I'm not sure," he said.

"What about the V.I.P.?"

His eyes widened, and he stroked his beard. "Yes. It could work. But it would take every single fairy to contribute and a lot at that... Even then, it's not certain."

Sydona held back a smile but nodded. "I understand."

He leaned in closer with a sideways grin. "I'll let everyone know. Go up to your room and lie above your covers. I'll send Lanie up."

"Thanks," she smiled soberly.

Her feet led her back upstairs with a tinge of excitement. She imagined she felt like Jubilee on her VIP day. It was hard to not get her hopes up because it could crash and burn. But at the same time, she kept envisioning all the times she flew above the treetops and houses. Her skin grew goosebumps again.

As she lay in bed, she stared at the ceiling and shook with anticipation. Soon, a lilac-winged fairy with short auburn hair flew into her room with a cup the size of herself.

"Good evening, child," she said. She landed on the side table, clunking the full cup down.

"Hi. Lanie?" Sydona asked. She had never seen her before. "What's in the cup?"

"Some tea. Chamomile and lemon balm. Plus, some stuff Faro put in it to knock ya out," she said with a high-pitched but raspy voice. "Needed to get ya a little extra 'cause, well... you about five-hundred of us." She giggled.

Sydona smiled. "So, how does this work exactly? I never get to see this part of it."

"It's quite simple, really. You just lay back and relax. Everyone will come by to donate their dust to you, just pile it on top of you, I guess. A bit impromptu. Normally, we have a whole thing. Then, when Faro comes in to start his chanting, drink the tea. You'll fall in a deep sleep. Then, when you wake up, you should be able to fly!"

"Should be," Sydona said, less enthusiastic.

"Well, dear. We've never attempted this before. Only fate knows what will happen next."

Sydona closed her eyes and took a deep breath. Fairies began to pile in her room one by one. Some brought candles to illuminate the room better. Raoul opened the window to let in the midnight breeze. A group of fairies sang an enchanting melody as the rest of them donated fairy dust. Once a fairy stopped by, they would touch her skin and whisper, "Svibanj vas lebdjeti s milost." She was not fluent in the ancient language, but Lanie said it meant "may you soar with grace". Grace of course, used in two different ways, which she greatly admired. She hadn't felt so relaxed in months; she thought she might not even need to drink the tea.

The ceremony lasted about an hour. Her lids grew heavy, and she wanted to drift off to sleep, but then Shaman Faro flew in. He wore robes created by silkworms, which complimented his ashen blue wings, and a large headdress twice his size. He floated down next to Sydona.

"It is time," he said. He slowly stretched his arm out toward the cup and bowed his head.

Her arms felt dead with comfort and struggled to reach behind her. The tea tickled her nostrils and soothed her throat on the way down. Even for as long as she lay still, the liquid still warmed her insides. The effect of the tea and magic went to work immediately. It was strange to feel completely void of weight while lying down. Normally, she would feel this way when she flew with her troubles far behind her. It was a feeling of absolute relaxation and euphoria. Her hopes soared.

After what felt like a year, the light from her bedroom window woke her up. A grin grew quickly on her face at the sight in her bedroom. Raoul lay on his bed on the window sill. It was the first time in a month he had slept in the same room as her. She let out a peaceful sigh and sat up in bed. The dust she remembered all over her body disappeared. Not a single speck was left behind. Only moments later, Raoul stretched out on his bed and perked up at the sight of her.

He flew straight up with hands on his hips. "You wanna give it a go?!"

"Try and stop me!"

She leapt out of bed and within seconds, she stood outside in the fresh morning air. Her lungs took in enough oxygen to give her a slight head rush. Quickly, the fairies gathered nearby to watch her. She positioned herself along the dirt road for a running strip. Her excitement overrode her worries of anyone seeing her.

With her feet locked into a sprinting position and fairies cheering her on, she took off. Her heart pounded harder with every step, and she swore she felt lighter already. When she felt she sprinted hard enough, she kicked her left foot off the ground and leapt into the air with her arms straight back.

It worked.

Her feet no longer depended on the ground to keep her up. Back to her normal self, she took another sigh of relief as she rose higher into the air. There would be no more feeling sorry for herself. With a huge grin, she thought about how she could go to Sparrow Island to see her father. She quickly pictured him making sand angels on the beach and drinking a cup of coffee.

But something felt wrong. Involuntarily, she slowly sank back down to the earth, and she felt like cement blocks hung off her legs. The feeling of weightlessness disappeared within only a few minutes. Her hopes were dashed. Normalcy had been within reach but quickly dissipated at her grasp. Raoul and the other fairies came to her aid and tried to sprinkle more of their dust on her. Her face turned beet red from embarrassment, and she waved them away.

It was done. She sat in the mud and cried. She lost all hope.

Chapter Four

Sydona ripped the heads off dandelions and crushed them in her hands, instantly staining her fingertips yellow. She memorized each petal smeared along her fingers, ignoring the attention around her. Tears soiled her face. Reflections of the glowing, mourning fairies bounced off her cheeks. The families pitied her as if she had lost a baby. Though she knew they meant well, it took everything within her to keep from running away.

The brown line around her wrist reminded her why she couldn't fly. It only angered her more. The doctor took something away from her that she was never able to get back. He stole a piece of herself.

Shaman Faro was the last to speak with her. "We did everything we could. I wish I could help you further…"

Sydona wiped her hands on her legs and cleaned her face. "I know."

"You're the same person you were, whether or not you can fly. A good person."

Sydona hung her head. "Thank you, Shaman Faro."

He flew off, back into the house with the rest of them. Raoul cleared his throat.

"I can't believe it didn't work. Everyone contributed so much…"

She stood up, her legs fresh with grass indents. "It's really okay. I'll be okay."

Raoul nodded. "Where do we go from here? Back home?"

A breath escaped her at his words. They were home, but it suddenly felt unknown. She took a closer look at the house. It was overgrown with vines and colonies of branches bundled into nests for fairies. Her home was now theirs.

Home. Giovonna. Silas. Willow. Time to go back, she thought to herself.

"Willow will want us back soon," said Sydona.

"But we just got here." Raoul looked back at his people.

Sydona sniffled one last time and glanced at Raoul with a sullen face. "I think they'll be alright. We don't belong here anymore."

A lump formed in her throat as she headed back inside to gather her things.

The goodbyes held them back another hour. In all her life, she never thought she would be saying a final goodbye to the fairies she lived with half of her life. But she saw no future for herself there anymore. She was a Sparrow now, a rebel who fought to end the discrimination of fliers. She mentioned Sparrow Island to the fairy families as well. As much as they had been sending fliers there, she assumed they sent fairies too; they were an essential part of being a flier.

As she headed back down the longer-than-she-remembered-driveway, she took one last look at the great blue house. A part of her wanted to say goodbye to it, but it was just a building after all. It wasn't like it could hear her or miss her in return. She lingered though, memorizing its every feature.

Trees and farmland whizzed by as they left. Her eyes glazed over the road, and her mind wandered the last few hours. Willow would be furious if they didn't leave in time, but she didn't care. She blasted rock on the radio, and they lost themselves in the music the whole way back.

A few hours passed and she pulled up to the house, which was a third the size of hers. She could almost hear Silas saying "size doesn't matter". She smiled. Immature as it was, it relaxed her. Willow's new used van was parked in front of hers, and she could already hear the lecture.

"She's back!" Giovonna called out as she ran from the house and straight over to them.

Sydona barely got her seatbelt off before she squeezed her.

"How did it go?" she asked.

Sydona turned to point to the truck.

"Oh."

"How long's Willow been here?" Sydona asked.

"Uh, yeah. She's not happy with you. Said we're gonna be late."

Sydona scoffed. "Willow can kiss my--"

"Syd! Where the hell you been?!" Willow shouted through the trees.

She rolled her eyes and grabbed her things from the truck bed. "You didn't tell her where I was?"

"We did. But she didn't care," Giovonna whispered.

They walked up to the front where Willow stood like a guard on the porch.

"Morning, Willow," Sydona said with sarcasm in her voice.

"Don't mornin' me, princess. Ya knew--"

"I know, I know." Sydona shoved past her to go inside the house.

Silas grinned as she walked through the door, and her heart raced. But she kept her head down at Willow's yelling and headed to her bedroom. She dumped her items in a corner of her room and repacked her bag of new clothes and essentials for the trip. She couldn't wait to sit in a car for another few hours.

Willow *finally* calmed down. She assumed Raoul talked to everyone and filled them in. Knowing she wouldn't have to explain gave her a wave of relief. As she got ready and opened her bedroom door, the three of them and Raoul turned to look at her with sad eyes.

"Oh, Syd..." Willow uttered.

"It's fine," she said softly. "Can we just go now?"

The group silently loaded into the van with Willow in the driver's seat. Giovonna sat up front as usual, and Silas, Sydona and Raoul sat in the back. It felt like when they went to Eagle Lake, but now she had someone to hold her hand.

"We gotta stop by an' pick up a few people. Might get a little cramped," Willow announced as they drove onto the main road.

Silas's and Sydona's fingers played with each other but not for long before Silas spoke up.

"You wanna talk about it?" he asked.

Sydona sighed and looked out her window.

"Come on. You can't keep holding things in. It's not good for you."

Why did he want to know her anger? About how absolutely defeated she felt? Talking about it would only make her more upset. But she soon realized she hated when Raoul kept things bottled up, and she was doing the exact same thing to Silas. She sighed.

"Shaman Faro did a Vila Prah, and I thought it was going to work. And it did... But then it didn't."

"I can't imagine what that felt like."

"I feel empty. And defeated. And not the same person I used to be..." She felt her face flush and tears trying to come up, but she squashed them. Her hands gravitated toward her lap. As much as she wanted to get angry, she was tired. All that remained was depression and sobriety. "I never should have gone. Should have just stayed home. None of this would have happened."

"Shoulda, woulda, coulda. You killed the leader of the pack. Why are you regretting that? You should feel proud of what you did. You saved so many lives. You found your parents! That wouldn't have happened if you decided to stay at home, silly."

Silas grabbed her hand again and squeezed.

The car came to a stop, and Willow yelled out the window. Lost in her head, Sydona rolled her window down for fresh air. Jet and Lacey walked toward the truck with a small, dark-skinned boy following them. Large backpacks weighed them down, while the child carried a vibrant multi-colored school bag on his back. Sydona met Jet and Lacey in the past, but the boy was new. His head hung low, making him look damaged. He dragged his feet and pushed up his black-rimmed glasses. She had a feeling he wasn't a flier like the other two or even closely related. Who was he?

"Hey guys!" Lacey called out. Devon ran ahead as Lacey waved.

"Hey y'all!" Willow shouted. "Ya excited for Chicago?"

"Chicago? I thought we were going just outside of Chicago?" Raoul asked.

"Yeah, but sayin' 'excited to go just outside of Chicago' just don't sound as fun."

"How are you, Sydona?" Lacey asked with a bright smile.

"I'm alright."

"Great job on your trials, by the way. I still got a bruise on my ass from you!" She rubbed her backside and nudged her through the window. "Hey, Gia! Hey, Raoul!"

"Who's the little guy?" Willow turned to greet him with a smile just before he got in.

"This is Devon. He's… going to join us today," Lacey said, her tone much softer.

Sydona leaned over Silas to get a closer look. Eyes were the first thing she noticed when meeting anyone, and his were brown. Could he be a human? Or had Giovonna been making contacts for other Sparrows?

Lacey bent down to level her face with Devon's. "Can you say hello?"

He waved his hand quickly. "Hi."

Lacey grabbed his shoulders and gently guided him to the back seat. "It's gonna be fun, okay?"

Devon didn't answer but moved to the back with haste and sat by the window, directly behind Sydona. She turned to face him.

"I like your glasses," she said.

He sniffed, wiped his nose and stared out the window without noticing her presence. She and Silas exchanged looks and silently agreed they should leave him be.

"Y'all got room back there?" Willow yelled back through the vehicle. Jet held a thumbs up. She put the van in reverse, and they headed out.

Lacey and Jet sat in the back. Sydona caught Jet from the corner of her eye taking a drink from a metal flask and hiding it back in his bag. Lacey bobbed her head to whatever music she was listening to on her Walkman, while Devon drew on a pad of paper.

Giovonna popped her head around once they were on a straight highway and whispered, "How do you suppose they know him? I'm guessing he's not theirs."

Silas shrugged. "He doesn't seem to really want to be here."

"Raoul. You think he's ever seen a fairy before? That might get him talking!" Giovonna said louder.

"We don't want him fainting like someone I know did…" Sydona added.

"A moment of weakness…" Giovonna said. "But really, try to talk to him, Raoul."

Raoul fluttered his wings with an expression of confidence.

"Hiya, Devon!" Raoul exclaimed as he puffed his chest out like he was a superhero.

He looked over the top of his glasses and then back down at his notepad.

Raoul exhaled and scratched his head. "Uh.. whatchya drawin' there?"

Devon continued drawing, ignoring the fairy. Raoul tried to sneak a peek by going behind him, but Devon turned his pad over. His nose flared with frustration.

"How old are you, little man?" Raoul asked cheerfully.

"I'm not a little man and leave me alone!" he cried. Every head in the car turned.

Lacey rubbed Devon's back, and she shook her head at the newbies. Raoul flew back up to Giovonna with arms crossed.

Lacey asked Devon with a hushed voice. "You wanna listen?"

He nodded his head and took her cassette player and headphones. He turned the rock music up so loud Sydona could hear it, too.

"What's his deal?" Silas asked with a lowered voice, still afraid he might overhear.

"He's a little fragile... Jet knows more than me."

They all looked at him. He stopped mid-drink and stared at everyone like a deer in headlights. "What?"

"Why is Devon with you guys?" Sydona asked.

"It's a long story."

"Come on babe. Just tell them." Lacey nudged him and swiped the flask out of his hand. "You'll get this back once you tell them."

Jet groaned and sat up straight in the seat. "You sure he can't hear?"

"He's good," Lacey assured.

Jet let out a loud sigh. "Me and Lacey stopped at a gas station for snacks or whatever. There was this kid inside that kept looking at my eyes. Just to have fun with him, I thought of something sad so my eyes would change color, and he loved it.

"Next thing we knew, some guy came in and held the cashier at gunpoint. I put the kid behind me. The kid's dad tried to calm the guy down, but he freaked and shot him point blank. His mom was next to him, and the guy shot her, too.

"He pointed the gun at me next, but then he stopped and took off. The cashier started to call the cops, and I bolted. When I was about to get in the car with Lacey, I felt something tug my shirt. The kid followed me out."

Lacey spoke up, "He's been with us ever since…"

"His parents were killed in front of him? How horrible!" Giovonna cried out from the front seat.

"Wait, so he just came along with you?" Silas asked.

Lacey replied, "We asked where his home was, and he didn't know. But we drove around until things looked familiar. We went inside with him and asked if he'd be okay by himself, but he said no. He already attached himself pretty hard to Jet and didn't want to be alone. So, we had him pack up his stuff and we left."

"No wonder he's so quiet," Willow added.

"They're going to be looking for him," Sydona said.

Jet grabbed his flask back from Lacey and chugged.

"You left the scene of a crime. And you're a flier. Aren't you scared the police are going to come looking for you?" Silas asked.

"Let them come. I didn't do anything wrong," Jet snarled.

"Why did the guy just take off when he saw you?" Raoul asked.

"I don't fuckin' know," Jet raised his voice.

Lacey tapped Jet's leg. "Okay. Calm down, babe."

"And in case you've been in the dark, humans hate us. I did you all a favor."

"Hey now!" Willow yelled.

"Jet!" Lacey slapped his arm.

"Are you serious?" Sydona asked with narrowed eyes.

"Just piss off," Jet snapped. He turned his body and took another gulp from his flask.

She thought *she* had some unresolved issues with humans. But Jet had more than a few screws loose. The boy was an orphan and witnessed his parents' murder. It was a wonder that he kept himself together so well. Jet seemed to be worse off than the ten-year-old. What would they do with the boy? And why would he cling to a complete stranger? She assumed in the few moments they had in the store were enough to build trust. Jet claimed to hate humans, yet, he took the boy in anyway.

The rest of the car ride there was silent. Tensions built up and didn't seem to come down. Not even with Raoul cracking jokes in lull times. He ended up falling asleep once no one laughed anymore. After a few hours on the highway, they arrived in the outskirts of the city. The buildings stood much higher than those in the city back home. She figured she could put fifteen of her own city into this one and still have room. How did people survive living so close to one another? How did they move? Or breathe? She wondered if being a flier meant she felt like she needed wide open spaces. Living in the city, for her, was like a bird living its life in a cage. She couldn't wait until they got out.

Finally, as the sun began to set, they passed the last industrial building. Her stomach filled with butterflies, and she couldn't figure out why. As a new Sparrow, she knew the tattoo was coming, but that wasn't why. Excited to meet the leader of Sparrows, she sat up straight in her seat and gripped Silas's hand.

"I don't think I've ever seen you excited, Syd. Like, ever," Silas said as he rubbed her back.

Sydona grinned. "Aren't you excited?"

"Mmm, I guess?"

"Really?"

Giovonna unbuckled her seatbelt and turned around. "I'm super excited!"

"That's no surprise, Gia. You love everythin'," Willow said.

"I don't love everything! I don't like… Uh…" she faded off and whispered. "Not a fan of Jet. Seems like kind of a jerk."

The group shrugged in agreement.

"We're here!" Willow shouted and put the car in park.

They exited the van one by one. Sydona grabbed her green tote and dagger as always and scooted across the seat. As she took one last look around the van to see if she forgot anything, she noticed the notebook Devon was drawing in sitting on his seat. She absentmindedly grabbed it to give it back. Curiosity got the best of her, and she examined the drawings. The image shocked her, and she almost dropped the pad. Two stick figures stood with holes in them, and red covered them and the background. He scribbled with the red pen so hard it went through to the next page. More than half of the notebook held crumpled, used pages, and each image was as disturbing as the next. Blood dominated all of them, covering the stick figures and the surrounding areas. A hooded figure appeared in some of them with a gun. Sydona wondered if Jet and Lacey knew of these and if they talked to him at all yet. Regardless, she felt she needed to keep a close eye on him. Witnessing both of his parents murdered in front of him already seemed to have repercussions.

Chapter Five

Sydona hid the notebook under her seat to remind herself to talk to Devon later. The way Jet drank, she guessed there wasn't much talking in their strange little family. But today was the day she was meeting Knox, the leader of the Sparrows. Her attention refocused. Raoul rode on her shoulder like he used to. They walked through the parking lot and toward a huge metal warehouse. It wasn't clear what it used to hold when it was active, but it seemed to be long abandoned. The number of cars parked around the lot made her excited. There had to be dozens of Sparrows attending from all over the country.

A man stood at the entrance holding a clipboard with everyone's names. Sydona noticed each person also had a notation on what race they were and had to reveal their real eye colors. Willow told her if they didn't have the right eye color, they weren't allowed in. It pained Sydona to see her name written down as a flier but with blue eyes. She was the only exception. The man nodded respectfully at her despite her unusual eyes. Perhaps he knew what happened.

After everyone checked in, her first thought was how happy Raoul would be. Not only were there tons of people but several fairies as well. His own family were the only other fairies he ever associated with. Chatter echoed loudly as folks were elated to see friends from the past. Willow gathered with several people outside of their small group, and her voice carried over everyone else in the metal building.

Sydona stayed close by Silas and Giovonna, and they talked amongst themselves as they observed the crowd from the sidelines. Jet, Lacey and Devon went off in their own direction to catch up with a few people, too. She saw, at one point, Jet and Lacey introduce Devon to their friends, and he was just as distant. Her heart ached for him. It wasn't long before Willow bellowed Sydona's name to come over to a large group.

Once her name hit everyone's ears, the loud chatter softened to whispers. Most of them turned their attention to her, and her face felt warm from the attention. Mumbles of the doctor made their way through the waves of conversation. If her eyes were normal, she was sure they would be turning brown. But for once, she was thankful her eyes were blue. She wore a fake smile as she walked through the crowd to get to Willow. Some people patted her on the back and congratulated her, while others gave her looks of pity because they heard she couldn't fly anymore. She didn't know what to think.

"Syd! Tell 'em how you took out the doctor! They been dyin' to know." Willow clapped Sydona's back with approval.

Her stomach twisted itself into knots. She never had to tell the story before, and knowing the outcome, she had to lie. And it had to be good, no holes.

"He's dead. Do you really need to know how?"

"Hell yeah!" Willow cheered, getting the people worked up.

She cleared her throat as she thought back to the horrific day. "It was dark. Very dark. I was looking for him in the woods because he was nowhere to be found.

As I learned of his location, a helicopter came out of the blue, shining a bright light on the field. That's when I saw him, running like a coward. So I ran after him and tackled him to the ground. I was just about to kill him when I was shot by someone in the helicopter. I lost my grip, and he got away..."

The crowd gasped.

"But I wasn't about to give up. I got up and chased after him again. He began to climb up the ladder, and I followed him up. He tried kicking me off, but I was so focused; there was no way to get me to let go. I grabbed my dagger, climbed as high as I could, and--I slit his throat. As he bled out, I let go, and watched the life leave his eyes before I hit the ground. The man who shot me probably thought he could be saved, which is why they flew off. But I saw. He was already dead."

The crowd burst out into cheers and applause. Sydona's jaw clenched, and she picked her nails nervously. Everyone seemed so happy, except for one. Raoul floated nearby with a skeptical face. He didn't believe her, but she hoped he wouldn't say anything. If anyone could see through her, it was Raoul. She dreaded having to talk to him later, but she needed to. He *had* to believe her story.

Soon, another voice shouted over the crowd. It was the Sparrows' leader, Knox.

"Silence, please," he bellowed in a deep, powerful voice. His voice matched his intimidating look. Sun from the high windows reflected off his bald head. A deep scar above his right eye contrasted his dark mocha brown skin, and Sydona wondered how he got it.

The crowd instantly hushed and turned their attention to him. He stood on a platform above everyone else. Standing next to him was a small but stunning Latina woman at least a full foot shorter. The jewelry on her arms and neck could have blinded someone with the amount she wore. Among the crowd of forest greens, blacks, browns and grays, her gold stuck out like a sore thumb. Sydona wondered what her role was since someone dressed like her could not blend in well at all.

"Thank you all for making it out on such short notice. You all should be aware of why we are here. There's been a change of plans thanks to Sydona Wilder."

He stared directly at her, parting the crowd to look at her.

"She single handedly took down the leader of the Vultures. But our work is not yet over. We still have much to do to wipe out the existence of their followers, the scum who killed our families, our friends, our own children!" Knox's voice echoed loudly through the rafters of the warehouse, building up excitement in the crowd. "Four new locations have been identified in Boston, Tallahassee, Austin and Chicago. The North and East District will go to Boston; West District, Tallahassee; South District, you're in Austin; Midwest, Chicago. Report to Avani tomorrow for your assignments and times. We need all wings on board. We lost a lot of Sparrows at Eagle Lake, so anyone who can, will help. Get all the rest you can tonight. And Sydona. May I please speak with you?"

Knox left the platform before hearing her answer. She assumed he was not the kind of guy who heard the word "no". She bit her lower lip and rubbed her neck. What could he possibly want to talk about? About the story she told? It had holes; even Raoul saw through it. But the only way to know was to just talk to him.

"Want me to go with you?" Raoul asked.

"Please."

"What do you think he wants?" Giovonna whispered.

"Who knows?"

Sydona sauntered to the left of the platform and through a set of doors Knox left ajar. Avani stood next to the door with a bright smile. Seeing her up close was like seeing a princess. Her hair and makeup seemed like they took hours to do, and the amount of jewelry took just as long to put on. Her elegantly braided black hair twisted to the middle of her back and was filled with jewels and decorations. The appearance of this woman put her at ease and made her feel almost like she was about to walk into a fantasy world.

"Sydona! Sweetheart!" Avani exclaimed and embraced her in a tight hug. She smelled like a field of roses on top of everything else. Avani pulled away but held Sydona's hands. "I can't believe I finally get to meet chu!" Her Hispanic accent was as adorable as herself.

"Uh--thank you," Sydona said.

"You're just as beautiful as everyone said!" She squeezed her hands.

"Oh?" Sydona blushed. "Who's saying that?"

"Everyone, my dear." She beamed brightly at Sydona, taking in her face and appearance. Clearly uncomfortable but flattered, Sydona released a nervous laugh.

"Go on ahead. Elias is very excited to meet you."

"Elias?"

"Oh, sorry. I mean Knox. He's so sensitive, he hates his first name. Makes him feel like a empollón. I said, 'Babe, with your stature and height, you could be named

Ernie, and people would still fear you.' But he no like that. So he go by his last name. Whateva. He'll always be Elias to me…"

"Okay…" Sydona said, barely moving her lips.

"Come on, go ahead. He's waitin' for you."

Sydona pushed the door open to reveal Knox sitting behind a desk, making himself look like a giant. Sheets of paper scattered the top layer of the desk, and he scribbled on forms with purpose. Large windows lined most of the room but were too high up to see out. Knox's desk sat on the left side of the room with boxes and papers everywhere. On the opposite side stood another tidier desk with several flower vases decorating it. Pens, pencils and every sheet sat perpendicular to the edge as if they were glued down. Avani's desk, she supposed. In front of Avani's desk, a long daybed held pillows and a teddy bear. She smirked at the bear. Sydona wondered how much more polar opposite the two could be

"Come. Sit," Knox commanded. His voice was so brash that it startled her.

She walked over to his desk and sat in a hard metal chair across from him. The chair across from Avani's desk had a luxuriously soft red cushion with armrests, engendering her jealously. Her hands shook, and her heart pounded. She wasn't sure why; she hadn't done anything. As she sat there for what seemed like several long minutes, Knox never once looked up at her.

"I'm sorry for your loss," he finally said in a softer tone.

Sydona relaxed. "Oh, thank you."

"Were you close?"

Her eyes shifted with confusion. She heard chatter that the rumor got around about her inability to fly. Could that be what he was referring to?

"Uh, yeah… I was close. Didn't last very long though."

Knox furrowed his caterpillar eyebrows. "Your relationship?"

Her foot tapped anxiously. "My… relationship?"

Knox put his pen down and looked up at her with intensity. She never felt so small.

"With your mother."

Sydona released a nervous laugh. "Oh! Yes. Close." She cleared her throat. "We were very close."

Knox shook his head at her buffoonery and looked back down at his work with a growl in his throat. Her pulse raced.

She sat in the chair, waiting for him to continue talking. Maybe he was waiting for her to say something? But he called *her* in; what would she need to say? She could talk about Avani. How different they were made her wonder about their relationship status.

"Are you and--"

"I brought you in today--" he interrupted, then stopped.

The awkwardness jabbed at every inch of her. She hoped Raoul would step in soon and say something, but she assumed he was just as nervous. He stayed hidden under her long hair.

"Sorry…" Sydona shuttered and looked down shamefully.

He took a deep breath and started again. "I brought you in to see if there is any information you can give me about Malik."

She panicked. "What?"

Knox looked back up at her with sympathetic eyes. "I know it's hard to talk about him after everything. But can you at least try?"

"Oh." She gulped. "What do you want to know… exactly?"

He pushed his chair out and stood up so fast he gave her a head rush. "Anything! He talked to you right? Did he give you anything about where other camps are, why he's doing this, if he already got what he was looking for?"

He stood only inches in front of her, and she leaned back in the chair, unable to focus on anything other than the large, murderous man. She dreaded uttering the next words.

"No." From his drive and body language, she imagined he would be able to take Malik down with a snap of his finger.

"Really? Nothing?" He leaned in more, his breath creeping into her nose.

She shook her head vigorously. "I'm sorry."

He slammed his enormous fist down on his desk, making her jump and expel a sound. "God damnit!" Knox swiped all of the papers off his desk in a fury.

Frozen, Sydona didn't move, unsure of what his temperament would lead to. As she was about to timidly get up, the door flung open.

"Elias!" Avani rushed in and ran toward him. "Dios mio! What happened?"

Avani stroked his chest and arms like she was petting a grizzly bear. Knox answered with a series of grunts and groans.

As Avani kept both hands on him at all times, she turned to Sydona. "I'm so very sorry you had to see him like this. You should go."

Sydona sat wide-eyed at the display of the two. After only minutes, Knox melted into Avani like warm butter. They sat on the couch and Knox curled around Avani. One minute he was Godzilla wanting to destroy the city, and the next he was the teddy bear on Avani's chair. Sydona stood but couldn't take her eyes off of them. It was the sweetest thing she ever witnessed. A brief picture of Silas smiling came and went, leaving her with a smirk. She left the room as Avani began to serenade him with a hauntingly beautiful melody.

As the door clicked shut, Raoul opened his mouth.

"What a whack job!"

Everyone greeted them outside with concerned faces.

"What's he want?" Willow asked.

"Just wanted info about the doctor. I'm as clueless as all of you," Sydona said with a shrug.

"What was he like?" Silas asked.

"He's uh... Large."

"And crazy!" Raoul blurted.

"What?" Giovonna asked with worried eyes.

"He's not crazy, Raoul. Just... uh… terrifying. He's terrifying."

"Man's psycho. Thought we was going to rip into us for nothing," said Raoul.

"What'd he do?" Lacey asked.

Avani walked through the door and gently shut it. The group stood patiently waiting on her words.

"Sydona? Can I talk to you un momento, por favor?" she asked with a loving voice.

She parted from the group, but Raoul rejoined her shoulder.

"Without el guapo little fairy," Avani corrected.

She stopped in her tracks, and Raoul flew up. Sydona could tell he tried not to look offended, but he had never been good at hiding his true feelings. He fluttered back over to Giovonna, and Avani made her way into a separate, smaller room that looked to be an old office or storage space. She closed the blinds of the empty concrete room and cleared her throat.

"Forgive my husband. He's not normally like that. Sometimes he has trouble containing his anger. But I've been trying. Ever since Eagle Lake and all the people we lost, he's having trouble adjusting. Blames himself for not going. But it wouldn't have changed anything..."

"Why would he blame himself?" Sydona asked.

"Well for starters, she went rogue. Didn't say anything to any of us about taking on that place. It was poor judgement and reckless."

"I don't think she planned on it. Gia and I were planning on going there from the beginning. She just happened to come with us."

"That's the problem. She is a member, and as a member, she needed to get permission to do something like that. Elias wouldn't have approved it because it was far too dangerous, and we had almost zero information about it. It would've been the same as her going to the I.D.F., which she is fully aware we've eliminated our chances there."

Sydona pushed her brows together. "The I.D.F.?"

"Yes, the Institution for Developing Fliers. A high security building where they keep children under the age of 8–before they can fly. We've lost many of our own trying to take it down. Elias forbid anyone else from going there. If he caught wind of that happening, they would be banned from the Sparrows."

"Wait, there's a place holding children hostage?"

Sydona felt her body get hot with anger.

"Sí… It kills me that we've given up trying to shut it down, but too many lives have been lost." Avani crossed her arms.

Sydona's nose flared, and she shook her head. She pushed the thought to back of her mind. "With Willow, are you saying she is banned now?"

Avani smirked. "The other thing is how she took on Eagle Lake. It was not a tactic neither Elias nor myself approved, ever. She rallied up Sparrows in a foreign district, and then got most of them killed. It was foolish… I never thought Willow would do something so stupid."

Sydona tilted her head and tried to understand the point of what Avani was trying to say. "So she *is* banned?"

"What she did would certainly lead up to that, but no. Willow is not banned. It's because of the outcome of Eagle Lake. She was able to eliminate most of the Vultures there and, thanks to you, Dr. Malik."

Her eyebrows raised. The news was not what she expected. "Oh, I didn't—"

"Oh, but you did. Despite the brash approach, you were still able to take down the leader of the entire NFA. Muy impresionante! Not trained or anything!"

Sydona took a minute to process. "What are you saying?"

Avani uncrossed her arms and shrugged. "I'm saying Willow should step down for a while… make room for a new leader of the Midwest district."

Sydona felt even more confused.

Avani's bright red lips curled up. "You."

Sydona gasped. "Me?"

"Why not?" Avani asked casually.

"Well--because--Willow would be devastated. She dedicated her entire life to this group. And when she finds out I'm replacing her…" Sydona's tone got louder than she expected.

"Señorita. No need to raise your voice. I'm simply offering you a chance to prove yourself. Again."

Sydona relaxed her fists. "I don't follow."

"Come see me tomorrow for your first assignment." Avani finished and stepped toward the door.

"Wait--" Sydona grabbed her arm. "What's going to happen to Willow?"

"Don't worry about her. Just worry about you." She opened the door and walked out.

"Avani! I'm not done--" Sydona stopped when she realized Avani wasn't listening anymore. She disappeared into their office. Willow and the gang joined her at the other door.

"What was that about?" Willow asked. Sydona couldn't help but feel bad for Willow. Sure, she didn't always get along with her, but Sydona never meant to betray her. A leader? She may have started the battle, but she didn't lead it. Why would they want her to do something so dangerous? Her mind flipped back and forth, self-doubting and kicking herself for self-doubting.

After everything she had been through in her life, this was just the next step. She couldn't help but to agree with Avani about Willow. Maybe it was time for her to step up, prove to herself she could lead and eventually take out the doctor with an army.

"It's nothing. Just going over tomorrow's mission."

"With you? Why wouldn't they talk to me about that?" Willow asked with open palms.

"I don't know, Willow. We should get to that hotel though, don't you think?"

"I'm tired," Devon said just loud enough for everyone to hear.

"Yeah, okay. Let's get going then, yeah?" Lacey replied and held Devon's hand.

Willow side-eyed Sydona, but she pretended not to notice.

The group headed out of the warehouse. Feet dragged and scuffled to the van. The moon shone bright above them, meaning it was midnight or later. No wonder the ten-year-old was tired. Her heart beat excitedly thinking of their mission tomorrow. Not only would it be her first mission, but she would be leading it. Things felt like they were going in the right direction, even if just for a moment.

Finally, they arrived at the motel and parked in the back where shadows were darkest. Willow left to talk to the motel attendant. Devon fell asleep in the backseat while waiting on her. She booked two rooms, enough for everyone to have space. Knowing Willow though, she would need a bed to herself. They joked that Raoul would be the only one small enough to share with her.

Willow handed everyone their keys with an acorn logo as a keychain. Lacey carried Devon who was dead asleep in her arms while Jet took their bags to the room. He stumbled on his way up the stairs. Sydona watched him as she trailed behind with her bags. It seemed like he finished off the flask. Giovonna, Silas and Raoul followed her to the neighboring room. Giovonna was the first to claim the bed next to the window and turned the air conditioner on full blast. Silas took the other queen bed and slipped off his shoes and socks. Everyone moaned.

"What?" He shrugged.

"Good thing you're small, Gia," Sydona snickered as she propped up her pillows.

Her face turned sour as Willow whipped her head around. "What's that supposed ta mean?"

"Oh, she didn't mean anything by it, Will. Here, you wanna sleep next to me tonight?" Silas interjected with a serious face.

"In your wildest dreams, boy!" Willow huffed.

Raoul made himself a bed out of a washcloth and laid it on the table between the two beds. Instantly, he curled up like a cat and fell asleep.

The room soon quieted once the lights turned off, but Silas's arm found its way around Sydona's waist. Her heart fluttered as she realized she was the little spoon. Surrounded by warmth and familiarity, her arm incased his and pressed it close to her body. They both wriggled in bed to better match up. His breath moistened her neck as her breaths got longer.

"You excited for tomorrow?" Silas asked at barely a whisper.

She grinned. "Yeah. I can't wait."

"Sucks I won't be there. Wish I could see you in action." He squeezed her tighter.

"Me too," she said. Her hand entwined in his.

As Silas fell asleep, thoughts of the day spun in her head. Where would they be heading tomorrow? And would Silas and Giovonna have to go home since they aren't Sparrows? Did Raoul have to go through the same process as her to become a Sparrow even though he's a fairy? Her brain conjured up a dream of the following day combined with a comic book she once read a long time ago.

Soaring over treetops and cities at a hundred miles per hour, Sydona felt like a superhero on her way to stop an evil villain. She wore a sleeveless shirt to show her badge of honor, the Sparrow's winged symbol on her shoulder blade. Planes and jets fell past her as their engines struggled to keep up. They shot their cannons and machine guns, but she weaved in and out of their path with ease. Her trusty blade somehow evolved into a boomerang, and she chucked it into the windshield of the planes. They both went crashing down to the earth in a huge explosion. Sydona kept flying and dove down into a huge cave carved miles into the ground. She was as nimble as a hummingbird as she flew around the stalactites and stealthy as a chameleon.

She landed on both feet, indenting the dense floor of the cave. In pure darkness, she was able to see a metal door at the end of a hollowed-out hallway, surrounded by guards. The guards were the same ones from the Lake and held semi-automatics. She took all ten guards out with karate moves she never knew she knew. She survived without a single scratch. A thick, soundproof door protected the prisoners. Her heel impacted it so forcefully, it flew off the hinges like a sheet of paper. Inside stood thirty or so fliers tied up by their hands. Her friends and family scattered around the prisoners, including Maverick and others she remembered from Eagle Lake. With her dagger in hand, she cut each bind with one swipe and set them free. As some of them began to flee and take off flying out of the massive hole, a dark clothed man stopped her. She held back the rest of her people from danger and looked the stranger in the eyes. His face was unrecognizable, hidden by a scarf and a hood that shadowed the rest of him. The only part of him she could see clearly was his cold brown eyes.

He held out his gloved hand and dared her to leave. Sydona laughed a mighty laugh. His ego inflated his head, making him think he was more powerful than her. She readied her fists of steel to take care of the pest. But then, the man's fingertips sparked with electricity that appeared from thin air. Her heart leaped from her chest in a moment of weakness. It was the one thing that could stop her. Her kryptonite. The unwavering confidence she had evaporated, and her forehead formed sweat the size of bullets. Bolts of lightning jolted at her feet, but she jumped quick enough to avoid it. One sliver of it touching her pale skin could paralyze her for eternity. Her mind rattled with ways to stop the evil being's powers until she saw a wooden bucket in the corner overflowing with water. Perfect.

The man tried shocking her again and failed as Sydona jumped backward, pushing the crowd against the wall. When the moment arose and he charged up the magic through his veins, she leaped toward the bucket. As he arched his back and parted his feet for balance, she effortlessly threw the bucket of water on him, covering him head to toe. In a magnificent display, the water mixed with the electricity and scorched his skin. His cries echoed in the cavern, and he melted to the floor. Only his blackened clothes and skin remained in a pile with smoke rising from the creature. Victory.

The prisoners lifted Sydona above their heads with cheers and laughter. As they were on their way out of the cave, a menacing laugh roared against the walls. The crowd dropped her and disappeared. He came back to life, more powerful than before. His heels clicked toward her, and she suddenly froze. Each step matched her beating heart. The man reached down to grab her and began to drag her away. She was unable to fight back. He would never be gone. Never.

Early the next morning, the alarm clock went off at six, but Sydona was already awake. Turning over in bed, she found Silas still there with the blanket over half of him and his mouth wide open. She took the quiet opportunity while everyone still slept to take a long, hot shower.

The door clicked shut, and she undressed. Hotel showers were not ideal. The water felt like a rusty hose was spitting water at her. But the car ride was so cramped and sweaty, she had to. It was the first time she had alone to herself in a long time, so she made the water extra hot. She stepped into the extremely relaxing steam that engulfed her entire body, and she let out a deep sigh. The water didn't bother her as much this time, and she stood underneath as it cascaded down. With each breath she took, she inhaled the moist air and let it settle in her lungs. The trickle of each droplet sang in her ears like a soft orchestra. She ran her fingers through her elegantly soft blonde hair that glued to her skin and wrapped around her arms. In the moment, she examined each strand of hair and playfully brushed them against her cheek.

As she opened her eyes, she looked up to see the shower curtains being pushed back and a naked Silas hopping in beside her.

"Silas! What are you doing?!"

He touched her hips and pulled himself close to her.

"Stop!"

"What's wrong?" he asked and wiped his face.

She stood wide mouthed at him. "I'm in the shower!"

"But you left the door unlocked…"

"So? That wasn't an invitation," she said, grabbing his arm and pushing him out.

"Syd, I've seen you naked before!" he said outside of the curtain.

"That was different! We had guns to our heads!"

He didn't answer.

"Are you gone?" she wondered, waiting for silence as confirmation.

"Yeah. I'm gone." He slammed the door.

She jumped at the strength of his slam and tone. His words dug deep into her. Was she unfair? It was hard enough trying to find a moment of peace, and everywhere she went, there other people were. She finished her shower quickly, no longer enjoying the loneliness. She didn't really want him to be gone, not forever.

As she exited the bathroom, the others were already packing up. Tension filled the room. She was sure their yelling was loud enough for everyone else to hear. Silas didn't acknowledge her in the room, and it made for an awkward ride back to the warehouse. Sydona and Willow sat up front while the others sat in back. Willow drove, while Sydona looked over a map of the area. Out of the corner of her eye, she looked back at Devon and then cleared her throat.

"How'd you sleep?"

He yawned, looked up at her and shrugged. Devon looked out the window for only a minute before he suddenly remembered his notebook. As he grabbed it out of his bag, along with a small handful of pens and pencils, Sydona's stomach twisted. She dreaded bringing up the topic, but maybe she could help him in ways Jet and Lacey couldn't.

She let him color a little bit before working up how to talk to the fragile boy.

"You know, I lost my mom recently too."

Devon glanced up quickly and then went back to coloring. She knew he was at least listening.

"How?" he muttered.

"In battle. She saved me."

He stayed focused on his picture.

Sydona cleared her throat. "I think your parents saved you too."

His pen paused while he stared away from his drawing.

"I know what it feels like… to lose someone. How does it make you feel?"

Devon pushed his glasses up. "Sad."

Sydona nodded but stayed silent. She wanted him to say more.

"It's okay to feel sad, Devon," Lacey whispered from the seat behind him.

"And I'm mad," he said lower.

He tightened his grip on the red pen.

Sydona replied, "I understand—"

"—Why did he kill them?"

"We don't know, Devon. We might not ever know…" Sydona answered.

"It's not fair. It's just not fair!"

"It's not, I know…" Sydona said and placed a hand on his tiny knee. From the corner of her eye, she noticed Jet staring out the window pretending nothing of significance was going on.

"Sometimes life just isn't fair, sweetie," Lacey whispered and also put her hand on him.

Sydona finished her sentence, "But it's how we deal with life that makes all the difference. When my mother died, I was very sad and upset like you. But I know my mom, and she wouldn't want me to live with that pain. She would want me to keep living life and enjoy it. I bet your parents would want the same for you, Devon."

Devon nodded and wiped his nose. "I can't stop thinking about it, though. I see them when I sleep."

"Is that why you draw them so much in your notebook?"

He shrugged. "When does the pain go away?"

Sydona felt a lump in her throat and had a sudden urge to comfort him. But as she was strapped in by a seatbelt, she simply squeezed his knee tenderly. Words escaped her. She caught Lacey's eye, and she looked just as speechless.

Willow spoke up from the front seat. "Darlin', my husband passed away over ten years ago, and I'll tell you one thing, the pain never truly goes away. But when I think about 'im, I don't think of the single day he left me. I think of the countless others we spent together. That's what ya gotta hold onto; that's how we move on."

A small smile grew on Sydona's face. Jet swallowed a drink from his flask again and made a cringing face as it went down. Her smile faded.

"So I just gotta think of the good times I had with my mom and dad, and it will go away?" Devon said with a more upbeat tone.

"Mmhm," Lacey confirmed. He turned to face her and wrapped an arm around her neck. Sydona smiled his way, and he returned it.

"Why don't you draw some pictures of things you did with your parents for me?" Sydona asked.

Devon gave her a quick smile. "Yeah, okay."

He put the red pen down, flipped to a blank page and grabbed a pencil.

Sydona faced forward again and composed herself. Her mother's face came to mind, both when she was a child and when she saw her at Eagle Lake. Every time she thought of her, her heart felt as if it were being pinched. Willow was right, the pain never went away, but somehow, she learned to live with it.

Willow pulled up to the side of the warehouse and everyone hopped out with their belongings. Only a motorcycle was present in the lot. With how strange Knox and Avani were, she assumed only a pair like them would own a motorcycle of that size. Most everyone exited the van except for Lacey, Jet and Devon.

Sydona knew they had to have a conversation with Devon about staying behind while they went off on a mission. Squeaks of crying bellowed from the open windows. They were leaving him behind with people he didn't know for several hours. She understood why he would be upset. But she guessed Knox made no exceptions with any Sparrow staying behind. All of the other groups had just enough people, so there was no one to fill in for either one of them.

She then focused her attention on Giovonna who hugged her tightly.

"I'll miss you! Remember everything we went through in training! You're gonna be amazing," Giovonna said as she squeezed her goodbye.

"Thank you, Gia. Couldn't have done it without you. I'll be back before you know it."

She couldn't help but notice Silas handing out handshakes and high-fives to everyone but her. He barely even noticed she was standing by herself. And just like that, he made himself comfortable in the driver's seat and got his seatbelt on. Sydona waved at him from outside the windshield, but he made himself busy by adjusting the seats and mirrors. Giovonna looked back and forth between the two and gave Sydona a shrug.

"Bye," she said to herself. Silas and Giovonna backed out, and Giovonna gave her one last, sad wave.

Sydona saw Devon wrapping his arms around Lacey's neck and tears soaking his cheeks. He then scampered up to Jet who was walking into the warehouse. Willow and Raoul were already inside.

Sydona stayed beside Lacey as they wandered slowly up to the door.

"He means a lot to you, huh?" Sydona asked.

"I haven't been away from him more than a night's sleep before. He may hate me, but I can't help but feel like his protector."

"Protector?" Sydona thought her word choice was interesting. Why not a mother or sister?

"Ever since we got him, Jet's changed. I've never seen him drink so much in my life. And I've known him a long time." Lacey faltered.

"Wasn't Jet the one who protected him though?"

"Yeah, but I think he may have regretted it. He didn't tell me the whole story. I know he didn't… Anywho, are you excited to go on your first badass mission?!"

Sydona chuckled at the sudden change in subject. "You know it!"

"We're gonna kill it!" Raoul chimed in.

The small group entered the warehouse again to see groups of Sparrows scattered around talking.

Avani soon called the group over, and she looked even more elegant than the day before. Silver and red was her theme that day, and her hair was in a different braided pattern. She embraced Sydona and pecked her on the cheek as she pulled away.

"You sleep okay?" Avani asked. Her hand never left Sydona's arm.

Sydona shrugged. "As well as can be expected."

"Are you excited for your first mission?"

"Yes… and no," she laughed.

"You gonna be fine, chica." Avani's teeth and lips sparkled. She then opened the door.

They went inside the big open room with both Knox's and Avani's desks. At his nearly seven-foot stature, Knox stood at attention in the middle of the room and met everyone's eyes as they entered.

"Good morning everyone," he began, almost smiling. His attitude seemed more in check today, to Sydona's relief.

"We have caught wind of a new Vultures hideout. Bravely, they have chosen a busy subdivision in Chicago underneath a building that was once a speakeasy. The surrounding area is filled with criminals, homeless, folks with nothing to lose. Best to blend in as much as you can. We're under the assumption it's not heavily guarded because of the dense population, but still be cautious. Sydona, you will be in charge."

"Say what now?" Willow asked immediately.

Knox paused and looked at Willow with piercing eyes.

"She just joined. Why is she leadin' us?" Willow raised her voice.

"Quiet, Willow," Knox responded at a temperate tone.

"I'm the one who led the dozens of Sparrows to Eagle Lake--"

"And you killed dozens of Sparrows in the process! Mind your place, Willow."

Even with Willow's large body, Knox easily towered over her. His stare calmed her back down, but Sydona could see veins emerging from her forehead. It was a strange sight to see someone getting Willow to stop talking; Knox could be Sydona's new hero.

"As I was saying, Sydona will be the leader so mind her instructions. I have all of your equipment ready to go in the other room including tranquilizers, pistols, walkies and clothes to help blend in. Don't use pistols unless you feel threatened. Since the base is close by, I want to bring in the leader or anyone else for questioning. Roll out when you're ready."

Knox relaxed and began to walk away from the group when Sydona spoke up.

"You don't want us to kill them?"

Knox sighed and turned back around. "No."

"But they deserve it…"

He released a bright white smile. "I agree. But we need more information."

Sydona nodded respectfully. His smile made her think that maybe he wasn't such a bad guy, just focused.

"Syd? Follow me please," Avani said with her arm outstretched.

"Ooh, you gettin' your tattoo, girl! Have fun!" Lacey teased and laughed.

Sydona gulped. "R-Really?" she asked Avani.

Avani nodded with a smile. "It's not that bad. Just stings a little bit."

Lacey, Jet and Willow headed over to the room with clothes and got suited up. Willow gave her a look she had never seen before, and it put a bad taste in Sydona's mouth. It wasn't her fault Willow wasn't a good leader. Sydona didn't know how she would be as a leader either, but at least she wasn't in charge of as many people.

Avani pointed to a chair next to her tidy desk and pulled out equipment for the tattoo. Gloves snapped on her manicured hands as she prepared her station.

"Lift your shirt up, por favor," Avani asked.

Sydona nervously grabbed the backside of her forest green scoop neck t-shirt and lifted it over her left shoulder. A cold dab of a cloth soaked her skin as Avani prepared the ink. The buzzing of the pen stung her porcelain skin, and the pain shot through her bones. Each time the needle touched her skin, her fist clenched. But after only ten minutes, Avani was done and cleaning up.

"Can I see it?" Sydona asked.

"Sí, claro!" Avani replied and handed her a small mirror.

A circle wrapped around a beautiful calligraphic wing that contrasted her reddened skin. All of her hard work paid off, and it was permanently etched into her shoulder blade.

"It looks amazing, Syd!" Raoul exclaimed, admiring it as well.

"Thanks," she said with a smile.

"Did it hurt?"

Sydona shook her head. "Not really."

"Really?"

She looked down at her wrist with the brown line caused from the metal bracelet. "I've had worse."

"You have other tattoos? Let me see!" Avani chimed in as she bandaged up the fresh one.

Sydona squeezed her wrist with the permanent brown, singed line and shook her head. "No, I don't."

Raoul and Sydona exchanged glances. It felt like the memories of Eagle Lake would never be put behind her.

Thankfully, Avani didn't press and moved on. "Okay, you're all set. When you're getting dressed, be sure to wear the jackets with our symbol on it. Since your tattoo isn't healed yet, something needs to indicate what side you're on. Especially with your… eyes…"

Sydona nodded. "Thanks, Avani."

They headed across the room to another door, filled with chatter.

Lacey was the first to greet her. "How'd it go?"

"Good."

Jet took a swig of his flask. "Did you cry like Lacey here?"

"Screw you, man! I didn't cry!" Lacey punched his arm.

"The hell you didn't! You were blubbering, like, 'Jet, Jet, it's hurts so bad. Jeeet!'"

She gave him two more solid punches in the arm. His jaw tightened, and he rubbed his arm with a glare at Lacey.

"God, I hate you," she huffed.

Jet let out a chuckle with a slightly high-pitched tone, almost mockingly so.

"You about ready, yet?" Willow asked Sydona, changing the subject.

Sydona paused and shook her head. "Uh, not yet."

"Get to gettin', girl. We ain't got all day…"

Willow's tone made Sydona uneasy. When they spoke about past missions, Willow would get fired up like she was a cheerleader at a football game. She usually had ideas flowing left and right, and she would speak words of encouragement to the others. But this time, she just looked as if she wanted it to be over as soon as possible. The mission was not going to go well if Willow refused to treat Sydona with respect. Sydona found a jacket with the wing symbol that fit perfectly. The whole group dressed in clothes that were worn, baggy or faded. She understood the reasoning of blending in but hoped the loose clothing wouldn't cause her to be grabbed easily.

As the group headed out with fully charged radios and weapons ready, Avani handed Sydona a piece of paper with the address.

Her heart dropped.

Of all the places and towns in the entire country, why did it have to be in her old neighborhood?

Chapter Seven

Pleasant memories of him appeared in her mind, and she reveled in them as she drove to the first location. Lacey sat across from her and caught her smiling.

"What are you so happy about?"

Sydona snapped out of it and frowned. "Nothing."

"I think it's somethin'. You look like you just took a bunch of painkillers," she said with a brass voice. She propped her feet up on the dash, blocking some of her view.

"Don't worry about it."

"Yeah, don't worry about it," Willow bellowed from the backseat. "So, what have ya got planned, *ma'am?*"

Her jaw clenched at the way she said ma'am. But she was right; she needed a plan. Without seeing the place, it was hard to know what to do. Knox said it was small and underground. They would need to cover the exits to make sure no guards or personnel escaped. That was all she had planned.

"I'll figure it out when we get there," Sydona said.

Willow laughed. "Oh ho ho! You don't have a plan, do ya? I'm so glad yer leadin' us. Can't wait to get slaughtered." She heard a slight chuckle from Jet who had been staring out the window.

Her grip on the steering wheel tightened, but she remained calm. "I won't get us killed, Willow."

"How am I supposed to know that when you won't tell us the plan?" Willow barked.

Sydona's face flushed with hotness as she tried to keep a level head.

Raoul spoke in her defense. "Willow, calm down. We won't accomplish anything if you carry all that negativity with you."

"Whatever."

The streets were busier than ever and nothing like the city she was used to back home. Lacey rolled the window down, fascinated with the cement and steel scenery. With the window open, the sound of honks, yelling and tires screeching intensified. Sydona's stress level heightened, yet at the same time, it strangely relaxed her. As she turned the corner, she released a smile, thinking of the time when she visited the neighborhood frequently.

"Is this…" Raoul started, wanting Sydona to fill in the rest.

"Yes," she answered. "Can't believe I'm back here."

"How amazing is that?! I wonder if Theodore is still around?"

"Oh, well, I don't know. Maybe?" Sydona replied, holding back a grin.

According to the map, the place was only a few blocks away. Sydona parked on the side of the road and fed a meter. Raoul crawled inside her green tote out of sight like he did in the old days. She took a deep breath in; the neighborhood smelled exactly as it did decades ago. A local Greek cafe across the street filled the block with an intoxicating lamb fragrance. Though she was a vegetarian now, she used to get food there every other day. Cracks in the sidewalks had stayed the same, including a shoe print she made when they laid the concrete. Theodore made one right next to hers with a slightly larger print. Two more very small divots were Raoul's feet. It looked like holes in the sidewalk, but Sydona knew what it was. She couldn't help but think of him and the last time she saw him.

She took a long drag of her cigarette as she waited on the corner of Main and Lester Street. Raoul stood by himself on the curb next to her feet as he wasn't a fan of her habit. A baggy brown jacket covered Sydona, and her hands shivered in the brisk January air.

Taking one last inhale of harsh, yet soothing smoke, she stomped her cigarette out and crossed her arms. Soon a man appeared wearing a suit with a brown Brixton hat. He walked toward her with swagger, and his head constantly swiveled around, looking out.

"What's good, Garrett?" Sydona asked with a slight slur in her speech.

He shook her hand and nodded his head. "Yo Eve, just livin', feel me?"

Sydona flipped her long hair back over her shoulder, and Raoul landed on it. "You got it?" she asked.

"You know it." He took one last look around the area. It was deserted, so he took his other hand from his pocket and slipped Sydona a stack of bills. She flipped through it, felt the weight, then took a small bag of green from her pocket and slipped it over to him. Without inspecting it, he shoved it into his pocket then gave a goodbye hand gesture.

"See ya next week, Eve." And he walked back into the shadows of an alley.

Sydona took one last glance around the empty corner, ran and jumped into flight. She soared over the tops of buildings until she arrived at the overpass where Theodore waited for her. Tilting her body upwards, she slowed and descended back to the ground. A smile grew on her face as she got closer to him. His red hair stood out among the rest of the group's dirtier brown and black hair.

"He finally show?" Theodore asked.

"Finally." She took out her pack of cigarettes and lit a match. She handed one to Theodore and lit his with her already smoldering stick. Raoul flew away from the smoke but still stayed by the two.

Theodore blew smoke into the air. "You try that stuff Omar picked up yet?"

"Theo, I don't even smoke the weed I carry around with me. What makes you think I'd try that shit?"

He laughed. His pearly whites were already tainted a little with yellow from tobacco. They were both still younger than eighteen but easily smoked a pack a day.

"It's not that bad, Syd. You don't know what you're missin'."

"I've seen what it does to you. I think I'll be fine." Sydona inhaled another drag.

Theodore took another drag but kept his violet eyes on hers. "He's gonna make us start selling it."

Raoul coughed. "What? Omar said that?"

"Yeah. Just now, while you were out. People are going crazy over it," Theodore said. He glanced over to the rest of their group huddled around fires under the overpass. Omar had his own area with tattered dividers and couches set up. He was like a king.

"Fuck that, man," Sydona blew smoke out and coughed. "I get marijuana, it's somewhat natural. But, what is it, cocaine? It's not natural, Theo. Shouldn't put that stuff in your body."

"You're one to talk, Syd," Raoul interrupted. "You smoke those sticks like they will cure you of cancer. I don't even use them, and I feel sick when I smell that smoke. They aren't natural either."

Sydona rolled her eyes. "Maybe you're right. But I just know that shit Omar has is way worse than weed or cigarettes, and I'm not getting involved. I'll sell this shit all day long, but I'm not touching that."

Theodore let his half-lit cigarette hang on his lip while he scratched his neck hard. "I don't think we got a choice here."

"We've always got a choice, Theo. We're fliers. We can literally go anywhere we want!"

Theodore shook his head. "It's not that simple, Syd."

"But it really is!" Sydona squashed her cigarette out with her boot. "I been thinking of finding a house soon. You, me and Raoul. Once I turn eighteen in a few months, I'll be able to sell my parents treasures, and we can live like fucking kings. –I wasn't planning to do this forever, ya know…"

Theodore looked at her sideways. He lifted his beanie, pushed his hair back and shook his head. "He'd find us."

"How? We can go all the way to Jamaica or Israel if we wanted. How would he even get there?" Raoul said.

"Exactly," Sydona said. "I got a few hundred bucks here, plus whatever you made today. We could just leave. Come on." She smiled, trying to convince him to leave.

Theodore stepped back from her. "I can't, Syd. I'm really sorry."

Her stomach ached. "He got you hooked already, hasn't he?"

He scratched his head. Sydona felt tears surfacing, and her breath quickened. She glanced over at Raoul who had sad eyes. It was too late.

"Look, let's just leave, and once you're not around it, you won't even think about it anymore. We'll get a fresh start. I could grow a garden and maybe get some chickens. Live off the land kind of thing. You won't even remember this place anymore."

Theodore kept looking at the ground, ashamed to look at his friends. "That sounds really nice, but…"

"But nothing, Theo," Raoul interrupted. "Who are we without you?"

"Please think about it, Theo," said Sydona. Her voice shook. "You're better than this shithole."

Theodore finally looked back up at her and gave her a sideways smile. "I'll think about it…"

"God, I miss you…" Sydona muttered under her breath.

"What's that, princess?" Willow shattered her thoughts.

She straightened up and side-eyed Willow. "The place is just up here." It wasn't much farther, but there were some folks hanging around nearby. The overpass looked just as it did when she lived there for a brief time. There weren't nearly as many people, but they looked just the same. They wore baggy, dirty clothes and slept on cardboard or sleeping bag on the sidewalks. A few were even asking for money from passersby. Some things never change.

The speakeasy stood at the end of the block near an overpass. Several homeless people hung around the area next to tents and makeshift homes. Her heart broke for them, having been in that situation before. As they arrived at the entrance that led down a flight of stairs, Sydona turned to the group.

"Everyone's walkies on?" Sydona asked as she flicked hers on and put the earpiece in as casually as possible. Willow and Lacey tested them and waited for her next instructions.

"Lacey, can you go to the back and tell me if there is an exit?"

"On it!" She made her way to the back of the building, watching her back with every step.

"Jet, you come with me."

He nodded. "Just cover you, then?"

"Yes."

"Willow, I need to you stand watch out here."

Willow shook her head and took a deep breath.

Sydona leveled with her. "Do you have a problem with that?"

"Nope."

"Good." Sydona surveyed the area and called to Lacey over the radio. "Find anything?"

"Yeah, uh, no. There's nothing back here. Not even a window."

"Copy." Sydona decided to look around one last time before she entered the building, but then she saw a familiar face.

Her heart dropped at the shaggy, red haired man standing across the street. He recognized her too as he made his way across the street with a smile. Yellow and black tainted the smile she remembered, but the essence was the same. His young, smooth skin from before was sickly and blotchy; some areas had sore spots.

"Syd?" he asked in a low, adult voice.

"Theo!" Sydona exclaimed and embraced him instantly. The odor radiating off his clothes and hair burned her nose, and she pulled away quickly but still wore a smile.

"How the heck are ya?" he asked. He pushed back his dirty red hair and scratched his full-bodied beard. If it weren't for his eyes and red hair, Sydona never would have recognized him.

"I'm doing good. How've you been?"

Theodore shrugged and shook his head. "Still here. You know…"

"Syd, we ain't got time for this," Willow muttered as she looked over her shoulder.

She acknowledged her but turned her attention back to her old friend.

"What happened to you?" she asked with sad eyes. His tattered appearance gave her a gut full of guilt.

He scratched his neck fiercely with long, dirty fingernails. "You know, this and that."

Sydona looked at the ground in shame. "Omar still around, then?"

"Nah, he got killed a while back. But I ain't dealin' no more…"

A lump formed in the back of her throat. What had she done? She left him there. "So what *are* you doing?"

He shrugged. "Whatever I gotta."

Sydona furrowed her brows. "I don't know what to say…"

"You don't haveta say anything, Syd. You seem like you're doin' good for yourself. I'm happy for you."

His words stung, even though he was being sincere. "Thanks… It was good seeing you again, Theo."

"Wait, why you here, anyway?" he asked before Sydona could walk away.

She turned back around and shook her head. She glanced back at Willow and met her narrowed, impatient eyes.

"I can't talk about it."

"Are you here for the experiments going on down there?" he asked, then his eyes brightened when he noticed the winged patch on Sydona's jacket. "Are you with the Sparrows?"

Her mouth twitched upwards. "You know of them?"

"Yeah! Some people who looked like you guys came by here a couple days ago. I'm the one who let them know about it. Must be why you're back. You're gonna stop them, right?"

"I'll certainly try," Sydona replied with a smile. Absorbing the conditions around them, how Theodore looked, and the guilt that still ate her up inside, she sighed.

"We found an island," she said at a whisper, making sure Willow didn't overhear.

He stepped closer to hear her better. His body odor was overwhelming, but she stood still. "An island?"

"Yeah. It's where we put the refugees from Eagle Lake. A safe place... I know I've tried to convince you before to leave here, but this place is real. It's remote, it's got beaches and sunshine. My dad is there, actually. Living out his retirement years." She chuckled.

Theodore smiled with wide, curious eyes. "Yeah. I might just have to do that... where is it, exactly?"

Willow sighed heavily behind Sydona. She put her finger up, telling her to wait. She sighed again.

"It's um..." Sydona looked back at Willow who looked ready to explode. "Just stay around here. I'll find you after, okay?"

Theodore's face changed suddenly. "Wait, Sydona. Don't – Don't go in there..."

"Why not?"

He fidgeted. "It's dangerous..."

Sydona relaxed. "We know, that's why we brought a team of trained people. We'll be fine."

Theodore paused for a moment but then nodded his head a few times. He walked away with his head low.

Her gut twisted. It was obviously dangerous, but his warning rattled in her head. She didn't have time to ponder about it as Willow was on the verge of popping a blood vessel. She jogged back to Willow who had already started walking back to the building.

Willow muttered under her breath, "Ya know I'ma be tellin' Knox about that, right?"

"I was catching up with an old friend. Leave me alone," Sydona snapped back and took the lead. Willow said nothing in response, giving her a small boost of confidence. She wasn't going to break, no matter what Willow did.

"Lacey, are you still out back?" Sydona asked over the radio.

"Yeah. You want me to come back up?" Lacey asked.

"No. If you can, hang out back there just in case. We should cover our perimeter."

"Copy that."

Sydona walked up to Jet. "You ready?"

"Yep. Been waiting here this whole time while you've been chit-chatting. I should be asking you the same."

Her bottom lip took the punishment at his backhanded comment. She knew he was right. She led the way as they walked down the rickety black staircase and stood in front of the door with chipped white paint.

Sydona had her gun full of tranquilizer darts at the ready and checked the doorknob to see if it was locked. The door was nothing out of the ordinary, unlike the doors in her test run through. It didn't have a digital lock or secret code to get in. She dug in her pocket and took out a small lock pick. Jet covered her as she picked the lock. With a click, the door creaked opened, and they stepped inside.

The first thing she noticed was how dark the room was, and then she noticed a velvet wall only a few feet in front of them. They shut the door behind them and followed the hallway down, slow as snails. Her heart pounded against her chest so hard she could hear it in her own ears. There could be a giant hole or something below them, and they would have no idea. There was no air circulation either, causing her sweat glands to suffocate. Every breath felt as if she were breathing inside of an oven. Once her eyes adjusted to the dark, she was able to see a little clearer. A dim light shone through a doorway, and she headed toward it. Cautiously, she pressed herself against the velvet wall and slowly peered around the corner.

A single floor lamp illuminated the bar. Upturned tables and chairs were scattered around the room, and broken glass crunched under their feet. Black and white photos from the 20's hung in broken and crooked frames. It was as if they had stepped back in time. It wasn't what Sydona expected; there wasn't a single person in sight.

Sydona listened closely for any sounds or movement, but it was eerily silent. She signaled for Jet to look around. He headed to what looked like a storage room in the back while she looked behind the bar. Her eyes widened and her stomach did a flip as she saw a woman lying on the floor behind the bar with a blanket covering her. Sydona bent down and whispered to her.

"Hey. Hey, are you okay?"

The yellow haired woman didn't move a muscle. Was she dead? Sydona's adrenaline pumped harder. She popped her head up over the bar to see if Jet had come back out yet. He was still investigating. Letting out a sigh, she crouched back down and built up the courage to reveal the potential dead body. The gun still in one hand, she peeled back the plaid blanket. She gulped and prayed the woman wasn't dead; maybe she was just asleep or unconscious. But if that was the case, the person who did it to her might still be in the building.

As she revealed more of the woman's body, her skin shimmered from the lamp in a strange, plastic way. Sydona narrowed her eyes. She whipped off the rest of the blanket and noticed a note taped to her skin.

No more death

Sydona's hands trembled as she detached the note. It was a mannequin; it was her. The note was from the doctor. It had to be. He was alive. He was looking for her.

"Fuck, fuck, fuck, fuck, holy fucking shit..." she breathed heavily. Her head spun. Spots formed in the corners of her vision. Even her stomach ached with nausea.

Raoul climbed out of her tote and inspected it for himself. Sydona crumpled the note so quickly she gave herself a papercut. Her jaw tightened, and she buried it deep in her pocket. No one could see this. At least not yet.

"Is that a mannequin?" Raoul chuckled.

"Yeah..." Sydona replied and cleared her throat.

Jet then joined them behind the bar and saw the doll.

"What the fuck is that?"

"I think it's a trap," Sydona said bluntly.

"What was the trap?" Jet asked.

Sydona cocked her head, asking herself the same question. "I'm not sure yet..."

"Trap?" Raoul asked. He flew over to the doll and stood on her stomach. "I think it's just kids messing around. Playing make believe."

"We got a report of the NFA bringing fliers here though..."

Jet examined the mannequin a bit more and scoffed. "She doesn't even look real."

He situated himself to look around the bar, and possibly under the doll for more clues. As he grabbed the doll's shoulders, Sydona noticed the slight glimmer of an almost invisible string wrapped around her slender neck. Her gut instantly warned her that something was wrong. Even though Theodore saw people going in and out, no one occupied the space but the doll with a note attached. The warning he gave her just before they went inside came back to her, and her heart sank.

"No, wait!" she shouted as Jet pulled the doll up into a sitting position.

The string triggered a sound similar to a match being struck. A small flame appeared on the bottom shelf in the back of the bar counter. Sydona's hairs stood straight up. Within seconds of the flame being ignited, the flame dropped down into something and instantly caught fire. Glass exploded from beneath.

Sydona screamed, and they all jumped out from behind the bar. The mannequin's hair quickly caught fire and escalated the flames by a hundred as if it was made of something other than plastic. Then, she noticed another string along the wall, but just as she realized it was another fuse, it burst into flame.

"What the heck is *that*?" Raoul panicked and flew around the room in a tizzy.

Sydona couldn't believe how scared she was. Her mind went in a thousand different directions on what was going on, what it was, what the next move was. Then, it hit her.

"Dynamite."

In mere seconds, she grabbed Jet's arm and pushed him into the storage room. The door would provide little to no protection against the impending explosion, but it was better than nothing.

Just as she slammed and bolted the door, a large explosion went off. Debris fell on top of them, and the walls vibrated. Sydona's ears rang, and she couldn't hear a single thing for a solid minute. Though she wanted to sit back and wait to hear if anything else was going to happen, she knew if they stayed in there much longer they would be trapped. Sydona pushed boxes and broken bottles off her and slowly opened the door.

A huge wave of dust and smoke burst through the crack, causing Sydona to cough and slam it shut.

"Syd! Syd can you hear me? What's going on down there?" Willow shouted through the walkie.

Sydona heard but couldn't answer with smoke invading her lungs.

"We're fucked," Jet said from the back of the room.

"Did you find any exits?" Sydona asked, even though it burned her throat.

He only let out several coughs while shaking his head. Smoke leaked under the door and got worse with every passing second.

Sydona couldn't stand the sitting and waiting. She looked around the room and found a pile of bar towels in the very back. Grabbing several of them, she gave a couple to Jet to cover his mouth and nose. Raoul climbed back into her bag, coughing like crazy. He dug his way to the bottom of her bag and wrapped his body up in a rag. The stench of moldy stale rags made her want to gag, but it was the only option they had. Sydona stood up and had one of the rags wrapped around the door handle to soften the burn. Her heart and stomach did flips as she quickly worked up the courage to open it.

But as she twisted the knob, the door shattered open and almost crushed them in the process. Once she waved the smoke away, Willow's face and body appeared from the smoke-filled room, and the giant woman grabbed her and Jet. They stuck low to the ground as Willow led them both outside. Sydona's lungs craved oxygen, and she gasped desperately as she lay on the hard concrete.

Lacey ran over to them. "Are you guys okay? What happened in there?"

Sydona coughed and grabbed Raoul out of his bag to breathe the fresh air. He fluttered and cleared his throat of smoke.

Willow yelled at a whisper and tried to block him from onlookers. "What are ya doin'?! He can't be seen out here!"

Sydona stuck up her middle finger and coughed one last time. "I'm not letting my best friend die because people can't handle seeing a fairy."

But as she spoke, she glanced around the area. At least fifty people gathered around them with shocked faces. They needed to leave. But Sydona had almost no energy left.

Lacey shouted at the crowd. "Alright! Everyone move out! Nothing to see here!" From the corner of her eye, Sydona saw Lacey take Jet in her arms, brush back his hair and wipe his face off with a wet thumb. He flashed her a small grin, and she kissed him on his charred cheek.

Sydona turned back to Raoul. "You okay, buddy?"

He cleared his throat and nodded his head. "We probably should go."

"Agreed."

Raoul slowly went back into her bag, and Sydona stood back up as her lungs regained their normal capacity.

As the crowd dispersed, the Sparrows made their way back to the car but not before Sydona spotted Theodore in the crowd. He was the one who told them about the speakeasy. He may know something.

"I'll catch up with you guys. Take Raoul," she said and handed Jet the bag.

Sydona made her way across the street as Theodore walked back to the underpass.

"Theo, wait up."

He turned and greeted her with a worried look. "Are you alright?"

"Yeah, I'm fine," she said and looked back at the building that had a stack of smoke coming out of the main entrance. She needed to make it quick before the fire department arrived. "Did you see those people only bring in one flier?"

"Oh, uh, no. I saw more," he said with shifty eyes.

Sydona narrowed hers. "How many, Theo?"

"I don't know," he looked at the ground and gave his neck a good scratching. "I don't have the best memory. You remember."

Her chest tightened. "No, I'm afraid I don't. You remembered me after all this time… You saw these guys only a few days ago."

Theodore stood still, thinking of something to say. "I didn't think they'd send you, Syd…"

Sydona sighed heavily. She grabbed his arm with force and pushed him in the direction of the car.

"Come on."

He was less fussy than Sydona thought he'd be, but it was still painful for her to turn in a trusted friend.

"Where you taking me?" he asked softly as they walked down the sidewalk and past the footprints. Her heart sunk as she took one last glance at them.

"Taking you to Knox."

Chapter Eight

A flier working for the NFA. Now she's seen everything. Why would he do that to his own people? She lived with him for five years of her life, and it was so unlike him. At least, from what she remembered. But seeing him now, in his condition, it looked like things had changed. It pained her to see her friend do this to her. Though she had all sorts of questions, she would leave it up to Knox. She hoped he wouldn't go rough on Theodore, but the hope waned with each passing minute.

After only an hour, they arrived at the Sparrows headquarters. Sydona was a little nervous to show Theodore to Knox; he might go ballistic on him like he did to her. He might be a rat, but he was still a good guy. He didn't even struggle on the way there.

He didn't struggle.

Why was it so easy to get him there? Maybe it was part of the plan, too. Sydona's heart beat faster with each step toward the warehouse.

She secured both his hands behind his back and gripped them tightly.

"Why, Theo? Why did you do this?"

"Syd… don't make me say it," he begged.

"Say what?"

He paused and hung his head even lower, revealing dirty skin on the back of his neck. She sighed; he was holding back.

"He's not going to go easy on you. Not like I would--I am."

His head didn't move from its tilted position. Her gut told her something was wrong, but she didn't know exactly what.

They slumped through the massive warehouse, and each step echoed off the walls and vaulted metal ceiling. Sydona led him over to the office and rapped on the door. She took a deep breath before the door swung open.

Avani greeted them first. "You're back fast."

"Yup. We sure are. ...This is Theodore. He has some information for us."

Avani looked him up and down with a sour face, then grabbed his cheeks. "You're a flier?"

He nodded his head and spoke through his smushed lips. "Yes, ma'am."

"Why you here?" She directed her question to Sydona for an answer.

"That's what we're here to find out."

She took a step back. "You armed?"

"No, ma'am."

Avani's eyes darted to Sydona. "You checked 'im?"

Sydona froze. She didn't. It never even crossed her mind. His baggy clothes could hide anything under them. If he had been anyone else in the entire world, she would've checked. Not Theodore. Not her second to oldest companion.

She answered with an unwavering expression. "Yes, I checked him."

Theodore glanced quickly at her, and she returned his look. She hoped she wouldn't regret her words.

"Alright," Avani said after giving him one more look over. "Sit over there."

An ear-curdling screech came from a metal chair Knox pulled over to the middle of the room. Theodore slumped over to sit in the chair with hands in his lap.

"Did you pull him out of a sewer or what?" Avani whispered to Sydona from the corner of her lips. Sydona kept her focus on Theodore while Avani went over to her desk to sanitize her hands. Sydona shook her head at the comment, but she had a point. Her attention switched to the whereabouts of Devon. Tapping Avani's shoulder, she quietly asked where he was.

"Devon's in that room over there, practicing some martial arts moves Knox taught him."

Sydona raised her brows. "Oh. How come?"

Avani shifted her weight while sitting on the edge of her desk. "When he came in, he started drawing in that little notebook of his. I asked what his picture was… he hid it from me. After a while I was able to peek, and it was some dark stuff in that book. I asked if he wanted to talk about it; he said no of course. I'm still unsure what's really going on with him, but I asked Elias to teach him some moves. Ya know, to keep him from drawing. I saw the pictures, Sydona. What the heck happened to that little boy?"

Sydona's heart ached. "He uh... witnessed his parents being killed in front of him."

"Dios mio!" Avani shrieked. "I had the worst feeling… poor boy. I'm certified in PTSD, and he is a classic case. I just hope with everything going on, he'll get help. I'll do what I can, but he'll need constant attention. No telling what could set him off."

"Thanks for looking after him, Avani. I'll be sure to keep an eye on him."

Their attention turned to the men in the center of the room. Knox stared at Theodore like it was going to burn a hole in him until he finally looked straight up at him. Knox took a deep breath, making his chest appear larger. Their eyes met.

"Why?" Knox asked, barely blinking.

Theodore's eyes flooded and looked away from him.

"Look at me when I'm speaking to you!" Knox roared and pushed his chest closer.

"I didn't mean to do it!" he cried out with a cowardly shiver. "I--I..."

"Speak up! Why would you do this to your people?!"

Sydona crossed her arms and stood sideways in case she needed to look away. Her instincts wanted to protect her old friend, but after the past encounter with Knox, she dared not interfere. With each word Knox shouted, her skin jumped along with her heart. Anything could happen now.

Theodore shook his head back and forth. Back and forth. Back and forth. And then, he smacked himself in the head several times so hard Sydona heard it clearly from her position. Knox's face altered at his behavior, and he stepped back with unsure eyes.

"No, no, no, no, no. No. No. NO. NO. NO! NO! NO!" Theodore chanted, getting louder and louder.

He then stood up quickly, reached into the inside of his jacket and pulled out a small handgun. As he pointed it at Knox, who slowly put his hands up in surrender, Sydona pulled out her tranquilizer gun. Glancing to her right, she saw Avani also had a gun pulled out, and her arms were buckled straight out toward Theodore.

Knox spoke in a calm manner. "Hold up now, uh…"

"Theo," he answered.

Knox treaded carefully. "We're not going to hurt you, Theo. Just ask a few questions."

Theodore's eyes shifted over to Sydona and Avani bearing arms at his head. Knox followed his gaze and spoke up. "Lower your guns, soldiers!"

"But, Elias!" Avani said.

"I said put them down!" Knox hollered.

Sydona and Avani exchanged a look and lowered their guns. They both kept their hands on them in preparation.

"See, it's all good, Theo," Knox whispered and outstretched one arm to try to grab the gun. "Now give me your gun."

Theodore laughed, exposing his hideous teeth and showing his crazy. What in the world happened to him?

"This gun isn't for you," he said evenly. He then redirected the barrel to his temple.

Sydona's heart dropped. Her gun went back into its holster, and she stepped toward him.

"Theo…" she said.

He turned his attention to Sydona with tears cleaning the dirt from his face. "I couldn't do it. I couldn't do that to my best friend. And I can't go back there…" He paused and squeezed his eyes tightly. "I missed you so much. Why didn't you come back? Why didn't you come back?"

Her lips trembled. She wasn't sure if his questions were rhetorical, and she struggled to find the right words to answer them. "I--I don't know. I'm sorry--"

"I'm sorry too. Forgive me."

His face relaxed to a blank stare.

There was a click and boom.

Theodore fell to the floor, his skull hit the pavement with a crack and screams shattered the room. Then, everything fell silent, aside from gasps and heavy breathing.

Sydona collapsed to her knees as her body turned to water. It felt like a deluge bursting through a dam, rendering her useless. Knox and Avani rushed over to the lifeless body while Sydona watched it all as if it were a television show. It wasn't real. Willow and the others came running in from behind her in slow motion. Raoul buzzed around her saying words, but she was unable to hear him. She knew Knox was yelling and asking what his last words meant.

Willow stormed over to Sydona and picked her up to give her a tight hug. She snapped out of her trance and came back to reality.

"You don't haveta say anything, Syd. Willow's gotcha..."

Her boa constrictor hug felt warm and tight, and she let herself melt into it. Sydona wrapped her arms around Willow and allowed her emotions to run wild. Willow moaned with each sob Sydona cried out. Her mother's face kept popping up in her head. She imagined Willow as her mother and squeezed tight. All the jealousy and anger the two women had for each other was squashed instantly.

Raoul flew over and buried himself in the hug. "I'm so sorry, Syd. I know how much he meant to you."

Sydona sniffed and pulled away to compose herself.

"You lied! You didn't check him. How could you be so ignorant?" Knox raged.

Her fingers curled into fists, turning her knuckles white.

"I didn't think I needed to," she said.

"Are you kidding me? He could have killed us all! Not to mention he was wearing a wire!"

Sydona paused and released her fists. "What?"

Knox continued his rampage as he paced the room, hitting things in his way. "What did you say to him?"

Sydona went from sadness to matching his rage. "I didn't say anything!"

"I don't believe you! He was your friend, yes? You said something to him..." Knox's eyes turned a fiery emerald.

"That's personal! And I did what I could under the circumstances."

"Under the circumstances? You put us all at risk for an old boyfriend? I don't fucking think so, Sydona. You're lucky I don't execute you for your extreme lack of perception. I put you in charge for a--should have been--simple mission, and this is what happens when I do?" He paused. "Leave. Now. Before I act on my thoughts."

Instinctively, Sydona yearned for Avani's words to calm her husband down. But she silently stood by with a heavy head, staring at the floor. Her friends had backed off slightly, and she never felt so alone. She messed up. Big time. But now may be the only time to make things right.

Her fingers found the crumpled paper in her pocket. Her pounding heart went back and forth on whether she should give it to him. She waited for him to calm down more before bringing it back up. He was already heading back to his desk when Sydona spoke again.

"I found something," she said somberly.

Knox turned back around with raised eyebrows. "I thought I told you to leave."

"Please. I just lost someone I really cared about. Can you just please look at the damn note?"

His brows raised even higher without moving any other muscles.

She held her arm out, waiting for him to take the note, but he didn't move.

"Dios mio. Give it here," Avani said as she clicked her heels over. She snatched the note out of her hand and whispered. "You better watch it, girl…"

Sydona silently thanked her with a little smile.

Avani's violet eyes widened with shock. "Elias… look."

He made his way over reluctantly. But as much as Sydona feared him, Knox feared his tiny wife even more.

"No. It can't be…" Knox uttered with a long face.

This was it. Her secret was out. They would know Malik wrote it and was after her. She really wanted to be the one to tell Raoul. She didn't want him to find out this way. Maybe she could tell him back at home, after feeding him the best fruit cake she ever made. With his belly so full, he couldn't fly away. But this was real and happening. She braced herself for whatever came next.

"Natalia…" Avani said and squished the note in her hand.

Sydona swore her heart stopped for a full minute.

"Who?"

"She's my sister."

Raoul flew over. "So she's a flier, too?"

"It's uh, difficult to explain," Avani said.

Why did the name Natalia sound familiar? She thought back to when they visited her house the other day. One of the fairies mentioned her being at the house when they burned it. Could it be the same woman? Sydona was certain it was Malik. But as long as they were still in the dark and blaming other people, she was in the clear. Still, a small part of her felt Raoul would find out at any time. She had to start formulating a plan to find him and finish what she started. Maybe this Natalia person could help, especially because she was somehow related to Avani.

"What are we going to do?" Sydona asked.

"I don't know…" Knox sighed heavily and dropped his head. "She's a little crazy, but Avani doesn't want to hurt her. All I want to do is wrap my hands around her fucking neck." A vein popped up in his thick neck.

"Excuse you, darling. She's still my sister. No matter how much you despise her," Avani said and stared him down.

"Honey, she could've killed more of our people."

"I understand that. But *chu* let *me* deal with her."

Knox sighed and walked away. It was clearly a sore subject.

"What do you think she'll do?" Sydona asked. Her heart had slowed. Maybe it really wasn't Malik. Avani cleared it up quickly and didn't seem to have a doubt in her mind that it was her sister. Malik could really be gone. It was one brick lifted off her shoulders.

Avani shrugged. "Who knows? But we need to be careful. If the Vultures are sending out fliers as spies, we gonna have a hard time knowing who to trust anymore."

She took the words right out of her mouth.

Avani couldn't be more on the dot about her own doubts. It broke Sydona's heart to know her old friend could do this to her. His suicide meant something more than being selfish, though. He apologized to her. Could his death have saved her? How would she have any way of knowing? She couldn't stop picturing the last look in his eyes before he squeezed the trigger, a look of desperation and guilt. He didn't want to hurt anyone. Especially Sydona. At least the mission was over, and it was time to head back home.

Devon wanted to stay with the group, and none of them saw a problem with everyone going back to their little house. Silas had gotten a bunch of food the day before, and they could enjoy a nice dinner. They piled out of the car like clowns, and her feet hit familiar soil.

She heard Giovonna yell out, "They're back!"

The voice gave her butterflies, and she embraced Giovonna with a tight hug.

"How'd it go? Did you put their asses in their place? Did you get your tattoo done? I wanna see! Where did you go? Was it nice there?"

Her head spun with questions coming at her like slaps of wind. "It was alright."

"That's it? That's all I get? Come on, Syd! I've been helping you train for months! Give me somethin'!"

"Gia, sweetie..." Willow spoke up. Her head whipped around. "We'll talk about it later."

"But!"

"Gia." Willow shook her head and extended her arm. "Come on. Let's get somethin' to eat for everyone."

Giovonna looked back at Sydona who didn't return her glance. She quickly got the hint and joined Willow inside.

A messy black haired, clean shaven man walked out onto the porch, and her heart fluttered. Silas leaned against a support beam and took a bite out of a green apple. As Lacey, Jet and Devon entered the house, he happily greeted them. Raoul flew up to him and gave him the cutest high-five. As Sydona approached with her baggage, Silas continued to look off in the distance, crunching his apple. Her throat tightened. The sound of the slamming bathroom door back at the hotel rang in her ears. She almost felt lucky she didn't have to see his face when she said it.

"Hey," she said, walking up the stairs.

Silas flicked his chin up. "Sup."

"How's it been here?"

He shrugged.

Her stomach knotted itself more. The next words spilled out. "I missed you."

Silas chuckled and took another bite. "Right."

"I did."

"It's okay. You don't have to lie to make me feel better, Syd."

Sydona furrowed her brow. "But I did…"

"Just stop."

Her heart pounded harder but for much different reasons.

"Look… I'm sorry for what happened back at the hotel."

"Are you?" he asked accusingly, chewed another bite and threw his apple off into the wilderness.

"Yes."

"Why do I feel you're only apologizing to me now because you missed me? Instead of when it happened?"

Sydona scoffed. "Because I was clearly upset, Silas…"

"Clearly."

Her lips and fists tightened. "Hey, I am still trying to get used to the fact that I am around other people twenty-four seven and *never* have a minute to myself anymore. Do you have any idea what that's like?"

"I do! Believe it or not. I'm usually the person around you twenty-four seven. But it's becoming pretty clear to me that you'd be better off without me." He straightened back up and started heading back inside.

"No, stop! I'm not done talking to you." Sydona grabbed his arm. He grudgingly turned back around.

"I--" She cleared her throat, trying to sort out the words in her head. "I am sorry about the way I've been acting. I just, I've had a lot on my mind. And I'm sorry that you get the brunt of so much of it." Her emotions felt like they were breaching a dam and about to burst open. "Ever since Eagle Lake, and the death of my mother and my father not being around anymore, I just… I joined the Sparrows to take my mind off all the bad shit that's been going on, to focus my attention on something other than the nightmares of my mother dying in my arms. Picturing the light leaving her eyes over and over again in my head... "

The dam broke. She wasn't sure when it happened, but she sat on Silas's lap sobbing. But she wasn't done, not yet. She took a deep breath to ready her lips for more confessions.

"I found Theodore… I found my best friend from Chicago and had to witness him shooting himself in the head." She let out ear piercing cries, well aware of what she sounded and looked like, but there was no closing the dam until she got every last drop out.

"And you… You've been there for me, for everything. I'm so incredibly grateful, and I'm sorry if I don't show it. But Silas, I need you to know, I really like you."

All she could see was blurriness from the tears, but she felt the stroke of his fingers brushing her hair back behind her ear. She spent the next several moments slowing down her breath and composing herself.

"About time you tell me what's going on in that head of yours…" he whispered.

She let out a laugh.

"I'm sorry about your friend."

"Yeah, me too…" she wiped her nose.

"Probably not the best time to ask how the mission went then, huh?" he asked as she sat up and straightened her clothes out.

"I think it goes without saying that it didn't go well." She chuckled, trying to bring her spirits back up.

"Let's get some food, yeah?" Silas suggested as they stood up to go back inside. "Oh, actually. Before I forget, you got a letter from your pops." He pulled out an envelope from his back pocket.

She gasped and could feel her face warming up. As she read the letter, she hung onto every word her father carefully wrote.

Dearest Sydona,

How are you, my daughter? I hope you're well and helping others like you wanted. I hear you were joining the Sparrows. I'm so very proud of you for doing something bigger than yourself. You have to let me know how your first mission goes. The island is beautiful. More coconuts and pineapples than I could ever dream of. Raoul would love it here! I've met a lot of interesting people, many of them my age. Sometimes I feel like a kid again, connecting with others who were also at the camp. Knowing I won't ever have to go back keeps my heart at bay. I only wish your mother could see me now. See this place. Oh, how I miss her and you. I do hope you'll come visit me soon. Show you the tan I've been working on.

Well, I'm sure you're busy training and saving the world. I won't bore you with my little things. I love you, baby girl. Tell everyone I said hello.

All my love, Dad
xoxo

Chapter Nine

The house felt warmer. It wasn't because Giovonna pulled back the curtains to let the sun in but because it was a full house. Lacey and Willow were in the kitchen cooking up something that smelled like garlic, rosemary and lemons. A sniff of meat snuck in, but it was still intoxicating. She presumed it was chicken. Giovonna and Devon were in her bedroom, and she was showing him all her robotics and gadgets. Sydona swore she even heard some laughing. Devon seemed to be opening up a little more, and she liked that. Jet planted himself on the couch with one leg stretched over the rest as he watched television. Silas must have finally gotten the antenna to work. The channels weren't crystal clear, but it was color and the sound wasn't bad. Jet probably flipped through every channel four times as there were only five to begin with.

Sydona saw a lot of herself in Jet. A loner. He spread himself out so no one would be tempted to sit by him. She wondered how he and Lacey worked out with how cold he had been lately. Silas sat down at the kitchen table with Raoul who was hard at work trying to peel an orange by himself.

"Why don't you just ask for help, man?" Silas asked with a smirk.

"I--don't need--help. I'm--just--fine," Raoul heaved. He had the orange wedged between the wooden wall and a heavy frying pan, and he used both hands to peel off a strip.

"This is embarrassing for you."

"Just let him be. He'll bite if you help. Trust me," Sydona said with raised eyebrows.

Lacey and Willow joined in making fun of Raoul. His face glowed red with embarrassment and pure pain from the simple task.

"Hey, you guys got a radio? I'm in the mood to dance," Lacey said while shaking her hips.

Everyone looked to Silas. "No, actually. But I can make some music up!" He tapped on the wooden table, making a mild tempered beat. Then, he threw in some sounds with his mouth.

"I want real music, Silas," she teased.

He stopped tapping. "Sorry. Didn't find any today."

"Oh no. You guys don't know Lacey," Jet said, entering the kitchen and opening every cabinet door. "She will dance with or without music. There's no stopping her."

"Whatcha lookin' for, baby doll?" Lacey asked. She danced on him as he searched for something.

"Cups and ice, suga' momma." He grinned.

"What is happenin' right now, y'all?" Willow stopped her cooking to be a witness to the heated footwork going on next to her.

"Come on, Willow. You wanna dance?" Lacey shifted her attention to Willow. She turned her back against her and grinded.

Willow just laughed and walked away to let Lacey and Jet have their fun in the kitchen. Sydona had no doubt in her mind they had been drinking. With such an emotional day, she couldn't blame them for wanting to let loose a little.

The thought crossed her mind a few times.

Alcohol had a place in her life once upon a time. She gave it up once she found a steady place to sleep every night. She would be the first to admit that when she was homeless for several years, she had a problem with it. No parents, no home, nothing to lose. She often took bottles from stores and passed out. They tasted good and made her forget her problems. It was hard to resist. Her poison of choice was whiskey. At first it burned, but after the first dozen gulps, it got smoother and worked quickly.

It had been a long time since she thought back to those days. Even Raoul drank with her. Of course, at his size, it took only a sip of her drink, and he was flying high. She remembered once, when she accidentally grabbed rum instead of whiskey, they pretended to be pirates. Raoul acted like a parrot on her shoulder. She laughed at the memory.

"What's so funny?" Silas asked with a concerned look.

She blushed for a second, then took a leap. "You didn't happen to find any liquor or beer out there, did you?"

His lips instantly grew to a wide smile. "Be right back." He scooted his chair out and swiped his hand across her back as he went to their bedroom.

Jet and Lacey's dancing became even more intricate. Lacey started singing a song Sydona had never heard of. Giovonna heard and joined them with Devon by her side.

"Is this what adults do when they tell kids to go play?" she asked with a giggle.

Lacey refocused her drunken attention to Giovonna and sang louder. Giovonna couldn't help but to sing along with her. The lyrics spoke to Sydona. They started over in unison, singing a song that seemed to change tempo with every few verses. Silas mentioned said it was called 'Bohemian Rhapsody'. The name was as unique as the song itself.

Sydona took a seat and listened to the words falling from their lips as if they memorized it long ago. Jet wasn't singing, but he was making the beat with his mouth, helping Sydona piece together the whole thing.

Silas soon joined her with two bottles of wine and glasses he pulled from the cabinets.

"Is this kind okay?" he asked sweetly. Sydona didn't care what kind.

"This is perfect." She grinned.

He poured her an entire cupful, and she took the first sip of the fermented grape concoction. She could feel her face scrunch up from the bitter taste, and she coughed.

"Is it good?" Raoul asked as he finished eating his orange.

Sydona laughed. The taste was much different than she expected. She wasn't an expert on wine, but she assumed since fruit was in it, it would be a little sweeter. Willow entered the kitchen again and finished cooking dinner. She was by herself now but didn't seem to mind. Everyone else migrated to the living. After finishing her cup of wine, Sydona joined the dancers in the living room. She narrowed in on Devon who sat on the couch, watching the adults drunkenly dance around him. Her hand outstretched toward him as her hips swayed in place. He grinned a smile with a missing tooth and jumped on the couch. She took both his hands and moved her feet in front of the couch while Devon jump-danced on the cushions. Sydona spun him around, and he let out a loud laugh.

The simple sound of a troubled child's laughter sent goosebumps all over her skin. The rest of the group turned their attention to Devon too, and soon he took turns dancing with everyone a little bit. Raoul flew around the group, sprinkling his dust over everyone and making them feel light as air. He then gave a little more to Devon, allowing his toes to actually leave the couch. He squealed with joy as he floated in the air in the middle of everyone. His hands were never let go of, otherwise he would have floated to the ceiling.

Lacey and Giovonna started singing something a bit faster and upbeat. Devon's giggles echoed through the house, each time getting a bit higher pitched. It was infectious. His happiness rubbed off on everyone.

She stood back to let everyone else have a turn with him and took a break. Her breaths were quick and heavy, but the wine had taken the edge off. A laugh from Silas caught her ear, and she whipped her head to him. She bit her lip, seeing him play with Devon. He never looked sexier to her. Once Devon switched partners, Sydona slyly grabbed Silas's arm and led him back to the hallway of the small house. He went without protest.

She couldn't stop smiling. Her warmed hands wrapped around both of his biceps as she stared longingly into his eyes. Without any control over her actions, she kissed him with so much passion it surprised even her. Silas only took seconds to understand what was happening, but when he did, his fingers quickly wove into her blonde hair, and he pressed her in closer. Her heart fluttered. She felt her hands shake and perspire. His hands touched her lower back, and he tugged her even closer. Everything happened so hastily, so she slowed down to remember the moment.

The first time she kissed Silas.

She had no idea how long she had been waiting to do it. It felt right. His lips on hers. His hands exploring her curves. His lips were so sultry, she couldn't stop touching them. Only her own lips could appreciate such a feeling. And at the same time, the kiss was forceful. They knew what to do, how to move perfectly. She held a feeling of pure vulnerability with Silas, yet he matched her raw, powerful passion. Her entire body curled with goosebumps.

Then, to her disappointment, cackles and whistling flooded her ears. For a moment, she had forgotten where she was. Their kiss was cut short, and their hands returned to their pockets. Willow stood at the front of the bunch, laughed the loudest and walked over to them.

"I wondered when this would happen…" She sucked them into a weird three-way hug.

Sydona couldn't help but let out a chuckle. Willow let go, headed back to the kitchen and yelled out that dinner was ready. The yelling seemed unnecessary since the entire house was only eight-hundred square feet. Everyone gathered around to eat dinner, but only four people could fit at the table. Jet, Lacey and Devon ate their food in the living room and turned on the television.

"'Bout time you guys made out," Giovonna said after taking a bite of carrots and potatoes.

Sydona couldn't respond. With a combination of wine and pure affection for the man sitting next to her, she had nothing to say. Her mind and body felt full of bliss.

"What'd your dad have to say?" Silas asked with a smile he was unable to shake.

"Oh, you know..." Sydona swallowed. "Everything's good. He's proud I joined the Sparrows, things like that. Oh, and that he's also getting a pretty good tan."

"Ian with a tan? No… I can't picture it!" Raoul said.

"Yeah, I guess he's really enjoying it. I'm just glad he's happy there. He made a good choice. Just hope someday I can go visit him."

The table mutually nodded and didn't respond. Sydona felt bad for bringing up the constant reminder of her handicap.

"This wine is really great, by the way. We need to get more," she said, breaking the tension and holding up her glass to toast with.

"What are we cheers-in' for?" Willow asked with a full mouth and held up her cup to clink.

Sydona took a deep breath, remembering all the good that had happened in her life. Too many traumatic things had been happening, and it was hard to focus on the good.

"To… a completed mission… amazing friends… new friends…" she turned to look at Lacey, Jet and Devon. "And people who can really surprise you. In a good way." She then turned to Silas and grinned. He took her position as an invitation and kissed her again.

Everyone then clicked their glasses together in laughter. As the group quieted down and ate silently, the television did something very bizarre.

The football game changed over to a podium with an American flag hanging proudly behind it. A line of words scrolled along the bottom, saying something about the National Fliers Association. Then, a man walked up to the podium. Sydona dropped her wine glass and heard it shatter on the ground.

"Hello. My name is Dr. John Malik. For those of you who don't know me, I am the lead scientist of the National Fliers Association. You may be aware of some of the projects we are doing around the country and perhaps of a recently disassembled facility in Oregon. The horrific tragedy we suffered because of the resistance group who call themselves the 'Sparrows' has hindered our studies greatly. This is a dangerous group; please inform yourselves of their doings. A symbol they like to use is this wing with a circle. If you see this anywhere in your area or see anyone wearing it, please call the authorities. They are very desperate to stop what we are doing. But more importantly, I urge you to memorize the name and face of the person I am about to show you…"

He held up a picture of Sydona's face, and her heart sank into her stomach.

"…This is Sydona Wilder. She is the leader of the Sparrows. She was the one who infiltrated our organization and killed several people. She and her group are terrorists and must be stopped immediately. There's no telling how far they will go and how many will have to die by their greedy hands.

"The NFA--no. I will offer a three-million-dollar reward to anyone who turns her into me. Keep in mind, she needs to be alive and well. If you find her, contact the authorities immediately, and you will be compensated for your loyal efforts. Thank you and God Bless America."

He stepped off the screen, it turned black and then went back to the football game.

Malik was alive.

Every single person in the house turned their heads toward her with the most gut-wrenching faces. The heart in her chest beat so hard she swore she would have a heart attack at any second. She tried to mentally prepare herself for the yelling, the backlash, the violence that was about to occur. But the silence pierced her harder than yelling. She wanted to run and hide so badly. Her entire body shook with intense emotions, and she couldn't figure out which one she should act on. Every pair of eyes felt as if they were burning her, and she couldn't look at any of them. The alcohol went straight to her head and mixed with the news. She couldn't help it. Vomit made its way through her esophagus and onto the kitchen floor.

Their silence felt deafening. Silas grabbed a towel and a glass of water for her. It was strangely calm, and she glanced around the room, noticing all the different expressions. Disappointment was the overall theme. Sydona almost wanted someone to yell because she deserved it.

Jet whipped the front door open but not before he glared at Sydona so hard she felt it across the room. Lacey followed behind him, shaking her head. Sydona flopped down on the hard kitchen chair and held her head as it started to pound. She covered the vomit with the towel and continued to stare at the ground, purposely avoiding eye contact.

The first person to speak was Giovonna, leaning against a wall on the other side of the kitchen.

"Why didn't you just tell us, Syd?"

Sydona shook her head. "I don't know. I didn't want to upset anyone. Make anyone worry." Her eyes drifted around the room as she searched for Raoul.

"Where did Raoul go?"

Silas helped look too. "I think he flew off. I saw his face. He looked like a ghost."

"I need to find him," she said as she took a step toward the door, but Silas put his arm out to stop her.

"Just let him be."

Sydona took a deep breath, still processing the news. Devon joined Jet and Lacey outside, while Willow turned the television off in case he made another announcement. Giovonna and Silas sat with her in the kitchen in silence. The quiet was killing her, but just having them nearby was comforting. She only wished Raoul was still there. Where would he have gone?

Jet came back inside and darted to the kitchen to refill his flask. Her eyes narrowed. She had no clue there was more alcohol in the cabin, and she suddenly felt the need for more.

"Where'd you get that?"

Jet turned toward her. "None of your business."

"Can I have some?"

"Hell no."

"Please, Jet..." She said with a sad voice, hoping that he would at least feel sorry for her.

He sighed heavily and licked his lips. "Only a little. I don't have much left."

"Can't make any promises." She snatched the bottle from his grip and chugged.

"Syd," Silas said from across the table.

Jet yelled, but she turned her body away from him, making the bottle out of reach.

Her eyes closed tight as she held the bottle up at a forty-five-degree angle and stuck her pointer finger out at him. She was parched. She swore the bottle was filled with water, water that quickly filled her insides with numbness. Releasing her lips from the bottle, she gasped for breath and made an audible "Ahh."

Jet shot her a dirty look and grabbed the bottle back.

"Don't worry. I'll get you more."

"Yeah, you will." Jet scowled and stormed back outside.

Giovonna seemed to have already left the table, probably while she was numbing her insides. Giovonna never witnessed this side of her, and Sydona didn't like imaging what she thought of her in that moment. She then flipped her neck over to Silas who had already started his way to the bedroom. Either he walked so fast past her she could barely grab his shirt, or the alcohol was hard at work already.

"Hey, hey, where ya goin'?" she asked with a slur. Words stumbled over her lips.

"Stop it." Silas paused but not because she tried to grab him.

"What?" Sydona whined, edging closer to him. Her hands began to wander around his torso.

"I know what you're doing. And I want no part of it."

Sydona paused and straightened up. "What am I doing?"

"Stop acting dumb. This isn't you," he said with a tense posture.

"How do you know… this isn't me? You barely know me, man. *Hick.*" The hiccups started. Her eyelids struggled to stay open.

Silas laughed sarcastically and started walking away again.

"Wait!" Sydona stammered. "Wait. I'm sorry… Silas…"

He sighed heavily.

"I'm sorry…"

And as if gravity was getting her back for a terrible deed, her entire body sagged to the floor. Her legs turned to mush, but her head must have still been solid as it was the last thing she heard as it slammed to the wooden floor. In the darkness, all she could feel was a throbbing headache. Something inside wanted out and didn't care how.

In what only felt like a minute, her eyes opened suddenly. The ceiling fan from her bedroom stared back at her. Just when she didn't think her head could hurt anymore, her eyes adjusted clearly, and she knew where she was.

"Ah, shit."

Chapter Ten

Morning came. How could so many hours pass without her even realizing it? She used to drink three times as much and be fine. Times had definitely changed.

Slowly, she turned her head to the side to look for Silas. He was no longer by her side. Events of the previous night rushed back, and she felt so embarrassed. Groveling like an imbecile, stumbling over her feet and words. No wonder he didn't stick around. Why should he? He's not responsible for her. But where was Raoul? Where was her best friend? He was the only one that could understand what she was going through. She lied to him though. To his face. For months. Why should anyone want to be around her? She would only cause them pain.

She sat up and touched her head. It was wrapped in a bandage. She felt around the throbbing area on the back side of her head, and a large bump made itself known. She winced and removed her fingers. They shook slightly, and she wrapped her other hand around them. Her lips and tongue cried out for hydration as if she was left out in the desert for a week. Her feet soon found their way to the wooden floor and stumbled across the hallway to the bathroom.

The light flicked on, and her eyes quickly shut. Using outstretched arms and wary feet, she felt her way to the sink and turned it on. She could use a glass from the kitchen, but it was much too far away. Cupping her hands, she slurped down at least ten handfuls of water. Then, she used the remaining droplets to wash her face and neck. Her hair kept getting in the way and became soaked. She arched her back and flipped part of it over one shoulder, and the mirror found her.

Normally, seeing herself in the mirror was no big deal. But one thing caught her attention other than her blue eyes: her hair. The mannequin at the speakeasy showed up in her mind as well as the photo the doctor showed everyone in the country. She had to do it. She had to cut it off. Change her identity. But the giant bandage on her head hindered such an act. The new do had to wait.

Where was everyone? Judging by the shadows outside and the angle of the sun shining in, it must have been about ten in the morning. She thought of Raoul again. He didn't say a single word during the announcements, and her stomach shriveled to the size of a raisin.

"Raoul?" she called out at a moderate tone. Too loud and it would cause her head to pound again.

No response. The house was empty. Her first instinct was to go outside and see if everyone took a walk or went hunting. Sydona wandered onto the porch, then went down the stairs to the edge of the forest. Morning birds and squirrels chattered in the trees. The wind blew oak leaves and clacked branches from the elders of the woods. A gust blew past her, and she smiled. The cold air felt good on her hot face after being wounded and hungover.

She was alone.

There was no one in the entire house. It was empty. Her smile grew, and she ran as best she could back into the cabin. If no one wanted to be around her, perfect. For weeks, she dreamt of the day when she would not have to listen to Giovonna's random spouts of singing everything she was doing, Silas's snoring and barging in on her in the shower, and Raoul's sudden emotional teenager phase. It was just her all by her lonesome self in a big empty house.

She took a shower that felt more amazing than back at her real home. An hour easily whizzed by. When she exited the bathroom, she wholeheartedly expected everyone to be waiting for her. The living room, both bedrooms and kitchen were vacated. A part of her began to worry, while the other part of her wanted to take advantage of the rare opportunity. She went straight for the kitchen table, which had a bowl of fresh fruit. Her hand dove for a banana and began to peel. Fruit was mainly put out for Raoul to have easy access to. As she directed the fruit to her mouth, she heard a knock at the door.

Confused by why someone from their group would knock on the door of their own house, she put the fruit down. She made her way to the door and opened it to find Dr. Malik standing in the entryway.

Sydona gasped. His dark, sunken eyes narrowed from the evil smile growing on his face.

"Found you."

Her body seized up. She was unable to even move a finger, but she was able to talk.

"Where is everyone?!"

And as if he knew she would ask, he turned sideways to reveal all her friends lying dead in the front yard. It was then she noticed the blade in Malik's hand. He casually took a cloth from his pocket and began to wipe it off.

"Is this not what you wanted, my dear? To be alone?"

"But you killed them!"

"How does that saying go? Be careful what you wish for?" His smile widened, then he cackled loudly, forcing it to echo all around her.

The door slammed in her face, and everything went black.

She suddenly felt the option to move again, and she gasped and sat up. The ceiling fan appeared above her once again.

Silas sat next to her in the comfort of her own bed. Her heart leaped and tugged with several emotions.

"You're…"

"You passed out," he replied.

She grinned. His face was only inches from hers. He wasn't dead. "I'm so happy to see you."

Her arms wrapped around him and squeezed tight. Silas let out a happy sigh, then hugged her in return.

"More nightmares?" he asked and pulled away.

She shook her head, still not sure if this wasn't part of the dream. "I swore it was real. I was… completely alone."

"Sounds like a dream for you."

"It was… at first." Sydona shook her head more. "I'm so sorry. I should have told you."

He shrugged and scratched the back of his head. "Yeah, probably. But… nothing we can do about that now."

Her jaw tightened, and she nodded her head fiercely. "I'll make it right. I promise."

"I knew you would say that. But how about you sleep for a little while more, and I'll go hide all the alcohol," he said light-heartedly and touched his lips to the top of her head. The bandage was there, just like in her dreams. The small detail made her heart jump. Sleeping felt impossible. No, she had to get up and do something. She had to officially kill the doctor. But first, she had to make things right with her friends.

Silas left the bedroom, and she made her way to Giovonna's room and knocked softly. When there was no reply, she pressed her ear against the door and heard some tinkering with metal objects and silence, then more clinking. She knocked again, a little harder.

"Gia?"

The clattering stopped, and there was a pause. "Come in."

The door creaked open to reveal a simple twin bed, white dresser and Giovonna sitting cross-legged on her carpet with a tiny screwdriver and something else Sydona didn't know the name of. A clutter of parts, tools and computer pieces sat in front of her. It was the only messy part in the whole room. Everything else was perfectly in place.

"Feeling better?" Giovonna asked in monotone without looking up at her once. She continued doing whatever it was in front of her.

"Yeah."

Sydona bit her lip, unsure how to talk to her. It had never been this difficult to speak to her before. She hated that she disappointed her so much. Sydona needed her unwavering optimism right now.

Her feet led her to the hard bed in the corner of the room, and she messed with her fingernails. What could she say to make the whole situation better? An apology didn't seem to cut it. She owed her way more than that.

Words weren't coming to her thanks to the throbbing headache she felt from the dream. Maybe it was another sign she was still dreaming, especially since Giovonna seemed to have all the sunshine sucked out of her. The feeling was extremely surreal. Her fingers pinched her arm so hard she involuntarily made a noise. It was loud enough to make Giovonna turn her head.

"Did you just pinch yourself?" she asked as Sydona rubbed a red spot on her forearm.

"Maybe."

She scoffed. "Okay, weirdo."

"Thought I might be dreaming," she managed to utter.

Giovonna stopped her work and slightly nodded. "Yeah. Doesn't seem real, does it?"

"No."

She went back to tinkering. Sydona sat on the bed and glanced around the room a bit more. A mirror with a frilly frame hung over the bed, and she saw her reflection. Her blonde hair reminded her again of the dream, and she had to look away. Anger began to bubble up inside her.

"I just don't understand why you couldn't tell me," Giovonna spoke up in the silence, making Sydona ignore her problems and turn to her.

She scooted around, giving Sydona her full attention while still sitting Indian-style.

"Have I not proven to you that I'm trustworthy? After everything we've been through? Giving you contacts of my own design to better hide? Lying for you to my parents? Finding out how to disable the bracelets? I mean… it's been three months, and no one knew. Not even your best friend."

Giovonna's eyes began to well up, awakening similar feelings inside of Sydona as well.

"You're exactly right. You have proved it to me. But… that's not why I didn't tell you. I was trying to protect you. Part of me really did think he was gone, and I didn't want to worry you. And, Gia… you're more than a best friend to me… You're… my family. And… I protect my family."

She hoped her words about family would receive some kind of smile or hug. But nothing of the sort came about. Just tears.

"I'm going to make it right. You watch."

Giovonna nodded again. "You better."

Sydona held back tears of her own. Guilt was becoming quite the shadow these days. Revenge was next on the list. She had to make things right. Everything had to stop. No more death, as Natalia or Malik put. No more suicide. No more people dying for nothing. She rose to her feet and headed for the door, assuming they didn't have much else to say.

"Do you know where everyone else went?" Sydona asked just before leaving,

"Um, I don't know where Raoul went. I think Lacey and them left, and Willow went back home. It's just us and Silas."

Sydona smiled as a thank you and walked back down the hallway. She hoped they would be around to talk to. She wanted to explain herself and ask for their forgiveness. She nearly forgot about Knox and Avani. Picturing his outburst upon finding out Malik still existed made her want to throw up. But then again, the couple glasses of wine and half bottle of vodka had the same effect.

The couch squeaked as she flopped down on it with both feet resting on the arm rest. Her mind pounded harder from the incident last night as she planned what her next move was. Last time she planned on stopping Malik, things didn't work out very well.

Cutting her hair was the first idea. And possibly dying it. Black, perhaps? With the bandage fresh on her head, she knew she had to wait a couple days to do that, though. Either way, she had to leave the cabin. She had been in one place for too long and it could be easier for him to find her. And not just him. That broadcast went out to millions of people who would have no problem taking her in to get their hefty reward. Three million dollars. That could set some people for life. Running was the only option. She couldn't stay in one place too long. But finding places to stay posed an even bigger threat. Her face was plastered all over the country. Going anywhere with other people was more dangerous than she ever thought possible. She thought Eagle Lake was problematic a few months ago, but now, it couldn't even shake a stick at the new threat. She hated thinking about it, but at least all this only concerned herself. For the time being, anyway, everyone else was safe. He only needed her. If he got her, everything else stopped.

But would she get to him? That was the real problem. She assumed police stations and federal facilities knew of his location. Otherwise, if some random civilian turned her into the authorities, where exactly would they put her?

As she lay there, staring up at the stained ceiling, her father popped into her head. They didn't know. He just sent a letter, and she wanted to respond to it as well.

Sydona searched for a piece of paper, sat at the kitchen table and began to write.

> *Dear father,*
>
> *I got your letter! I'm so happy to hear you're doing well. I miss mom too… every day I think of her. And you. I wish I could go there to see you, see how you're doing. And don't get me wrong, to live on a tropical island sounds amazing too.*
>
> *The reason for my letter… I wanted to tell you something that happened that I should have mentioned before. Now that I'm forced to deal with the truth, I thought you should know what's going on here. Our television broadcasted a nationwide announcement with the doctor alive and well. He's put an award out for my capture. I wanted to let you know that you and everyone else are still okay. They just want me.*

She held the pen up, shaking. A tear hit the parchment as she worked up her next words.

> *I'm going after him. Alone. In case I don't make it, or he kills me, I want you to know… You have been with me every day since you two left. I can't believe I actually got to see you again, and I loved every minute we spent together. I urge, whatever you do, don't come back. Stay on the Island, where you're safe. Don't come try to stop me. When I do what I need to do, I need to know that you'll be where I can find you when it's all over. I love you so much, and when I see you again, we will all be free.*
>
> *Forever yours,*
> *Sydona xoxo*

She folded up the piece of paper, stuffed it into an envelope and wrote "Ian Wilder" on the outside. Her fingers glided across the sides of it, and she tapped it on the table a couple times. Just then, Silas spoke up from behind her.

"That for your dad?"

She wiped her eyes and face, knowing she probably looked like a mess. "Yeah."

"Can I read it?" he asked with a hand on her shoulder.

"Oh," she sniffed. "Just personal stuff. Father daughter things. You know."

He squeezed her shoulder. "Oh right. Yeah, I know all about that."

Sydona laughed.

"You hungry?"

A smile curved on her red cheeks. "Let's go pay Willow a visit. That way I can send the letter, too."

He nodded and agreed. "I'll go get Gia."

"Thanks."

Once the three of them got dressed, and Sydona took her bandage off, they loaded up in the car and drove to Willow's. Only a few miles down the road, they arrived at the much too familiar home of Willow the Widowed. Sydona thought back to the time she, Giovonna and Raoul took refuge from Harold and his goonies. As Harold's face came to mind, she couldn't help but shudder. His holey, stained, white shirt matched his holey, yellow-stained smile. His southern drawl was worse than Willow's; she could still hear it in her head. She was glad she'd never have to see him again.

As she pulled around to roll down her driveway, she noticed a familiar truck sitting next to Willow's vehicle.

But no… it couldn't be. He hadn't been seen since Eagle Lake, according to Willow anyway.

The three exited the vehicle, and Giovonna was the first to run up to the door. She knocked loudly and called out her name in a sing-songy tone. Her mood had certainly perked up since their last encounter. Then again, Willow didn't betray her. Silas and Sydona walked up behind her, and the door opened slowly.

Bright crimson, curly hair creeped through the opening followed by Willow's face of shock.

"The hell y'all doin' here?" she whispered loudly as if she would wake something inside.

"Can't we stop by to say hi?" Giovonna asked less cheerfully.

"You couldn't call first? Damn…"

"What are you doing in there?" Sydona peered over Giovonna.

"None of your damn... business…" she paused to laugh and closed the door slightly. "Stop it!" She giggled more.

The three of them stared at one another, perplexed by her flirtatious chortles. Sydona had a horrible feeling she knew who was in the house with her, but she needed proof. She leaned in to Giovonna's ear.

"It's Harold."

Giovonna whipped her head around in disbelief. "No it's not!" she tried to whisper. "How do you know?"

"You don't recognize the truck?"

Her neck bent to look in the driveway. "How do you know it's his truck? Why can't it be someone else's truck?"

"It's his," she confirmed and forced the door open, tired of the games.

The door swung open, and both Willow and the man stood like statues. It was Harold alright. But something was different about him. His boney, tanned skin was all too much exposed because his white and blue boxers were the only thing he hid behind. Scars and dark hair covered his legs and chest, a vision Sydona hoped to never see. The permanent anger lines that littered his face seemed to have dissipated. The only smile she knew of his was evil and selfish, but now it was much more carefree and innocent. It was a description she never would have picked for him.

"Wha--" Giovonna uttered and glanced quickly back at Sydona who had a smug smile on her face. "You were right."

Sydona relished in the satisfaction of being correct, but then she remembered who she was dealing with. "What's going on here, Willow?"

Willow and Harold made a point to stand apart from each other. Her face transformed from a blushing high school girl to a feisty woman remembering the events of the previous day. "I thank I'll aks the questions, princess."

Aks? She had been around Harold too long. Sydona rolled her eyes and shut the door after letting everyone else in. Silas made his way over to the kitchen while Giovonna stayed by Sydona's side. She didn't trust Harold either. Sydona taught her well.

"How could ya do this to us?" Willow crossed her arms.

Sydona's mouth gaped open wide as she stared at Harold. It was hard for her not to burst out laughing.

"Me? You're sleeping with Harold! Talk about betrayal, Willow."

Harold looked up with an innocent face and blubbered. "I-I thought he was gone…"

The sudden change in behavior from Harold shocked her. Why would dirty, scruffy, gap-toothed, rude Harold be messing around with Willow? They had been neighbors for a long time but also mortal enemies. What happened in Malik's office three months ago? It was like he was neutered.

"Welcome to the club," Silas said from the kitchen.

Giovonna seemed just as upset as Sydona with him being there, and her face hardened. "Why is he here?"

Willow's expression changed as she turned her attention to Giovonna. "Well uh… Things just kinda happened, ya know?"

"But you're Willow the Widowed, not Willow-- newly single," Giovonna joked but sounded strangely serious.

Silas stayed on topic. "He's with the Vultures, though. This is as bad as that guy who you all brought back to Knox. How do you know he's not a spy?"

"'Cause! I'm done with that shit," Harold spoke up, finding his backbone.

Sydona huffed and rolled her eyes.

"I'm serious. John only wanted numbers. Didn't care about us or me. 'Specially once that bitch Natalia joined and brown-nosed her way to the top." He sounded relieved rather than vengeful.

"What are you talking about? He loved you, his 'right-hand man'," Sydona said with air quotes.

"You got a hearin' problem? I said once Natalia joined, he forgot 'bout me," Harold retorted with a snip.

Sydona's fists began to curl at his familiar temper. "Oh, how sad for you, Harold. You want me to bake a you a cake?"

"Shut it, princess," Willow snapped. "He's tellin' the truth. He's done. No need to waste more of your precious breath convincin' us he ain't. He's been, uh, hidin' out here, actually."

"Why here?" Silas asked.

"Willow an' I go way back," Harold confessed.

Willow didn't interrupt as Sydona thought she would. He took a seat on the edge of the mustard-colored, flowery bed top.

"I knew Noah, Willow's late husband. We was buddies. He was a good guy, always doin' the right thing. Well, we was out drinkin' at a bar we went to a lot, and that's when we met John, lookin' all spiffy in his tight pants and jacket and tie like he was from Wall Street or somethin'. He stuck out like a gold thumb. Yeah, we was intrigued by him, and he bought us a roun'. Well, we got to drinkin' and talkin', and John told us he was lookin' for new people for his comp'ney. Said he was in sales but didn't exactly say what. Anyways, he ends up offerin us both a job, but Noah turned 'im down. But the money was too good to pass up.

"Later on, Noah and I fought about it, sayin' he was scum and that I shouldn't trust him... I didn't care. He was offerin' a ton of money, like, a lot. So, I end up takin' the job, and Noah joined the military 'round the same time, thinkin' he would make more of a difference that way. 'Course that's where he met Willow. He came back after a couple years, and he moves in with her. Coincidentally, she happened to live pretty darn close to me, and I run into Noah again. He, Willow and me used to hang out all the time, and we all got even closer.

"One day, it slipped what my job actually was, and it was all downhill from there. Willow and Noah joined the Sparrows, and we grew apart again. Eventually, Noah's heart went out, and she blamed it on me, a best friend who stood for everythin' he was against. Naturally we became enemies, and she never forgave me, until recently…"

He grabbed her hand, and she massaged his fingers with her thumb.

Sydona slipped a smile but then quickly hid it behind her hands. "So, why did you do it all if it killed your best friend? Why didn't you just leave?"

Harold's face melted. "I 'unno. John made me feel like I was really contributin' to somethin' extraordinary. Like, yeah, maybe a few people might get hurt, but imagine what the final product would be."

Silas interjected. "Killed, man. Not hurt, killed people."

Harold's eyes darted over to him, and he no longer held Willow's hand. He needed his for protection.

"It wasn't supposed to go down that way… Things got way out of hand."

Sydona burst out laughing.

"Alright, alright, stop this. I already forgave the man; leave him alone. He ain't the problem anymore. It's Malik we need to worry about," Willow said, calming her tone.

The room filled with silent agreement. Sydona still hated Harold, but maybe she would have to forgive him, too. He did work closely with Malik for several years. He might be her only chance of finding him. Sharp pains entered her stomach at the thought, but she had to give it a shot. The letter crinkled in her pocket, and she shoved her hands inside. She suddenly remembered why she was there.

"Oh, right," she said and handed Willow the letter for Ian. "Almost forgot to give this to you."

"For yer daddy?"

"Yeah..." she replied with a pencil line smile.

"Fairy should be by tomorrow for the mail. I'll let 'em know." Willow patted her shoulder.

"Speaking of fairies, is Raoul here? Or did he go straight to the pantry?" Sydona asked.

Willow shook her head. "I ain't seen him. He didn't come here."

"Well, maybe he's gone back home by now," said Silas.

"No, I don't..." Sydona took a deep breath. "I don't think he's coming back this time..." Her chest felt tight and heavy. She didn't want to say it, but she'd been thinking it. He never left her for very long willingly. She worried something happened to him but...

"As you know, fairies aren't--equipped--to feel extreme anger. It can be so harmful to them it can sometimes be fatal. Luckily, he knows where a shaman lives, and that's the best way to overcome it."

"You know where he is?" Silas stood up, seemingly confused.

Sydona returned his look. "Yeah."

"Well, then why haven't we gone there?"

"He doesn't want to see me, Silas. He's trying to get over his anger, and I will put him into relapse."

"Of course he wants to see you, Syd," Giovonna argued. "You're his best friend. He'll forgive you. Look at Willow the Widowed and Harold here. If they can get over their qualms, you and Raoul certainly can! Come on…" She flashed Sydona her adorable, full-toothed grin, making her cheeks so big her eyes closed.

She couldn't help but smile back. Giovonna was right. If two people as polar opposite as Willow and Harold could get over their problems, she would be alright.

Chapter Eleven

Everyone agreed to go back to her old home but not before Willow fed everyone a huge lunch. Sydona made a point not to rush; it was good to let Raoul have his alone time with his family. But she was part of his family, too. On the road there, she thought of everything she wanted to say to him. How she never meant to hurt him. How she just wanted to protect him and spare him the stress of knowing the man who tortured him was alive. How she didn't know who she would be without him. He was her subconscious, her parrot, her life companion.

Since three of them didn't want to speak much with Harold there, they arrived at the house after a long and silent ride. The blue Victorian still looked as she remembered, and she never got tired of coming back to it. Technically it was still her house, but the fairies made it obvious it was theirs now. The interior appeared even more like the outdoors than during their last visit. A path on the stairs was still large enough for people to walk through. Twisted branches, leaves, lights and cubbies of new homes covered the walls, ceiling and everything in between. As Harold walked through the door, his mouth was wide open and speechless, and Sydona smiled. It was nice to see him fascinated by something he tried to destroy. Sydona didn't exactly want Harold inside, but Willow promised to keep an eye on him. She felt she should've checked for a wire though.

All the fairies welcomed them into the home with open arms. If Sydona was with them, they were a friend of the fairies. The happy faces faded once they knew the reason for her visit.

"He's upstairs," said a fairy with turquoise wings.

"How's he doing?" Sydona asked.

He shook his head with saddened eyes, and all the fairies around him did the same.

Her feet and lifted chin led her upstairs through the forest with everyone following her lead. Her ears heard the rumble of feet behind her, climbing the creaky wooden steps. It was so loud that she was afraid it would bother Raoul and set him off. She shushed them, and they slowed their steps. Her first instinct was to go into her bedroom. Not only was Raoul not in there, but everything looked destroyed. And from what she recalled, it wasn't from the first time they stopped by. No. This was from Raoul. From what he was able to do. He put holes in her pillows, blankets and mattress; and tore up letters, pictures and papers with nothing written on them. It was like a baby tornado had ripped through her bedroom. It wasn't massively destroyed, but Raoul made it clear he was livid. But where was he?

A psst came from behind her. She turned around to see Harold pointing to inside the bathroom. His brown eyes were so wide she could see yellowish whites around them. What the hell was in the bathroom? As she peered around the door frame, the light from the window illuminated Raoul floating around in a sink full of water. His tiny body was completely submerged aside from his face and tip toes.

Sydona's eyes narrowed as she tried to figure out what he was doing. Raoul's face looked relaxed and didn't move, making her think he didn't know she was in the room. She had to a take moment to realize how peaceful it was in there. The tiles on the walls were also taken over by branches and vines, and some yellow flowers bloomed near the open window. She made a seat on the toilet next to the sink; Giovonna and Silas sat on the bathtub on the opposite side of him. Willow and Harold stood outside the door looking in and just as speechless as she was.

With all her knowledge of fairy history and tradition, she couldn't think of what this was a part of. Raoul looked peaceful enough, so whatever it was he was doing seemed to be working. Soon a swift breeze squeezed through the window, strong enough to open Raoul's eyes.

"Ahh!!" he shouted, and his head ducked under water, causing him to splash everyone and cough loudly. "What! What are you doing here? And… him! Why is *he* here?" He pointed angrily at Harold.

Sydona wiped off her arms and explained. "I was worried about you, buddy."

He swam to the edge of the sink, shook off and grabbed a washcloth set aside like a towel at a public pool. "Syd, why is Harold here?!"

"Don't worry about him right now. I'll explain it later."

Raoul dried off by running the towel all over his body and hair. His brunette locks were a mess and not at all the look the rest of them were used to seeing. He mumbled things under his breath. "Worried, pah! Then she goes and brings the doctor's lead man into *my* house?"

"Raoul!" Sydona broke his rantings. "Are you better?"

Raoul threw the towel down with his tiny, angry grip. "Better? You come here asking if I'm better while that guy is standing in my bathroom? Are you delusional? Have you been smoking the stuff we planted way behind the corn fields?"

Silas perked up at his last comment.

"Raoul, please…" Shaman Faro flew in through the window, landed by his side and grabbed his shoulders. He stood in front of him, trying to catch his eyes. "Remember what we talked about?"

Raoul adjusted his head, closed his eyes and took a long deep breath. He did that three more times in unison with the Shaman.

"Now," Shaman Faro released his shoulders. "Focus on the positive."

Raoul opened his eyes again and stared at everyone staring at him. "I can't with everyone looking at me, Shaman."

The Shaman nodded and agreed. "Could everyone please leave us be?"

Sydona understood and reluctantly left the room along with Silas and Giovonna. Not wanting to stray far, the group hung out in the hallway. When no fluttering wings were around, it was eerily tropical and quiet. Small animals had even found homes inside including squirrels, raccoons and a couple of songbirds. In a way, the fact that her home was now home to the many critters who lost their shelter in the oak made her heart warm. She missed it but wouldn't be comfortable forcing the fairies to go someplace else.

Her ear stayed close to the bathroom door to possibly overhear what he would say.

Silas whispered from across the hallway, only an arm length apart, "So nosey."

"I'm curious," Sydona whispered back, but she couldn't hear anything.

Giovonna, who stood next to Sydona, changed the subject to get her mind off Raoul. "Hey Silas, do you know where Jet and Lacey went?"

"Yeah, they went home," Willow answered. "They hadn't seen their fairies in a couple days."

"Oh, they have fairies, too?" Sydona asked.

"You ain't the only one, dear," Willow said.

"I know that… but, why didn't they come to any missions?"

"Not everyone is as brave as Raoul," Silas added. "My fairy never would want to be a part of this. She was too dainty."

Sydona wished she could've met his fairy. With the bond she had with Raoul, she thought it would be adorable to see him with a cute female fairy by his side. Maybe Raoul would have liked her. She felt her stomach twist as she thought of Raoul being alone all this time because of her problems. Raoul was never the type to settle down, but now he really couldn't if he wanted to because he was too busy being by her side. She felt so selfish sometimes. Even now, she was eavesdropping on him, though she was sure she was the last person he wanted to see. He left to get away from her, but here she was, crowding a furious fairy who needed the powers of a Shaman to calm down.

Sydona headed to her room while everyone else moseyed about the rest of the house. Sitting on her bed, she stared out the window that once showcased the large fairy tree. All that remained were the fields of corn and the forest behind that. It was still a great view, but it turned her insides. Raoul's bed grew dust on the windowsill, and she smiled. She thought of the many mornings of waking up to his snoring and mumbling. The rooster would crow and jolt him awake every single morning. A lump formed in her throat.

"Okay, I'm done," Raoul called from the bathroom.

Sydona treaded lightly on the wooden floorboards as she got closer to him. Her insides were jumbled up. She hated the feeling.

"Well?" she asked at barely a whisper.

He took a deep breath with closed eyes. "Shaman Faro said that I need to talk to you in a controlled environment. He said the best way to get this horrible feeling out of me is to talk it out." He rolled his eyes and stuck his tongue out.

Sydona smirked slightly, not because he had to do something he didn't want to do but because she agreed with the Shaman, and Raoul had to tell her what was on his mind. "Okay."

The door clicked shut, and Sydona made herself a seat on the toilet with a towel.

"Thank you for wanting to talk with me--"

"No, no... let me start with you. *You* made me do this, Syd." He flew up and paced in front of her face with animated arms. "I don't think you understand the level of danger you put me in. I had to fly back home when I thought my heart was going to explode. I don't know if you've noticed, but I'm much smaller than you. When you drop a *bomb* on me, you may as well have literally dropped a *bomb* on me!"

Tears started to form in her blue eyes, and her lips shook. She had never seen this side of him before, not in the sixty years she had known him. "I'm sorry--"

"No! Not done yet. Let me talk!"

"Raoul--" Shaman Faro spoke from outside the window. "Breathe, Raoul. Remember to breathe."

Raoul stopped ranting, formed fists at Shaman Faro's words, but then relaxed and took another breath.

"I'm trying to understand why you kept this from me. *Me*. I've been there for you through everything, Syd. Since before I could even fly. I risked my freedom for you, went through torture and then you tell me you killed the man who tortured me, only to find out that he was never actually dead. And then I find out that Jubilee was captured… Of everyone I lived with, why her? Every time I think of what they could be doing to her, I think of..." He paused to put the horrible thought behind him. "Ever since this trip, I feel like I've only begun to really know you. Everything is always about you. Well, what about me? I'm not your sidekick. I have needs; I have ambition. I always do what you want to do."

Sydona understood his pain, but the last part irked her. "I'm sorry Raoul. And I wish I could turn back time and tell you the truth about Malik, but… Raoul… you've never spoken up about that other stuff before. And you're not a sidekick. You're my family, my best friend."

"I don't feel like it sometimes, though," he said. He was calmer but still pacing around in the air. "And you've never asked me. Ever! You've never asked me what I want in life."

"I'm sorry! What *do* you want, Raoul? Tell me!" Sydona replied strongly.

Raoul paused, seemingly unprepared to be asked the question he felt so strongly about. "I want… I want to be treated like someone with goals. Not just along for the ride."

Sydona furrowed her brows. She wanted to sympathize with him, but not even Raoul really seemed to know what he wanted in life. He was just still upset and feeling unwanted and betrayed.

"Do you want to be a Sparrow?" she asked, thinking maybe giving him options would help narrow it down.

"I--I don't know!" he threw his hands up. "I want to be like you…" Raoul admitted and stopped pacing.

"What?" Sydona shook her head, thoroughly lost now.

"I just… I want your passion. I want to be able to do stuff like you. But I can't. Because… I can't even peel an orange by myself! You saw something that needed changed, and you're doing it. I know you didn't mean to lie about the doctor; you were doing what you thought was best. But I mean, of all people, you could have just told me. You know I wouldn't have judged you."

She saw a hint of a smile creeping up on his reddened face. "I know; you're right."

"I'm what?" His smile grew.

"You're right, Raoul. About everything. I can be selfish, and I hate it. I don't want to be. I guess I feel by keeping things to myself I'm protecting others. I know I have trust issues that I'm also working on. And honestly, if you weren't there for me, none of this would have happened. I never would have met Gia, who I consider to be, well, a daughter. And Willow who I never thought I would like, but she's growing on me. And Silas who, well… he's the first person I've known in a long time that I have real feelings for. None of us would even know each other if you didn't come along. You're more than my sidekick, Raoul. You *have* to know that… The day we left the house for Eagle Lake, and I was driving away; I was

150

just upset. I could never leave you behind. You're my rock."

They both smiled wide through the tears. The air that was once stiff and tense now felt clear and light. Raoul flew to her shoulder and hugged the side of her head. He whispered in her ear.

"I'm sorry I scared you."

Sydona swallowed and nodded slightly. "It's alright. Are we okay now?"

"Yeah…"

"I've missed you, buddy…" She wiped her face of an embarrassingly large number of tears that soaked her cheeks.

"Missed you too, Syd."

"And we'll find Jubilee. I promise. I know how much she meant to you."

"Thank you," Raoul said. His chin raised a little higher.

Sydona composed herself and exited the room.

"Did you see your bed is still in the window?"

Raoul buzzed over to her bedroom. "Holy cow! It is! Can we take this with us?"

"What, you mean you don't like sleeping on washcloths and hand towels?" Sydona winked.

"Not if I could have a bed instead," Raoul replied as he flew over and straightened the covers. "I'll make Silas carry it."

Chapter Twelve

It was time.

While Raoul took everyone on a tour of the house, Sydona found the scissors and began boiling water. Stains from black tea constantly soiled her countertops, so she figured it would stain her light hair, too. She moved the hot water into a large bowl and steeped ten tea bags to a deep amber color. It would be a darker, more dramatic change but not permanent. She carried the bowl up the stairs, which she later regretted. Carrying a full bowl of boiling water upstairs covered in branches and leaves was extremely difficult. She was thankful no one saw her trying to juggle it.

The bathroom door clicked shut, and she hushed her heart. It was silly to be anxious over cutting hair, considering worse things laid ahead. She grabbed a chunk of silky blonde hair and stared at it as if she were already mourning it. The scissors snipped and snapped. She didn't much care if things were even. Just to getting it off her head would help her disguise herself even more. Once all her hair stopped just above her shoulders, she stopped. Her lungs filled with air, and she let it out as she admired her work. It didn't look half bad, but it wasn't her anymore. She threaded her fingers through her short hair, still able to feel the length it was only a minute ago.

Once the bowl of black tea cooled enough for her to dunk her hair in, she let it soak for several minutes. Her mind wandered off. She took in the smell of the dark tea through her nose and breathed out. Her ears found the sounds of chirping birds enjoying the warm weather. Wood from the branches made its way into the aroma, and it made her feel like she was in the forest. The warming water helped her relax as well.

When she thought it had soaked enough, she flipped what hair she had left back and washed her hair quickly in the shower. She examined the new color and cut in the mirror.

Unrecognizable.

If she barely knew it was her, certainly no one else would be able to tell either.

Sydona made her way downstairs where she heard everyone. The tour must have ended. As she turned to face the living room, everyone stared at her. Her cheeks turned red, and she bashfully tried to twirl a piece of hair around her finger. It felt weird.

"What'd you do to your hair?!" Silas quickly stood up.

"I cut it," she said with a shrug.

"It's brown!" Giovonna shrieked.

"It's just hair you guys. What's everyone talking about?"

Just then, someone knocked on her front door.

Everyone stopped in their footsteps and chatter. They looked at one another with wide eyes. They thought if they all stayed perfectly still, they would go away. The fairies immediately hid away in their cubbies, and some flew to the backyard. They sensed something wasn't right.

Then, another louder knock came followed by: "Police, open up!"

Sydona's heart plummeted to her gut. She looked at Willow with desperate eyes. Willow shook her head and stepped back. When she denied her, Sydona glanced at everyone else to open the door. Giovonna and Silas both did nothing. With their purple eyes, she couldn't fault them. They might be tortured for information about her. Suddenly, Harold lifted his scruffy chin and stepped forward. He patted her shoulder and headed for the door.

What was he doing? No hesitation. He knew them, the police. He planned it all along. Adrenaline pumped through her veins, and she began to lunge toward him. But before she took two steps, Harold swung the door open just enough for the cops to see him. Everyone else hid in the corner of the living room.

Harold cleared his throat before speaking to the two men at her door. "Yes?"

"Good afternoon, sir. Is Sydona Wilder home?"

She could see the right half of his face and sort of read his facial expressions. He seemed calm and collected. Thankfully.

"I'm afraid not." His accent seemed to almost disappear. Sydona almost smiled.

"When will she be back?" the policeman inquired with a steady tone.

Harold chuckled. "Your guess is as good as mine. She been gone over three months now."

A pause.

"Do you have any idea of where she went?" they asked.

"Nope." He scratched his balding, ash-colored hair. "Sorry I can't be more help to y'all."

"The reason we're here is to find… this girl." Harold leaned out to examine something. "Name is Giovonna Carr. Her parents are Frederick and Denise Carr."

Harold's head slightly turned as if to match it to something, but then he turned his attention back to the cops. "Never seen her."

Sydona's eyes widened, and she turned to Giovonna with the same look. She scooted closer to her and hugged her as she could tell she was about to cry.

"She was last seen with Ms. Wilder. She's been reported missing. Since Sydona is a fugitive, we have a warrant to search the premise."

"Now, hang on. I don't know who in the blazing saddles that little girl is, but I do know someone's already been here looking for Sydona. Destroyed the damn place!" Harold's tone got louder.

"Who's been here?"

"Them folks from the NFA. Couple days ago. I've been watchin' the house for her like she asked, but I ain't gotta clue where she at or when she comin' back. Now, I'd like to be left alone to watch my shows in some peace and quiet!"

Another pause. Then one cop spoke up. "We're very sorry sir. But, if you happen to see her or Ms. Wilder, please let us know."

Harold grabbed something and nodded.

"Have a nice day, sir."

He shut the door and sunk his head. He held a piece of paper in his hand and looked at it again. Sydona peeked out of the curtains and waited for the cop car to get back on the road before moving another muscle.

From the corner of her eye, she watched as Giovonna stormed over to Harold and ripped the paper from his hands. Her fists wrapped around the edges so tightly it almost tore in two.

"Bullshit!" she gasped and hit the paper over and over again. Her eyes flooded with tears, and she collapsed onto the floor.

"God! I can't believe they reported me missing! They couldn't give two shits about me."

Sydona couldn't believe the language she was using. She had been a bad influence on her. Giovonna's anger was justified, though. After months of not hearing from her, they just now put in a missing person's report? What horrible timing. And they used Sydona as an excuse to come looking.

Giovonna sobbed so hard she fought for air. "And I'm with a fugitive now? Like, come on guys."

"Sorry, pumpkin…" Willow sat on the edge of the couch and rubbed Giovonna's back. Just then, she looked down at her hip and lifted her shirt. A small black device was clipped to her jeans, and she read it carefully.

"Knox wants us," Willow announced calmly.

"Is that a pager?" Silas asked.

"Yep."

"When did you get one of those?"

"Avani gave it to me. It's how I been keepin' in touch with 'em," Willow explained as she pulled up her pants. "We should prolly get goin'."

Sydona listened to both conversations on either side of her. She knew Knox would eventually want to see them again, especially after the news.

Giovonna could only focus on her parents. "What am I gonna do?"

Sydona lent Giovonna a hand and she grabbed it, and Sydona pulled her off the floor. "We'll figure something out, don't worry." Sydona side hugged her and kissed her on the temple.

Giovonna wiped tears from her face with one hand while the other wrapped around Sydona. She didn't want her to go back to her parents. Sydona needed her. She wanted her. It would be so hard to keep going without her around. But having her around meant the authorities would be constantly searching for her. Neither one of them would be safe as long as Giovonna stayed around.

Sydona made a point to sit across from Giovonna in the car. Several minutes passed before Sydona tried talking. Giovonna needed time to figure things out for herself first.

"I don't want you to leave, Gia, but I understand if you do."

Giovonna sighed heavily and turned to her. "I don't want to either. But if I stay, you know they're going to be constantly looking. And if they end up finding me, they'll find you and…"

A dry spot formed in Sydona's throat. She wasn't sure what to say to make anything better. But the fact was, nothing about any of it was a good outcome.

"It's just the police. It's not like it's the NFA coming for us. They have laws to abide," Sydona said.

"Yes, and you're a fugitive, Syd. You basically have no rights," Giovonna said. "Just like me."

Her words stung. "The cabin we're staying in is so far in the middle of nowhere they aren't going to find us…"

Giovonna wiped her nose. "But what if they do? We have running water and electricity. I'm not an adult like you all, but don't you have to pay for that? And if you have to pay, someone knows we're here."

Willow cleared her throat. "Yes, darlin', but it's not in Syd's name or your name. They won't even think of comin' here. We'll find a way out of this, okay?"

Sydona caught Willow's eye in the rearview mirror and flashed her a smile. It seemed to have calmed Giovonna a little. She pulled her knees up to her chest, wrapped her arms around them and stared out of her window. Sydona squeezed Giovonna's arm lovingly and then gazed out of her own window. Her eyes welled up, but she squashed the tears. The rest of the ride was quiet. No one knew what else to say; there *was* nothing else to say.

Reality eventually sunk in as she remembered where they were headed. Sydona wasn't looking forward to being yelled at again. Her time in the Sparrows so far hadn't been ideal, and she wouldn't be surprised if they kicked her out. Not being in the Sparrows might benefit her though; she could go find the doctor on her own.

They pulled up to the warehouse, and her heart did somersaults all the way to the office door. She knocked. Heavy footsteps grew louder, and she took a deep breath with hands shaking.

The door flew open. Knox's eyes were dark and fuming, and he lunged at her with bared teeth. Sydona instantly hit the ground with his large hands squeezing her neck. She pried and gasped for air. His body crushed her as she squirmed to get him off. Everyone screamed at him, but his face and eyes stayed glued to Sydona's bulging eyes. Her lungs felt as if they were already shriveling like a deflated balloon. No matter how hard she fought, he didn't budge. Silas, Willow and everyone else tried to grab him off of her but were unsuccessful. Her head swelled and pounded so hard she swore her heart moved positions. Her vision began to blur. Nothing Avani said or did convinced him to let go of her.

She was going to die.

Her murderer would be the man who lead a rebellion to stop those who wanted her dead. A man who swore to protect those like her.

But her mission wasn't over.

She needed to live to kill another. Doctor Malik would not stop the trials until he found someone else like her. Not today, Knox.

As she felt herself fighting for life and gasping for air, her hand suddenly found her trusty dagger on her hip and gripped it tightly. But it was stuck. Whimpers escaped her opened mouth, and no matter how hard she tried, it wasn't coming out. Her fingers went limp.

Suddenly a scream from what sounded like a little boy called out her name. It was Devon. The boy exposed his tiny teeth and bit down on Knox's forearm as hard as he could. Knox was forced to let go and get Devon off him, and when he released one hand, Sydona used her body to maneuver herself out of his grip. When she was able to free herself, Silas and the others instantly grabbed him and dragged him away. The stale warehouse air never felt so rejuvenating as it quickly filled her lungs. Her heart returned to its normal place in her chest, and her vision cleared. Giovonna stayed by her side and helped her sit up. Devon bit Knox so hard it made him bleed, covering the boy's mouth in red.

"What the fuck is your problem? You could have killed her!" Giovonna yelled at Knox who was slumped against the wall, gripping his side.

"Hijo de perra!" Avani screamed in his face. "Too far, Elias. Too far!"

"After what she did, why wouldn't death be reasonable punishment? She's killed us all!" Knox bellowed.

"She's the only one he wants, sir!" Willow joined. "If you'd have killed her, we would be right back at square one."

Sydona didn't give Willow enough credit. She was right on the money. Sydona wanted to add to the conversation but didn't want to give up any of the precious oxygen she just acquired.

"How do we know? How do we know that once he gets her, he will stop everything else? What if he fails and continues on?" Knox's voice reverberated against the walls and through her skin.

"He won't fail," Harold said.

Knox turned his head to Harold who he seemed to have just noticed. "Who are you?"

Harold didn't answer. "John don't fail. Not in anythin'."

Knox narrowed his eyes and cocked his head inquisitively at Harold. He winced slightly as Avani was hard at work patching his wound. His green eyes, slowly turning back to violet, studied Harold's brown eyes.

"You're a Vulture, aren't you?" he asked, with a confident tone.

Harold dropped his head.

"Get out," Knox scrambled to his feet. "Get out before I fucking kill you too!"

"Nu-uh. You sit your stupido ass down right now," Avani said. She pushed him back down on the ground as she wrapped up his arm.

Sydona turned her attention to Devon. Of course she was upset that Knox tried to kill her, but she decided to focus on the fact that this little boy just saved her life. Jet and Lacey appeared from the doorway. She released a smile, and the two of them returned it. Lacey made Devon rinse his mouth out, and although she was upset, she still patted him on the head. Her thoughts changed about Devon's new attitude. He was willing to risk his own life for her. But why?

"Thank you," she said softly.

Devon said nothing but nodded.

Knox's grunting forced her to deal with him. She crawled back up on onto her feet with Giovonna's help. Her patience was wearing thin. His anger was a force to be reckoned with and needed controlled. Avani wouldn't always be around to control him, and Sydona knew that. She needed to speak with him privately.

"Can I talk to you?" she asked with a stern tone, glaring down at him on the floor.

His eyes narrowed. He leaned to one side, pressed his massive hand to the ground and stood up to tower over her. Sydona's eyes stayed glued to his, not looking away for even a second. She knew his tactic; it was pure intimidation with just his stature. It wasn't going to work. Blinking only twice, Knox eventually curled his lips slightly. He was amused, and Sydona loved the feeling of winning the staring contest.

"Let's go outside," he said and broke eye contact to exit the building.

She looked at everyone who seemed curious about what may happen and winked. Raoul stayed behind with them as her boots echoed across the metal walls and out the door.

Several feet in front of her, Knox continued to wander far past the warehouse and cars. He took large strides with his beefy legs and wide arm swings. He seemed to go everywhere with a purpose.

"What'd you wanna talk about, Miss Wilder?" he asked while still walking. His voice was so loud and low it sounded as if he spoke right next to her.

Her jaw tightened at what he kept calling her. It reminded her of the doctor.

"Call me Syd," she stated just as loudly.

Knox turned around to face her and acknowledged her request. He sat down on a tree stump. Sydona mirrored him and made herself comfortable with another stump to the left of him.

"How'd you become leader of the Sparrows?"

Her question made Knox perk up, and he cleared his throat. "You don't think I'm fit, do you?"

"I think you have issues."

Her heart pounded like a jackhammer in her chest. She could tell he liked strong figures and wouldn't tolerate indecisiveness. Bluntness and quick thinking were the only ways to talk to this man.

Knox let out a sigh at her comment. "I can't help it sometimes. Ava has helped me tremendously though, believe it or not. Don't know what I'd do without that woman…"

"You should learn to deal with it yourself. She won't always be around."

He dropped his head. "I know."

Sydona made him feel guilty enough, and so she tried changing the subject. The massive scar on his face triggered a new conversation. "How'd you get the scar?"

Knox absentmindedly touched it above his right eye, causing his jaw to tighten. "I was captured, like you, a long time ago. I was there for roughly six months or so. I'm not sure actually. Time doesn't exist in places like that. But when I met Avani there, I made a decision to escape. The leader of it at the time, a man named Alejandro, was brutal. Practically starved us. Only gave us enough food to not die. Anyways, once I finally got the chance to overthrow the camp, I targeted Alejandro. I didn't want to kill him right away. I wanted him to suffer. I wanted him to feel what he put us through. Some of us for months, some years. We fought. Glass from the window we fell out of shattered everywhere. He grabbed a piece and sliced my head open. It was the last time he hurt me before I shot him." He paused and quickly smiled. "Wish I had more time with him."

"Jesus... "

"Is this what you wanted to talk to me about?" he asked.

"No..." Sydona said. "But that's how you met Avani?"

His smile grew wider and his eyes gentler. "Yes. She saved me as much as I saved her."

At first, he didn't seem like much of a romantic, but deep down, he really was. Silas and his kindness rattled around in her head. He saved her countless times, but it puzzled her on what she actually did for him. He left his life behind only to be captured, then lived with her in a cabin with a teenage girl. She didn't know why he stuck around. Maybe it was about time she did something for Silas. The silence broke from Knox's clearing his throat.

"What about you? You know me. It's only fair I know you, too. While we're still breathing that is."

Her stomach ached. He wasn't fully over it yet. She took a deep breath. "My parents were taken from me at a young age. I grew up fast; I had to. Luckily, I had Raoul by my side the whole way. Survival is all I know." Her thoughts became dark as she quickly lived through the day her life changed to the day her mother died to now. She closed up.

"I'm sorry. No one should have to go through that," Knox replied.

Sydona shrugged and evaded his eyes. Tears were fighting to come up, but she held them down.

The two sat quietly as the conversation reached an end. Knox could tell Sydona had said as much as she wanted. Wind blew her darkened short hair in her face. It was a mild annoyance. She was no longer able to pin her hair into a ponytail to keep it out of her face. She pushed strands of it behind her ears, and Knox noticed.

"You changed your hair."

Sydona smirked and tried not to laugh because it was like he read her mind. "Yep."

"Smart."

Her heart fluttered. For some reason, the word offered more than the surface. Knox was starting to respect her, and it felt good.

He continued. "What do you plan on doing?"

Her legs and position shifted on the wooden seat as she was ready to finally talk business.

"I plan to kill him."

Knox let out a chuckle. She could tell he was choosing his words carefully to avoid saying something harsh. "No offence, Syd, but haven't you tried that already?"

Sydona's cheeks turned pink, and she smirked. "Yes, well, I have a new approach. That guy we brought with us, Harold, he was Malik's best man. I bet he knows where he lives."

She bit her lip with excitement, almost surprising herself on the flawlessness of her new plan. Plus, she had impressed the leader of the Sparrows. So she thought.

"You expect us to trust a man who worked for someone as vindictive as Malik?"

"Do you trust Willow?"

"Yes, but not as much as I used to..."

He was referring to Eagle Lake, and her heart sank.

"Well... I do. Do you trust me?" As soon as she asked the question, she immediately wanted to take it back. Knox just tried strangling her to death; he wouldn't change his opinion of her that quickly, would he?

"I don't. But I respect you. And what you're doing. You just need to get your emotions under control."

They looked at each other seriously. Sydona was a tad speechless from his last words. In unison, Knox and Sydona burst out laughing. She found herself a little like Knox as well. He was emotional too but sprinkled with much more rage. Laughing heartily relaxed her and seemed to do the same for Knox. Something had changed in their relationship, and she felt her blood pressure lower.

Knox let out a quick sigh; he seemed more relaxed as well. "So, what now?"

She shrugged but remembered she needed to be decisive. "I'm going there. I need to kill him."

"Need, huh?"

Sydona nodded slightly with tight lips.

"I'm finding us more alike than I thought. No longer a want. Wanting things is selfish, childish.

Needing is much more. It consumes you, leaving it as the only thing you can think about, pushing everything you ever wanted in the darkness. Needing is power. Needing is everything."

His fists rounded and whitened. She noticed how much he sunk into his words, feeding off them like they were food to a starving man. Then, he came back to her eyes. "I'll go with you."

She wanted to smile, glad that he was finally on her side and knew what he wanted, but she couldn't. "No. I can't let you do that."

"Excuse me?"

Sydona gulped, afraid of the words she said out loud, but she meant them. "He only wants me. He would probably just kill you."

Knox roared a ferocious laugh. "Let him try."

Chapter Thirteen

Avani's voice rang through the barren lot and into the trees of the forest. "What the hell you two doing? We're all over here thinking you're both dead!" She walked toward them, wobbly in her six-inch heels.

"We'll be right there, darling. Please, don't wear out your pretty little feet!" Knox said.

Sydona raised an eyebrow. She didn't think she could ever get used to how his words and tone changed when he spoke to her. It was almost comical at times. Avani heeded his advice and swiveled back around to the warehouse where everyone else waited.

"'Bout time! Thought Avani was gonna bring you guys back thrown over her shoulders," Jet said.

Raoul zoomed right up to her hairless shoulder with a concerned expression.

"What happened?" Willow asked.

Knox glanced at Sydona. "Nothing. It's all good."

"We should go back to the cabin. Harold, you know where Malik is?" Sydona asked.

He flashed his black and yellow teeth. "Hell yeah I do."

"Alright then. Let's go."

Sydona and her group split up from Knox and Avani. The car ride was short as Sydona went over in her head what she would do when she came face to face with the doctor again. He wouldn't have a way to escape this time. He would already be at home. Picturing the look he gave her when she had him pinned down in the grass made her grin. She imagined a look of pure shock that he could be overpowered. Malik was weak. Without his army, he was nothing. Sydona was confident she could take them out, especially with Knox and the others beside her. Even Devon would prove helpful if he bit someone for her.

Sydona dropped everyone off at their homes. At first, she wanted to go alone, but these people were her family now. They wouldn't stand idly by while she did all the dirty work. Giovonna, Silas, Sydona and Raoul opened the door to the cabin and immediately began to gather up their things. They dropped everything by the door once they packed and left a walkie buried in the mess. The sun was going down, and she decided they should get a good night's rest before setting out on the long journey.

In no rush to get to sleep, she cuddled next to Silas in bed. Her arm stretched over his torso while he had his under her head. She admired how close Knox and Avani were and wanted to be that way with Silas. With everything he had done for her, she kept wondering what is was she had done for him. With nothing physical to offer him, she thought simply talking would help.

"Crazy day, huh?" she began with a deep sigh.

He laughed, moving her head up and down. "Yeah, you could say that."

His fingers moved through her dark hair like a wave. A tremor of nervousness spread through her body, and she wasn't sure why. She had been in bed with Silas a hundred times, but this was the first time they had been really close. With so much on her mind, she realized being intimate was never at the forefront. Until now. But not unless it came up naturally.

"Oh my god. Your feet are freezing, girl," Silas said and jerked his legs away.

Sydona blushed and grinned. "No they're not!" Her feet chased after his, and he failed at getting away.

"No! Stop! They're like ice cubes!" His defense was to tickle her, making her laugh so hard her abdomen ached.

"Okay, okay! I'll stop!" she surrendered. "They're still cold though… you don't want to warm them up for me?"

That smile she loved grew on his pinkened cheeks. His eyes never seemed to leave hers. Silas's toes made their way toward her frozen bare feet and warmed them as best they could.

"Thank you." She smiled and went in for a soft kiss. He kissed back, and it sent a tingle down her spine. She soon found herself engulfed inside his arms and body. Heat quickly spread to her feet, allowing them to thaw. Fingers from both bodies gripped each other's backs and shoulders. As much as she wanted to let go of everything, let herself into him, she stopped. This wasn't what she meant by giving him something. And in a house full of people, it felt wrong.

She pulled away reluctantly and pushed her chin down to tell him she was done. He understood, probably for the same reasons. They once again held each other close but this time fused together like a freshly molded dagger.

"How come things ended with your last girlfriend?" It wasn't the question she originally wanted to ask, but she was genuinely curious.

He took a deep sigh. "Oh. Um… we just drifted apart. Ya know?"

"That's why you didn't want to marry her?"

"Yeah. That and… I kinda had a feeling she was cheating on me. I never said anything though…"

"Why did you think that?"

"She was starting to come home late after she started a new job. I gave it a few months, but it was always the same. When I asked her what she was doing, she would always say she was out with her friends. Just the way she answered, so vague… I knew. It was a guy. I waited for so long for her to tell me. But she never did."

"And she was still expecting you to propose?" Sydona asked with narrow eyes.

"Yep." He moved his free hand to the back of his head. "She had no idea I knew. People think I'm ignorant because I'm simple. They don't realize I'm just observing."

"I'm sorry, Silas." Her hand rubbed his chest back and forth through his blue t-shirt.

"What about you? You and that Theodore guy? Were you a thing?"

His name shot through her heart, and she swallowed forcefully. But it was only fair; she asked about his ex.

"Not… really, no."

"What does that mean?" He laughed. "You gotta give me more than that."

"We ran in a gang together. He was the only other flier besides me. We were able to cover more ground."

"A gang? What kind of gang?"

"We were drug dealers, marijuana mostly. Until Omar took over and wanted harder stuff. That's when I got out. But Theo stayed. He's a really good guy but weak willed. No matter what I said, he wouldn't leave. Then I go and rub my inheritance in his face like an asshole…"

"Wow, Syd. I had no idea…"

"Yeah… We never dated or anything. He just meant a whole lot to me at that time in my life. Sucks that meth took him over. Omar would've killed me if I came back though. I was one of his best dealers."

"Damn. Why didn't I ever know about this?"

Sydona shrugged. "I don't really like to remember things like that. I'm not proud of what I did. But it was the easiest way to make money and feed myself."

Silas rubbed her back without a word.

"What about your parents?" It was the question she really wanted to ask.

"Psh... I wish mine had been taken away. Nah, nah, just my dad..." His muscles and jaw tightened.

"Not your mom?"

"My mom… was an angel who fell in love with the devil. When my dad would come home drunk off his ass, she would immediately go into the kitchen and start making me hot cocoa with those rainbow-colored marshmallows and real milk. It was amazing. Helped me forget about the hazard in the other room. She made it for my brother and me. If my dad passed out soon enough, we would watch a movie in my room, usually a funny one…"

He smiled briefly but then stopped. "I wonder how she's doing now."

Sydona squeezed him tighter. "I'm sure she's doing fine, Silas. She sounds like a wonderful person."

"She was. Just like your mother."

A tear slipped out as she lay sideways on his chest, but she quickly wiped it away. The crickets and cicadas soon serenaded them outside their window, and it was like a lullaby for her. They both yawned.

"Ready for bed?" he asked at a whisper.

She kissed him in response and turned the lamp off. She loved that she was able to connect with Silas more but could only think of her mother now. And her father. She felt blessed that she had two wonderful parents who loved her but saddened that not everyone did. She wondered what her mother and father would be doing on the island if they were together. She let out another deep sigh as she knew she would dream about her mother again.

Early the next morning, she awoke with Silas's arms wrapped around her. To her surprise, she didn't dream at all, and she felt extremely refreshed which was great because it was the day she was going to end everything about the NFA.

Before she could get her feet on the ground, however, a loud knocking on the cabin door startled her. She glanced back at Silas who was just as clueless as her. Willow had a key and wouldn't have to knock. Then, fear set in. Was it the police? Or was it someone searching for her? She could turn herself in and end the war. As she battled in her head as to who they were and what to do, they knocked again.

"Police! Open up!"

A rumbling barreled down the hallway, and their bedroom door swung open. Giovonna and Raoul burst in with anxious looks.

"Oh my god. They're back!" Giovonna whispered, gripping Sydona's hand.

"It's alright Gia, just calm down," Sydona said. She wanted to bolt out of the back door, but they could be waiting there. The fact was, they couldn't answer the door. It had to be Silas. The three looked at him suggestively.

"Alright, alright. I'll get it. I'll just tell them I don't know anything," he sighed but stood up quickly.

"Good plan!" Giovonna said.

Silas slipped on pants over his boxers and threw on a wrinkled tee. They knocked again, and Silas bellowed back.

"I'm coming!"

As he stomped his way up to the door, Giovonna collapsed down on their bed in a full-blown mental breakdown. She sobbed harder than Sydona had ever seen her cry before. She kept mumbling how mad her parents were going to be and how she felt horrible for putting Sydona in jeopardy. She went back and forth for what felt like an eternity.

"Just breathe, Gia. It's going to be fine, okay?" Sydona said, making breathing motions with her hands.

"Yeah, you don't have to worry about them. Silas will make them go away, and then we're gone!" Raoul said, helping with the motions.

"But they'll keep coming back! And if you're caught because of me, I couldn't live with myself, Syd! I just couldn't!"

"Breathe. I'm sure it will be fine," Sydona said with a smile. She took her own advice and breathed deeply over and over.

Giovonna shook her head. "It won't...." She stood up and wiped her tears. "We've already come too far to have me be the reason it all goes to shit."

"What do you mean?" asked Sydona.

"This is just something I have to do. For you. For the Sparrows. For our people… I have to leave."

"What?" Raoul gasped. He buzzed around, unsure of how to feel. "No, Gia! We'll figure something else out!"

"Gia," Sydona grabbed her arms and tried to calm her down. "Listen to me. You don't have to leave. And you're right, we have come too far. Too far to let you go."

Giovonna began to sob again and hugged Sydona so tightly it caused her to cry, too. It was all happening much too quickly. Giovonna couldn't leave. But she already made up her mind. Raoul joined in the hug.

"What will we do without you?" he said through sobs.

"I'm sorry guys…" She let go and took another deep breath. "I have all of my things packed. I'll continue working on the bracelets. Here's my home number if you ever need to call, okay? I won't really be gone." She smiled through her red, soaked cheeks.

"Be safe, Gia," Sydona said.

Giovonna nodded with a sad smile.

Sydona took one last look at the teenage girl who changed her life, unaware of when she would ever see her again. She wasn't dying, but it hurt just the same.

The police and Silas were getting loud, and Giovonna was back in her room packing up. Sydona had a feeling it wouldn't be as easy as Giovonna simply turning herself in. If they knew Giovonna was hiding there, they might think she was too. She had to hide.

The voices became instantly louder, and Silas could no longer keep them outside.

"—she won't mind if we ask her a few questions then, right?" said a man with a much deeper voice than Silas.

Sydona panicked. She gathered up a dirty pile of clothes and threw it to the side of the bed facing the door. She squeezed under the bed, scraping herself on the dirty carpet on the way, and then hooked the clothes under the bed to disguise herself. It wasn't the cleverest idea, but it was the quickest, and she hoped they wouldn't search too hard. They were getting Giovonna back; it was the reason they came by.

Her knees tucked into her belly, but her back felt so exposed. She hoped that more clothes littered the ground on the other side of the bed. Willow couldn't complain about them being too messy now; it might save her life.

A whiff of dirty clothes and body odor invaded her nose, and she was forced to plug it. Muffled voices spoke in the living room and hallway.

"—We have to look, sir. She was the last person she was seen with. She's a danger to Ms. Carr, and she's a danger to you. We're just trying to do our job."

"Bullshit! That man is a damn liar! She saved lives," Silas lashed out.

"Whatever your opinion, sir, it's irrelevant to the real danger. Now, please let us look. And if you don't calm down, we'll have to—"

"Yeah, I know. I'm calm…" Silas said and lowered his voice.

Sydona swallowed hard. She heard someone enter the bedroom and mumble to himself. Silas tried to talk to them as they began to pull items of clothing from under the bed.

"Just gonna find more clumps of clothes. Bit of a slob…"

She smiled. It seemed to work, and they stopped and stood back up. She heard their joints pop. Giovonna talked louder than usual, answering their questions with attitude. She told them the time her parents saw her at the house was the last time she saw Sydona and that she just hated her parents and wanted to leave. She didn't give them exact details, but she was smart. Giovonna knew not to say too much.

A small section of the clothes gave her a window into the hallway. She could see feet walking past. It killed Sydona to be hiding under a bed when Giovonna was on her way out. She could only see her poorly tied, black and white shoes and hear a backpack clanking with materials.

But Giovonna whispered into the room, knowing full well Sydona was in there. Her voice was cracked and empty. "Goodbye."

The front door soon slammed shut, and Sydona felt her face get hot with tears. "Bye, Gia…"

Chapter Fourteen

A clap of thunder made Sydona jump. The sky darkened, and she hadn't even noticed. It was as if the universe knew her hurt and wanted to cry too.

"Come on, let's go inside," Raoul said. "Willow should be here any minute."

Sydona slowly rose to her feet and slumped indoors. Visions of Giovonna's face clouded her mind, making it hard to see anything else. She missed her already.

Knowing they still had a long journey ahead of them, she made everyone breakfast. It also helped to keep her mind occupied. She cooked up scrambled eggs with peppers, onion and mushrooms with a side of turkey bacon. Lacey, Devon, Jet, Harold, Knox and Avani were also on their way, so she tried to make enough for everyone. Silas was kind enough to make coffee, and she slipped a bit of Jet's leftover vodka in it. It tasted awful, but it numbed her sadness.

Two vehicles pulled up to the house, and Sydona's heart dropped. She took another swig of her coffee.

The front door flung open to reveal Willow in all her army gear and a shot gun in hand. "Y'all ready to go huntin'?!" she bellowed as loud as she could. She strutted inside the cabin, which quickly filled with people. Her nose was high in the air that was pungent with frying fat, and she grinned.

"Aw, you cook all this for us, Silas? So sweet." Willow ruffled his hair.

"What? No, I cooked it, actually," Sydona answered.

"You did? Wow, I'm surprised, princess! You must be in a good mood. Can't imagine why." She elbowed her arm enough to hurt.

"Gia's gone." Her words were short and still.

Willow's face melted into a gaping mouth. "What?"

"About two hours ago... She insisted." Sydona gulped down more vodka flavored coffee.

"It's 'cause her parents?" Willow asked.

"That and she didn't want to risk me getting caught."

The group got closer in the kitchen, but Devon spoke up. "She's gone? For good?"

Raoul shrugged. "We don't know. I hope not, though."

Devon looked down to the floor.

"Do ya think we could still get her back?" Harold asked from behind the group.

"She won't come back. Her mind was set," said Silas.

Sydona looked up at the wood ceiling to clear her eyes, then turned back around to serve breakfast. No one spoke, but Sydona could tell Willow was clearly upset. Harold squeezed her tight. Knox and Avani didn't know Giovonna as well but still comforted each other. In the living room, Devon sat on Lacey's lap with his head on her chest and played with her necklace. His mouth moved every once in a while, and Sydona knew he was talking to Lacey about his feelings. Her hand stroked his back while he wiped his nose.

She pushed the fork around the eggs on her plate, thinking of the last words Giovonna spoke. So alone. So small. But certain. The entire meal passed in silence; no one looked at one another. Raoul didn't eat a single slice of banana. A dark mist invaded the empty space, and they were the rain. It was all she could think about.

Sydona gulped her coffee hard enough for it to burn on its way down. After half an hour, people were finally starting to talk. She knew they needed to get a move on. They had Jubilee, and every second mattered. At last, she spoke up.

"Harold. You said you knew where he lives?"

"Yeah, uh, he's on a beach front in California."

"Is it large?" Sydona asked.

"Yes, ma'am. Reckon it's 'bout forty acres or so. Lot of security."

"I think we can handle it," Knox said with a smirk.

Harold drew out a rough sketch of his house and the layout. It had been a while since he visited his ex-boss's vacation home, but his memory was spot on. He even knew where most of the guards frequented and where to hide.

"You never been sexier to me than you are right now my bugga lugga," Willow said in a baby voice and kissed Harold passionately.

Everyone scrunched up their faces with disgust, except for Avani who thought it was adorable.

"Enough of that," Jet said with a swig of his special coffee. "We good to go now?"

"What about niñito?" Avani said. "He's coming with us?"

"He wanted to come," Lacey answered.

"If this turns into Eagle Lake though… he could be in real trouble."

"He'll be fine." Lacey narrowed her eyes at Avani.

Avani saw this and snapped back. "Okay, but you're responsible for him, chica. If he messes up our plan--"

"Stop talking like I ain't here!" Devon yelled from the kitchen table with a squeak in his voice.

Everyone turned their heads toward him and stopped bickering. Devon's personality was slowly leaking out of him each day, and Sydona respected him more every time.

"Well, if we're all set, we should get the cars loaded up," Knox said. He folded up the map and put it in his long, black trench coat.

"Oh, um, actually I was thinking instead of driving there, we could fly," Sydona said shyly.

"Fly?" Raoul asked. "What about the other day when you shot us down when we tried to help?"

Sydona glanced over at Silas, still feeling guilty about that day. "This whole–thing--is bigger than me. I'm pushing my stubbornness away. It's the fastest way, and we need to get Jubilee back, right?"

Raoul perked up with a smile.

Suddenly, Willow chuckled like a nervous school girl.

"Nooo, no. No, no, nononono. Absolutely not. Not in a thousand years am I flyin'. No offence to y'all, but I would rather have a hive of bees sting me all over than fly."

"I gotta say, I'm with Willow on this one," Harold added. "I'm scared ta' death of heights."

"What a shocker; the two rednecks don't wanna do nothin' but sit on their asses and chew tobacco," Jet said in a mockingly southern accent.

"Excuse the piss outta me?" Harold huffed, walking over to Jet who took another drink of his coffee.

"You're the only two who seem to have a problem with flying, you racist mother--"

"Jet, stop it!" Lacey yelled.

"This ain't a race thing, boy," Willow made her way over to Jet. "It's a 'I don't want to be thousands of feet away from the ground and worry about fallin' on it' thing, ya prick!"

Sydona interrupted, not sure how the conversation got away from her so quickly. "Hey, no, I just thought it would get us there quicker. Driving is going to take too--"

"--ever since you joined us, you took Willow back to her old roots. She was better off without you, Harold." Jet whiplashed back.

Willow and Harold both stared at him with murder in their eyes. Willow answered, "Who do you think you are telling me who I am, Jet? You barely know me, you drunkard. Go on, take another drink!"

Sydona stared wide eyed from the kitchen. Taking another drink didn't sound like a half bad idea. She gulped down more coffee and added more of the special ingredient.

"That's enough, Willow!" Lacey cried out. She was holding onto Devon who opted out of the conversation a long time ago. They, along with Knox and Avani, exited to the porch.

"Guys, come on!" Raoul flew into the middle of the fight. "We need to be on each other's side!"

Jet waved his arms around. "Exactly! We need to be on each other's side. Harold is a Vulture! Did you all forget that?"

"He knows where Malik lives, Jet. Why would he do that if he was on their side still?" Silas argued, getting as upset as the rest of them. "And where the hell have you been this whole time? You sit there in the background like you don't even exist, and you only come out to start shit?"

Jet didn't back down. "He was a Vulture, Silas! A Vulture! How the fuck are you all trusting him right now? How do you know it's not just a set up? Especially you, Sydona! I was told you were the hardest person to get to trust, and here we are only, what, a day later? And you give him permission to have us all killed?"

Sydona furrowed her brows. "What?! No! I trust Willow, so I trust Harold! Why is this my fault now?"

She caught Willow giving her an approving smirk.

"Because I guess you're the leader of this gang of misfits, and you're calling the shots on what we're all doing."

"I'm not the leader; Knox is!"

Jet shrugged. "Doesn't really seem like it."

Her words fell short. Was she the leader now? She only wanted revenge on Malik. Everyone else coming wasn't really in her original plan. All she knew was that she wished Giovonna was there to lighten the mood. She would just start singing or dancing or something silly to stop the fighting.

Silas spoke up. "Knox is the leader of the Sparrows. But this isn't a Sparrows mission. This is something she needs to do... It's something we all need to do."

"And we can't spend all day fighting about it," Raoul said. "I trust Sydona with every bone in my body.

And if she trusts Harold, then I trust him too. Now everyone just shut up so we can go already!"

For such a small creature, he sure had a way of capturing an audience. Jet slammed the screen door open and stormed down the wooden stairs. Willow rolled her eyes and huffed at his behavior. Harold and Willow both caressed each other, but Harold caught Sydona's eyes. He held his hand out with a closed mouth smile.

She took his grimy hand and shook it.

"Thanks, Sydona. I appreciate you havin' my back."

Her stomach did flips. As much as she did stand up for Harold, Jet's words stuck with her. Maybe she did trust him a little too quickly. But there was no turning back now. She needed to keep two eyes on him, just in case.

"You better not be lying about this place," she whispered out of earshot from Willow.

Harold shook his head but gave no verbal answer.

The response made her uneasy, but there was nothing to be done about it now. Flying to California was still a question floating in the air.

Raoul took his position on Sydona's shoulder as they faced Willow and Harold. "With my dust and everyone else here, you both would feel so light you wouldn't even feel like you could fall."

Sydona smiled wide. "It's a feeling unlike no other. I know you guys would love it."

While they were discussing the flying situation, the rest of them out front were strapping things to themselves. Sydona joined them and saw Devon with a huge grin on his face while Lacey helped suit him up.

"Are you excited to fly with us?" she asked and crouched down to his level.

"Yeah! I'll be like Superman!" he exclaimed.

When his excitement showed through, he reminded Sydona of Joseph from the farmers market with his unstoppable energy and positivity. She admired children who could experience such traumatic events in their short lives but still have a sense of wonder and curiosity. The tragedies he went through would never go away, but the fact that he didn't let it keep him down long was admirable.

Lacey side-eyed Willow and Harold who soon came out with everyone. "See, even he's looking forward to flying with us. We'll all be like Superman."

Willow laughed and noticeably gave in. There was no winning an argument about flying with a whole group of fliers.

Sydona grabbed her black backpack and green tote and secured everything as best she could around her back. From the corner of her eye, she saw Jet get in Harold's face and accidentally overheard his threat.

"You make one wrong move or even look at my girl wrong, I will personally make sure to watch you as you fall back to the ground."

Harold hacked up something from his throat and spit it out near Jet's boots. Their noses almost touched as Jet challenged him.

"That would never happen. I got everyone here on my side now, and they wouldn't let me die. Plus, I'm the only one who knows where we're goin'. You kill me, this whole thing was for nothin' and y'all still be in the dark. Best to stay away from me, kid."

Harold turned his back, but Jet clearly had too much to drink despite the early morning hour. He shoved Harold in the back so hard he bumped into Knox and Avani, throwing them off balance. Harold whipped back around to size up Jet, and his eyes grew dark with anger. He lunged at Jet with such force it pushed Jet backwards, then the punches started.

"Damnit," Lacey said. Her tone made it sound like Jet did this on a daily basis.

"Dios mio! Shouldn't someone stop them?" Avani asked with manicured hands over her mouth.

Willow watched the brawl from afar with everyone else. "Nah. Best to let them get it out. You know how men are...."

"Tell me about it!" Lacey scoffed. "It's one of the reasons I hate going out with him anymore. Always used to get kicked out of bars because of this crap."

Knox entered the conversation. "Bars? How old are you?"

Lacey widened her eyes. "Uh, twenty-one."

"Yeah, sure you are," Knox guffawed.

"Alright, I'm only nineteen," Lacey said. "But I'm not the one on trial here."

Devon stood in front of Sydona watching them like it was a UFC fight match. He mimicked their punches and grunted with each swing he took to an invisible opponent.

"Oh, Devon." Lacey noticed too. "Don't watch this. Come on, let's get some food from inside."

As Lacey and Devon went back inside, Avani leaned over to whisper into Sydona's ear. "She don't want him watching a fight, but she's okay with him going on this mission where we could die?"

Sydona shrugged. She had a good point.

"Do you think we should break them up now?"
Raoul said.

Sydona nodded. "Yeah, I guess we should. Do it
your way though."

Raoul perked up. "Okay!"

A trail of red and orange dust followed behind him
as he quickly flew to the brawl. He waited for a moment
when they both took a short break from beating on each
other, flew up their shirts and tickled them.

The once stressful, bloody fight was instantly
turned into a giggly, high-pitched laugh fest. Jet's laugh
was so high pitched it crushed his manly tone he worked
so hard to get. It caused everyone else to laugh along with
him. Raoul exited his shirt, and his smile went to a frown
instantly. His face turned twenty shades of crimson, and
he stormed off to grab his stuff. Jet didn't speak a word to
Harold the rest of the time.

"Hope you all had your fun. Do you think we can
get going now?" Knox said.

Jet wiped his nose, smearing blood all over his face
and matching his skin's new color.

"That should be yer new nickname, Raoul. Raoul
the Diffuser," said Willow.

"Not nearly as catchy as Willow the Widowed
though," Sydona added.

"Your nickname is Willow the Widowed?" asked
Knox. "That's so wrong…"

Willow shrugged. "Gia gave it to me." She sighed
heavily.

Lacey and Devon came out with more supplies and
whatever food was left inside. Sydona made sure to pack
extra fruit for Raoul in her tote. After several more
minutes of packing and strapping things down so they

wouldn't fall out of the sky, they were finally ready to take flight. Lacey took hold of Devon since he was small enough to carry. The others got in formation from left to right: Avani, Harold, Silas, Sydona, Knox, Willow and Jet.

Raindrops hit the pavement and her skin. Sydona took a deep breath of the fresh rain on dirt smell and exhaled. The bigger group gathered in the road as it was the only place big enough for everyone to run together. Lacey and Devon stayed behind. Once everyone was ready, they took off running as fast as they could; Raoul helped to dust everyone as much as he could. Willow started out slow, but the more dust she received, the easier it was for her to make strides.

Soon, everyone's feet left the earth, and they flew over the trees. A plethora of reactions surrounded her. Devon's contagious laughter rose up from behind, Willow cursed and laughed, and Harold kept asking questions like: "Have you ever gotten bugs in your teeth like a truck grill?" and "What if I need to use the bathroom?" The rain was rough at first, coming at them as they soared easily at sixty miles per hour, but it soon faded into humidity.

Chapter Fifteen

Sydona looked to one side and studied Silas's wind bearing profile. He looked hard and brave. His lashes fluttered to keep his eyes from drying out. She had heard of some folks buying goggles. Some even had helmets in case they ran into something like a bird or worse, and others had kneepads for rough landings. It was fun to picture Silas with that attire; he looked like a pilot on his way to end the war.

To her left, Knox held her arm with his, and with its massive size, she felt there was no way she could fall. His look mirrored Silas's but with a bit more smirk on the edges. She was proud to have him by her side. She couldn't help but feel envious of his bald head, which was shiny from the rain. He had no hair to whip him in the face from the unyielding, icy wind.

Occasionally, someone in the group would ask how the humans were doing, while others would yell out when they saw too much traffic below. They would either turn the line or go up higher. She didn't know how high they were, but she imagined about eight-hundred feet. It was enough to have people on the ground not question what it was they were seeing in the air.

Sydona wondered how Raoul was doing. They had flown roughly two-hundred miles, and he had been sprinkling dust the entire time. He would inform her when he needed a break, but they also had to calculate if they would be able to land with a group so large. They avoided cities and towns of any kind and stayed near the forests and farms. The larger cities were dangerous and full of people who might spot them, and they took an extra thirty minutes each time to go around them. Landing would also give them the opportunity to check the map and make sure they weren't going in the wrong direction.

Sydona had never flown for so long at one time. It sometimes felt she was in a dream with the scenery she encountered. Her eyes closed, and she pretended she wasn't being held onto. She swore she could smell the mountains, streams, rivers and fields of yellow and purple flowers far below. They reminded her of her home. She thought of Raoul again.

"Hey." She looked around for his glowing orange light. "Raoul, you okay? Do you need a break yet?"

He joined her and stood on her shoulder blade, clearly out of breath.

"You need to let me know if you need rest, buddy. I don't want you overworking yourself," she said over her shoulder.

He patted her on the head and focused on breathing. She took his pat as confirmation for a break.

Sydona yelled as loud as she could to either side of her. "Hey guys, let's find a landing. Willow, Harold-- Raoul's not going to dust you anymore, but you should be fine. As long as you keep a hold of us, you won't fall. The weightlessness will gradually fade off, though."

Knox replied, "Over to the left looks like a good spot, in that field."

"There's a farmhouse over there though," yelled Harold.

"It's far enough away from where we're going. It's fine."

The party began to descend as they slowly angled their body vertically. The speed decreased dramatically, and the ground grew closer every second.

"Whoa, whoa! Slow down! We gonna crash!" Willow screamed.

Silas yelled out, "Level out everyone!"

The formation was falling apart. Some of them were straight up and down, while others flattened themselves out to prevent landing too fast. Harold and Willow especially spazzed out. Sydona didn't like the feeling either since she was no longer in control. She couldn't break away from the group and do it herself. They had to work as a team.

Sydona shouted, "Everyone stop! We need to work together. Look at the person beside you and match their positions. If we mess this up, we could get seriously hurt! All together at the count of three, we slowly go vertical. Got it?"

Everyone verbally agreed, but the landing strip was running out. Raoul regained some energy and took the lead to see everyone in front of him and correct them if needed.

Sydona counted down. "Three."

"Willow, you're going too fast!" Raoul shouted. "Look at Jet next to you and do what he's doing!"

"I'm tryin'!" she spat with a groan.

Jet howled a laugh.

"Two," Sydona continued.

"Avani, you are still too vertical. We need to slow down," Raoul corrected with a softer tone.

"I know what I'm doing, muchacho. You try doing this with people strapped to either side of you!" she argued.

Sydona yelled irritably. "ONE!"

"Alright everyone, nice and easy." Raoul held his arms out as if he were an orchestra director helping everyone play the right notes.

But it worked. Eventually they all got on the same page and landed smoothly on the blue grass below.

Willow rolled on the ground back and forth, thanking God profusely that she was still alive. She pulled up tufts of grass and kissed them. Lacey and Devon landed just after them, and Devon had a smile plastered on his face.

"Is Willow always so dramatic?" Lacey asked as she brushed her auburn and pink hair out with her fingers.

Sydona nodded with a snicker. She copied Lacey and groomed the knots out of her hair. Everyone took a few minutes to catch their breath and enjoy having their feet back on the ground. Knox wasted no time in pulling the map out from one of his many pockets.

"Alright, we just passed this river, and that mountain is to the north of us, so I think we're right about in this area."

Willow finally came back to reality. "How much more flyin' we gotta do? I don't know if I can do it, y'all…"

Jet laughed loud enough for everyone to hear.

Harold took notice and couldn't bite his tongue. "You got somethin' to say, slick, ya better just say it!"

Silas marched over to Jet and went chest to chest. Sydona couldn't hear what Silas said, but whatever it was, it calmed Jet down. The two men glanced over at Harold. Jet hung his head, and Silas gave a nod.

"Harold," Knox called. "You know how much longer?" Harold joined him along with Willow and Avani as they took a look at the map, figuring out the time and distance. Sydona wanted to be included in the plan, but she also wanted to see how Devon was doing.

Lacey greeted her with a bright smile as she made her way over. Devon picked flowers he found randomly sprouting about and showed them to Lacey. Most of them were white flowers with petals that delicately flew off with a gentle breeze like summer snowflakes tickling his nose.

"How ya doing, girl?" she asked.

Sydona shrugged. "I'm more tired than I thought I would be. Watching Raoul fly around like he was on speed was exhausting. I knew he would be too proud to tell us when he was tired."

"He's a special guy. Our fairies would never do anything like that. We wanted to bring them, but they don't really do things like this."

It suddenly dawned on Sydona why Devon never seemed surprised to see Raoul in the car; he lived with two of them. Raoul was just another fairy. "What do your fairies do?"

Lacey shrugged. "Oh, ya know, they *love* to sing. Everything revolves around them singing, learning new songs, vocal cord stretching. It's fun but gets kinda old after a while. They need a place to showcase their talents."

Devon groaned. "They sing soooo much. It's so hard to sleep sometimes!"

Sydona laughed. She was somewhat happy not to have that issue with Raoul. He couldn't carry a tune if his life depended on it. Sydona lowered herself to Devon's level and balanced on her toes. "Did you enjoy flying with everyone?"

"It was such a blast! When are we going again? Soon, I hope!" He jumped with so much excitement his glasses almost fell right off his nose.

"I hope so, too!" Sydona grinned. She rubbed the top of his head and stood back up. She talked softer so the ten-year-old wouldn't be able to hear as much. Devon soon got bored though and ran off to find more flowers for the bouquet. Sydona bit her lip and fidgeted with her nails as she worked up the courage to talk about a sore subject.

"Hey, um, can I talk to you about Jet?"

Lacey looked over to quickly search for him. He was by himself, somewhere far away from the group. He lifted his arm, and it was clear he was drinking from his flask again.

"I know, I know. He has his problems. I'm working on it..." she said with her head low.

Sydona furrowed her brows. "Lacey, let me just say, you shouldn't be the one working on anything. He should be. This is *his* problem. Not yours."

Her face turned away, embarrassed. "I know."

Sydona licked her lips and took a deep breath. "We're not in the best position to take him to AA meetings or anything... but if he doesn't get his alcohol problem under control, he could be a danger to more than just himself."

Lacey whipped her head back to meet her gaze with angry eyes. "You think he's the only one with an alcohol problem? I don't recall Jet getting so wasted he passed out and knocked himself unconscious."

Her breath quickened and the incident before her blackout came rushing back. "That was different, Lacey…"

"How?"

"I--" Sydona paused, trying to understand why she was suddenly being put on trial. "Well, you saw. I thought I killed him… I think that was reason enough, don't you?"

"Reason enough? You know what you sound like?" Lacey said and pointed sternly at her boyfriend, stumbling around in the grass.

"Are you serious right now?" Sydona said louder.

Silas walked up behind her. "What's going on here?" he asked innocently. Lacey rolled her eyes and flounced away from the conversation.

"Lacey's accusing me of being an alcoholic like her deadbeat boyfriend over there!"

Her muscles began to tighten. Silas avoided her gaze. Her heart dropped into her stomach.

"Do you think I am?" she asked Silas, almost forgetting about Lacey.

"No! Not at all. She's known you for a little while, and this was the first time you got drunk like that, right?"

Sydona furrowed her brows. "Right! That was not me. You know it wasn't."

"I know. You—had a reason to," he said softly.

Sydona's rage shifted. For a moment, she knew she should be angry with the doctor. But it flowed over her so strongly she had to release the rest of it. She stormed back over to Lacey.

"I know you don't know much about me, Lacey, and I won't deny that one night I had too much. But if you knew all the crap I have been dealing with lately, you would want to drown it in anything that made you feel even the tiniest bit numb. Like nothing could touch you."

Lacey listened to her words, but it didn't seem to change her mind much. "I like you, Sydona. I really do. But please stop acting like you're the only one who has problems. We all have them. Don't make excuses and start blaming others for something you are equally guilty of... Come on, Devon, let's go see Jet. See how he's doing." She guided the boy's head and took one last glance at Sydona before walking across the field.

"What is with everyone today? Is it a full moon tonight or something?" she asked Silas who took a seat on the ground.

He shrugged. "Yeah, I dunno."

"Why didn't you defend me back there?" She knew she sounded like a woman with a boyfriend who needed to stand up for her no matter what. She didn't need him to defend her, but it would've been nice to hear. He could have at least showed he was on her side.

"Come on, Syd, just let it go..." he lay back with arms out.

She sighed heavily. This was their biggest difference. Sydona was stubborn, hard-headed and had a hard time letting anything go, while Silas hated confrontation, was easygoing and didn't like to argue. She wanted to know why though. Her display in front of Lacey was embarrassing, and he made it worse. Maybe she should have taken a more direct approach and talked to Jet himself. But it was too late for that now.

"You know me better than that..." she said in a soft tone.

Silas's chest expanded, and he let out an irritated breath. "I do know you. And I know there was stuff in your coffee this morning. My dad was an alcoholic, Syd. You gotta try harder to slip things past me. I can smell that shit on your breath from a mile away."

Her nostrils flared, and she suddenly felt hot all over. She wasn't slick. It was hard to hear Silas now compare her to his father. It seemed worse than being compared to Jet. The grass tickled her neck as she lay down next to him.

"I'm sorry…" she said.

"We all cope with things differently. Alcohol, punching things, running away… I just don't want this to get worse. We need you. I need you. You're not the same when you drink."

"There's a lot of things that aren't the same about me lately." She paused to let a tear roll down. "I don't even know who I am anymore. I can't even look at myself in the mirror without wanting to cry."

Silas tenderly grabbed hold of her hand and entwined his fingers between hers.

"You're Sydona Fucking Wilder. You are… the most passionate, the most hard-headed, loyal and focused woman I've ever met. That will never change. You have to know that. Your 'flaws' are what make you amazing. I wish I had that fire. You care so much. And that's what makes you the best person for what we're doing right now."

Her head turned sideways, and she smiled wide at Silas. He turned his head too and leaned in for a kiss.

"Can that be my new nickname?" Sydona asked in between their kisses.

"If you want it to be," Silas said and rotated his body so he could wrap his other arm around her and squeeze.

"Ew, god, ack," Raoul spat. "In broad daylight? In the middle of a field with all these people around? Seriously you guys?"

Silas and Sydona broke apart and sat upright. "We weren't doing anything, Raoul."

"That's not what I saw. God, gross!"

Sydona rolled her eyes and stood up. She held out her hand to help Silas off the soft grass.

"What's the expression? Get a room?" he continued.

"Okay, Jesus, Raoul. We're not even touching anymore."

Sydona made her way over to Knox and Avani who were still looking over the map.

"How's it going over here?" she asked timidly.

"Bueno," replied Avani. "We're only in Iowa right now, so we still got a ways to go. Might get there by tomorrow night as long as everything goes as planned."

"How many breaks like this would that include?"

"Maybe two," Knox said. "I know you want to get there as fast as we can, but we can't risk overworking the only fairy we have. We may be able to do it without him, but I don't want to take that chance."

"Yeah," Sydona nodded. "I agree…"

Yelling and screaming echoed throughout the valley, and Sydona saw Devon jogging toward her. Jet was especially raising his voice at Lacey. What the hell was his problem today? Sydona wanted to go see what the problem was, but after the last conversation with Lacey, she thought it might be best to not interfere. They all looked at each other as if to say: who has to deal with the drama couple now?

"I'll go," Knox said with the most unenthusiastic tone.

The two of them weren't so far away that they couldn't be overheard.

"...I don't want to keep traveling with these people if they fucking hate me, Lacey!"

"We can't go without you, Jet! We kinda need everyone to go in order to get there," Lacey argued.

"Why should I care? This isn't a Sparrows mission. This is because of Sydona's blind revenge. This isn't our fight!"

"This is all our fight!" Knox roared over them.

They turned to face him with sour faces.

"Knox, I can't go with you anymore. I don't want to be with people who hate me."

"If I recall, you're the one who started this whole mess. You brought it upon yourself!"

"How did I start this? It's Sydona who thinks I'm a danger to the group because of my drinking. I have it under control, man. And who is she to judge me? She's the one who took my bottle of vodka and passed out. You still owe me, by the way!"

He pointed at Sydona. Her eyes would be green if it was possible.

"Enough!" Knox's voice rang out so loudly birds flew out of the trees from a nearby forest. "I'm tired of everyone's anger. Give me your flask, Jet."

Jet stared at him with wide green eyes. "What? No! No disrespect, sir, but this is not going--"

"I said give it to me." Knox held his hand out steadily.

"Or what?" Jet challenged.

Lacey took Jet's shoulder to ease him off their huge pit-bull leader. "Jet, just do it. Come on."

He shrugged her arm off while still keeping an eye on Knox. "What?" He waited for an answer from Knox.

From where Sydona stood, it looked like Knox hadn't moved a muscle or blinked an eye. He calmly held his arm out and stared back at Jet.

In a matter of milliseconds, Knox's open palm curled into a ball, and he shoved it straight into Jet's torso. Jet instantly hunched over and fell to the ground coughing. Knox composed his previous position, retracting his arm as if it were on a spring. Jet whimpered, and Lacey went to his side. Knox's feet finally moved. He stood over Jet like a statue.

He looked down at Jet, and only his lips moved. "We are going with or without you. If we go without you, it won't be because we left you here but because you would not be among the living anymore. Your choice."

Lacey comforted Jet, and he slowly rose back to his feet. He didn't say another word. Knox gave the group walking back a wink.

"That was mucho bueno, baby," Avani hugged him.

Raoul raised a brow. "He punched him. You saw that, right?"

"Si, but just once. I'm so proud of you, papi," she grinned and gave Knox a long kiss.

"Thanks to you, sweetheart." Knox grabbed her bottom, and she shrieked.

"Alright. Think we could go soon?" Sydona asked.

"Yeah. We should be good now," Knox said. "You guys ready?"

"Yes, sir!" Harold was the only one to answer.

Knox rolled his eyes. "Alright. Same formation."

Jet dragged his feet on the way over and lazily grabbed Willow's arm.

"Let's try to pay attention and listen to one another this time people!" Raoul called over the group like a coach.

Everyone groaned as they listened to the fairy give orders.

Knox looked over at Sydona and spoke up. "He could be a great Sparrow someday, Syd."

"Oh no, don't say that." she said.

He laughed along with everyone.

Soon they were all back in the air. Raoul went straight to work to make the non-fliers comfortable. She wished she had a camera to capture all the beautiful landscapes out there. She just had to try to remember all of it: the colors, the feeling of crisp air in her face and hair, the feeling of being above it all. It was the best high. Better than alcohol. Flying and the feeling of flying never had any consequences. She hated the tension she brought to the group by doing something so stupid, something she thought she put to rest decades ago. Bad habits die hard.

Flying went smoothly for the next few hours. She hoped they had gone at least another state over. The sun was at its highest point in the sky with not much cloud coverage. It was nice that it wasn't very cloudy. It would be like driving through super thick fog. Anything could be inside. Sydona looked ahead rather than down to avoid the sun rays and saw a massive city on the horizon. As usual, the group veered to the edges of it even though it set them back a lot. It was better to be safe than sorry. After the city was behind them, they turned back to where they were originally flying.

Then, Sydona heard something from the ground that resembled a firework or gunshot. Others from the group heard it too, and Knox and Silas both looked at her with puzzled looks. When it didn't happen again, they calmed down and kept going. But then, another shot rang out, and it was clear what it was.

"Whoa!" Harold yelled out, causing turbulence in the formation. "They almost shot me!"

Sydona looked down at the ground, but small clouds had appeared. Still, she could see a large vehicle with a sniper gun. The gun was almost as large as the truck itself.

"Go, go, go! We need to move faster!" Sydona shouted.

They flattened themselves out as much as possible, now going almost one-hundred miles per hour. Lacey kept following them, but at their new speed, Devon was now screaming, and Sydona's heart leaped from her chest. The shooter down below paused for a while, but Sydona kept an eye on him even with her eyes watering like crazy. The driver sped up with them and pulled the trigger again.

Silas yelled out in agony. He pulled Sydona down to her left so hard she almost couldn't breathe. Her heart stopped as her grip almost lost Silas, but she twisted her arm to adjust her hand. She grabbed his bicep as hard as possible. Willow was on her other side freaking out even more than Silas who had been shot.

"Willow! Stop!" Knox shouted.

"I-I can't. I want down! Now!" Willow bellowed.

"We can't! Not now!" Knox answered.

Silas screamed out in pain again. Sydona looked back at his body, and his leg was covered in blood.

Another shot was fired, and it must have gotten too close to Willow or Jet. All she could feel was a massive pull from her right. Knox slipped out of her reach, and her arm still stuck out as if it was still attached to him. Her heart pounded in her ears like a jackhammer.

"Knox!" Sydona screamed. They were separated by clouds, and it felt like they were miles away. She whipped her head back to Silas with a worried expression.

"Silas, are you okay?"

"No…" he said through a closed jaw.

Soon, her right hand was grabbed again.

"Knox!"

Willow was still screaming and shouting. Knox spoke up. "We're going to land. You go on without us. We still have the walkies. We'll keep you updated."

Her face dropped. "What? No, you can't--"

"We have to, Sydona. See you on the ground."

"Knox! Wait!"

He let go again. Another gunshot rang out. They had to maneuver around the shooter. She hated that Knox separated from them, and she didn't have anyone on her other side, but she would manage. It wasn't as if she had never flown before. With less people, it would be faster to weave in and out of the clouds, confusing the person below.

"Where's Elias?!" Avani cried out. She must have just realized they took off.

"We'll meet him on the ground," Sydona said.

"He can't be serious!"

"No time to debate this, Avani. We need to get to a safe place and help, Silas."

A million thoughts ran through her head on how the hell they would get out of this situation. They couldn't out-fly the shooter, and Silas needed to land. His leg was getting worse, and she couldn't take his cries anymore. "Raoul! You think you could help me fly. Just you?"

"Uh… are you sure?" Raoul asked.

"Silas needs help, and I think they are after me. I could fly ahead and let them land."

"Okay. Yeah, let's do it!" Raoul shouted.

Sydona looked to her right at Avani, Harold and Silas. "You guys okay with that plan?"

Harold spoke up. "Anything that gets me out of the sky."

Avani and Silas agreed.

Sydona looked over at Silas one last time, wrapped her free arm around his neck and kissed him.

"I love you."

Silas stared at her wide-eyed and frozen. Sydona pulled away and took a second to realize the words she uttered aloud. As her entire body blushed from embarrassment, she let go of Silas, and he disappeared into the clouds.

Chapter Sixteen

Raoul dusted every inch of Sydona's body as she flew stiffly at a thousand feet above the ground. That was the first time she ever uttered such delicate words to Silas. She wanted to cry and hug him so badly it hurt. If the shooter wasn't just after her, maybe the ground was the last place to be. They could be hunting down the others right now. She watched as the three descended to the earth, far away from the truck on the white dirt road. A cloud of dust still rose from the road, which meant they were still after her. Why were they trying to shoot her? Didn't the doctor want her alive? Judging by Silas's injury, they weren't darts like she experienced before. They wanted to kill her. But why?

"I'm going down, Raoul."

"What? Why? They're going to kill you!" he shouted.

"No, they won't."

"How do you know?"

She didn't. But if she wanted to protect the rest of her pack, she had to stop the attack at the source.

"Stop dusting me."

Raoul looked her in the eye. "But you'll fall!"

"It's alright. I know where I'm going."

He did as he was told, but she could tell he was confused by what she meant. She spun her body around to direct herself back toward the shooter. Straightening her body out like an arrow and keeping her head level, she flew toward them with narrow eyes and teeth clenched. The truck and the person standing in the back became clearer and clearer.

They shot again, and she dodged it with one quick turn of her body. All that Sparrow training really paid off. As she got closer and closer, she pulled out her trusty dagger. She kept it down at her side but with the blade resting on her forearm. They shot again. She heard it whistle past her, but it still missed. Raoul dusted her quickly to slow her landing, but she still made direct contact with the shooter, shoving them over the edge of the truck.

The two women rolled out over the truck and down a hill on the side of the road. Branches, shrubs and stumps hit her as she rolled down. They both finally stopped at the bottom in a large puddle of mud. Every inch of her body felt like it went through a shredder. As she tried to get to her feet, she kept slipping on the mud. She heard the other woman grunting as she attempted to stand up. Once Sydona was able to stand on two feet, her heart sank as she noticed her dagger was nowhere in sight. She was defenseless. She panicked.

Just then, the shooter stood up and their eyes met. A young Hispanic woman stood hunched over with a snarl on her dirt-covered face. Her natural black hair was wild and dirty, matching her clothes. She had shorts that didn't conceal much and a black shirt that tied in the front to expose her stomach. Sydona didn't know who the woman was, but it was clear she knew who Sydona was.

"Who are you?" Sydona started.

The young woman cried out a tribal cry and lunged out toward her. Taken off guard, Sydona didn't stand in her way and ran. But she continued to slip on the unyielding mud and fell. Down on her hands and knees, she crawled away from the crazy woman, but not for long. She grabbed Sydona's hair so hard she had no choice but to let her.

"Get off me!"

The woman pushed Sydona down in the mud and put her hands around her neck.

"Stop!" Sydona cracked. She wanted to kick her off, but with the weight she put on top of her and the slippery ground, it was nearly impossible. Next thing she knew, Raoul pulled the woman's hair back, allowing Sydona to breathe again.

"Es eso un hada?" she asked in Spanish.

It was all the time she needed to get the upper hand again. Without her dagger, she had to rely on her own strength. With the woman knelt at the right distance from her, Sydona did a sweeping kick to her jaw, pushing her back into the mud.

"Tu puta perra!" she yelled. She clumsily got up but was able to grab ahold of Sydona again and punch her in the face. Sydona tightened her jaw as the impact made her vision go black for a second, but she socked her back just as hard.

While they took a short break from hitting each other, Sydona asked, out of breath, "You work for the doctor?"

"Fuck you." She spit in Sydona's face.

Sydona wiped it away, smearing more mud and blood over her face. "That's a yes."

She angrily pushed Sydona back to the mud with a frighteningly loud growl. Sydona knew her tactic already and would not let her do the same thing again. Using her hips and knees, she pushed the woman over and had the upper hand. She bound her hands to the ground and sat on her legs.

"Why are you trying to kill me?"

She didn't answer and Sydona asked again. "Why do you want to kill me?!"

"I don't have to answer to you, la punta."

Sydona slapped her so hard the woman's lip split open. All she could do was wriggle and growl.

"Syd! Raoul!" A voice that sounded like Avani echoed through the trees.

Sydona glared down at her. "No, but you'll answer to Avani."

"Over here!" Raoul called out.

Avani and Harold barreled down the hill with Silas limping close behind.

"Avani?!" the woman called out. A slow, menacing grin took over the woman's entire face, and her eyes sparkled. She stopped squirming underneath her. The three met them down in the mud pit.

"Dios mio, Syd! You are filthy! And… oh my god, is that…?"

"Hermana! You came!" the woman bent her neck backward just to see Avani.

Sydona only knew a tiny bit of Spanish, but she remembered "hermana" meant "sister". What did she say the name of her sister was?

"Natalia!"

That was it.

"¿Estas loco? You could have killed me, you cabron!" Avani shouted and began to hit her sister in the head. Too close for comfort, Sydona backed up and out of the mud. Harold halfway held up Silas. He smiled at Sydona but then winced.

"You okay?" Sydona whispered.

He nodded but hobbled, trying to balance on one leg.

"What are you doing out here?" Avani asked.

"What the hell do you think? Trying to capture the celebrity over there. Why you with her?" she gasped. "Oh my god, Harold? Que carajo? You here too?"

"Nat…" Harold said flatly.

"Malik is super upset with chu," she laughed. Her teeth looked blinding white against the blackened mud on her face.

"I don't care. He's wrong. You're all wrong."

"Of course it's wrong. But it feels so right!" Natalia squeaked. She stood up and splashed off some dirt. "Hey. That your fairy?" she directed to Sydona.

Sydona's nostrils flared. "Yeah. Why?"

Natalia shrugged. "Just curious. He's gonna love seeing him coming in with chu. Maybe give me an even bigger bonus." She danced.

The group stood around watching the woman who had more than a few screws loose. She may have been Avani's sister, but they were nothing alike.

"Ben--Benji? Where's Benji?" Natalia asked looking up the hill.

"Benji's gone, Natalia. You're stranded. Just give up," Avani said.

"You killed him? Maldita sea… told him I'd split it with him. But, whatever. More for meeee."

"You're psychotic," Silas said.

Natalia turned her attention to him and cleaned herself a bit. "Oh shit, did I hit you? My bad. I'll try to aim higher next time."

Silas grunted, propelled forward and tripped. Harold regained his balance. "Don't waste yer energy on her, Silas. She's nothing but a huge disappointment."

"Oh, do you need help carryin' such a big word? And I'm far from a disappointment, Harold. You're the one who turned your back on Malik. He's gonna kill you, hombre."

"I thought he was dead. We all did."

"You musta shit your pants when you found out then, huh?" She chortled.

Sydona grinded her teeth and curled her fists again. "Enough with the bullshitting. You're coming with us."

Natalia laughed more. "Oh, where we going? Disney World? I've always wanted to go there. So magical. Or Fiji? Either way, both are pretty rad."

"Cállate, Natalia!" Avani yelled. "You're in our custody now." She reached out to grab her sister.

Natalia quickly reached for a handgun in Avani's holster and aimed it at her and the group. "Mmm, I'm thinking not."

Avani and Sydona put their hands up. Sydona's heart pounded, and adrenaline pumped hard through her veins.

"You're too trusting, hermana. These are desperate times," Natalia said and clicked her tongue.

Without realizing it, Harold was already pointing his gun at Natalia.

"It's five against one. Drop the gun," Harold said.

Natalia smiled cunningly. "Four and half, technically."

"Just shoot her already!" Silas belted out.

"No!" Avani threw herself between Natalia and Harold. "No one is shooting anyone. Nat, would you *please* put the gun down?"

Natalia looked her sister in the eye, and then back and forth between everyone else. "What chu gonna do to me?"

"Kill you," Sydona said.

Natalia aimed the gun at Sydona.

"No! We're not going to kill you," Avani corrected and flashed Sydona a dirty look. "We're just keeping an eye on you. For now…"

"Oh no… not that…" Natalia with a toneless inflection and dropped her arm with the gun. Avani swiftly took it back from her and put it back in her holster.

Avani bound her sister's hands behind her back with handcuffs she had in her bag. As she led her up the steep hill, Harold and Silas followed behind. Sydona stayed behind to grab everything she dropped. After several minutes, she was finally able to locate her dagger, which was caked in mud. She found a clean area of soft grass and wiped it down the best she could. The engravings appeared once again on the blade, and she absorbed the words. "Love without fear."

She loved Silas. It felt strange to even think and say the words to herself. To have a feeling so strong about a person, to be that vulnerable and to say words that bind two spirits together was exhilarating. Silas asked her about Theodore, and while she may have had strong feelings for him, it was never love. It took over fifty years to truly understand the meaning her mother engraved on her dagger. Evelyn had no fear in loving her father, and she had no reason to fear loving Silas. And when she loved without fear, fighting for them came naturally.

Sydona scrambled to grab the rest of her things that fell with her down the hill so she could help Harold with Silas. She secured her backpack and tote around herself, and Raoul joined her on her shoulder.

"Hey," Silas said as Sydona put her arm around him.

"Hey."

"You okay?" he asked.

Sydona smiled. "Am I okay? I'm not the one with two human crutches."

"Oh this? This'll heal. The image of what you look like right now will never heal from my brain."

Her fingers pinched his side.

"Ow! Hey!"

They finally made it to the paved road and the truck. She wasn't sure where they would be going next, but it needed to be somewhere with running water and a bed for Silas. Raoul sprinkled some dust on Silas to help him walk a little easier.

"Thanks buddy," Silas said, his face back to normal.

Suddenly, Sydona heard Knox's voice faded and electronic. She opened her bag and pulled out the black walkie.

"*...Is anyone there? Copy,*" Knox said again.

"Sydona here. You guys okay?"

"*Finally. Been trying to reach you for over ten minutes now. We're fine. You?*"

"Uh, yeah. We ran into… someone."

"*The shooter?*"

"Yeah. It's Natalia, Avani's sister."

Natalia gasped. "Oh my god, is that Knoxy Poo? Ooh, can I talk to him?"

There was no answer on the other side. Sydona could only imagine what his reaction would be. He probably threw the walkie off into the abyss.

"Knox? You still there?" Sydona asked.

"Hi Syd, it's Willow. Knox is... busy."

Sydona chuckled to herself. "Are Devon and Lacey with you?"

"Yeah, they're here. You guys find the assailant?"

"Yes. We have a vehicle now, too."

"Thank the heavens. Don't think I can do this flyin' thing anymore."

"Copy. We'll discuss it when you get here."

"Copy."

Sydona clipped the walkie to her hip for quick access. Silas held onto Sydona while Harold went to the truck and pulled it off to the side of the road. A body lay to the side; that must have been Benji. Natalia and Avani were far ahead of them, but Natalia had some colorful words for him.

Sydona wanted to know where they were, but Knox had the map. The truck would be helpful for Willow and whoever else didn't want to fly, but it would take so much longer to get there. Plus, Harold was the only one who really knew the place well enough. There had to be a group discussion on what to do, especially since they had a member of the NFA who wanted Sydona's life.

Avani put Natalia in the back of the truck, and she sat down. Sydona had a glimpse of her crazy, but she seemed too calm about being captured. Perhaps she had a soft spot for her sister as Avani did for her. As Sydona

Silas and Raoul approached the truck, Silas cleared his throat.

"So, uh… You said something… up there…"

Her heart raced. "Yeah…"

"I just wanted to say…"

"No. Don't say it," she blurted.

Silas stuttered. "W-Why?"

"Because… if you say it, I might start crying, and I don't want that maniac in the truck to see."

"Okay…" Silas said and looked away from her.

"Sorry."

"No, I get it."

Raoul flew away from them, clearly uncomfortable with the subject matter.

"Hey, Avani. I got a question for you. How are you related to her? She's insane! You're nothing like her."

"Don't you dare fucking answer her," Natalia growled.

"What? What if I do?" Avani said.

"Ava, lo juro por Dios. It's none of their goddamn business! Después de todo lo que pasé…"

"She's my sister, alright. Same parents. Same brothers…"

Natalia struggled to get the handcuffs off, and her face reddened. "Ava, detener! They don't need to know!"

The group watched in silence, waiting for what Avani didn't want to say.

"She a flier," Harold said, breaking the tension.

"Gah!" Natalia growled again. "Fuck, fuck you Harold! Who told you?!"

He slipped out a smile. "Malik told me a lot of thangs… she ain't never been able to fly."

Avani glared at Harold. Sydona noticed a rollercoaster of emotions pulsing through her.

Silas spoke up. "Wait, what? How is that possible?"

"It's extremely rare," Avani said. "But it *can* happen."

"Shut up! Just shut up!" Natalia screamed almost desperately.

Avani stopped talking, and Natalia kept her brown eyes glued to her sister.

Sydona felt sorrow for the woman even though she was a borderline psychopath. It suddenly made sense why she was the way she was. She was a flier but never learned something so natural for all other fliers.

"I feel bad for you," Sydona said.

Natalia moved her glare from Avani to her and bared her teeth. "Fuck you, bitch. You don't ever get to fucking feel sorry for me. None of you!" She looked at everyone else who seemed to all feel somewhat the same as her. "Don't feel sorry for me puntas 'cause once I get out of these fucking handcuffs, I'm killin' all you motherfuckers. Then none of y'all can fly again."

Harold spun his gun to face the butt of it outwards and hit Natalia in the head so hard she passed out in the truck. Avani stared wide-eyed at him.

"Sorry… did you not want me to quiet her up after she threatened to kill us? I could hit her harder if you want."

Avani sized Harold up. "You don't ever touch my hermana again."

Harold moved his jaw around while clenching his fists. His head whipped away from her and he walked toward the forest. Sydona couldn't believe she was on Harold's side for once. Still, she admired Avani's unwavering love for her family; she knew exactly what it felt like. She would do the same for hers, even if they were off their rockers. Right?

The rest of the group sat around the truck, waiting for the other half of their party. Sydona went through her bag to make sure everything was still there. She took out some food and handed it around as it was past lunchtime. Silas sat in the front seat of the car, and Avani began to look at his wound. She only carried basic medical supplies and did what she could. Using a pair of strange looking tweezers, she carefully pulled out the shrapnel from his thigh. He used his outer shirt to bite and scream into. Sydona stayed by his side and let him squeeze her hand until it tingled. Avani dressed it with medical wraps and gave him some pain killers.

"Do we need to take you to the hospital?" Sydona asked as she watched from the opened car door.

"No, I'm good. Not dying today." He forced a smile.

It was clear Silas would not be flying anymore. He could barely walk. She sat by his side in the truck for what felt like forever. Her lids drifted off for just a second before she jerked back up and shook her head. Grabbing the radio from her pants, she called for Knox again.

"Knox, Willow, come in."

The radio clicked a couple times and went to static.

Suddenly, in the distance, gunshots rang out through the fir trees.

"Shit. Willow," Harold said with his head sprung up like a prairie dog.

Sydona and Avani both looked out toward the sounds of battle.

"Damn. Did I forget to tell you guys I called in reinforcements? I am sooo sorry," Natalia mocked as she finally woke from her beauty sleep. "Hope they don't kill my Knoxy Poo before I get to see him again. I miss that big guy."

Sydona gritted her teeth and grabbed a gun laying on top of the console of the car. Pulling her arm back to hit her again, Natalia flinched.

"Please, no! I'll shut up. I promise." She looked up at Sydona with the most serious face she had seen since they met. Her shoulders hunched, and her eyes became submissive.

"Fine." Sydona sighed. "Silas, keep one eye on her, please."

"No problem. Go. They need you."

Sydona smiled and handed him the gun. "Be careful."

Silas returned her smile and nodded. "Go."

"We're coming to help, Elias," Avani radioed over.

There was still no answer, but they heard more shots fired.

The three of them and Raoul sprinted through the forest as fast as they could, heading toward the gunfire. She then heard muffled crying. She assumed it was from Devon, and Lacey was busy trying to stifle it. They crouched behind a large boulder, out of harm's way. It was only Knox, Jet and Willow fighting against about five or six Vultures. Each person hid behind a separate tree for cover.

"You guys okay? Any wounds?" Sydona asked, then quickly pivoted around the tree base to shoot before retracting back to her position.

"We're fine! These assholes came outta nowhere," Knox replied. He took a break to look at everyone who joined him. Focusing in on Avani, his face changed.

"Babe! Take Lacey and Devon out of here! You know the way back!"

"I'm not leaving you, Elias!" she pled and shot clumsily. Her effort was admirable, but she would no doubt be the first one to get wounded. Sydona agreed with Knox.

"I said now!" Knox bellowed.

Avani threw a sour face his way but did as she was told. She ran back to Lacey and Devon behind a fallen tree. Sydona made her way back to cover Avani in case the Vultures used the opportunity to shoot a defenseless child.

"Go! I'll cover you!" Sydona yelled. She ducked back behind the tree, and Devon gave her a hug.

"No, just take Devon. I need to stay and help," Lacey said.

"What?" Devon cried. "You're not coming?"

"Avani will take you to safety, Devon. I'll be right there," Lacey said.

"No! I'm not leaving you!" Devon cried harder and grabbed Lacey tightly.

Sydona shot a couple more times. "Devon, she'll be fine. Avani will take you to Silas. It's not far. I promise."

Avani took Devon's arm, and he screamed harder than ever. He clung to Lacey like glue.

"Devon, please!" Lacey said. She pushed him off as Avani pulled. He finally let go of Lacey, and Avani got ready to leave the safety of the tree. Sydona moved closer to cover them. She shot again, sending someone to the ground. One less worry.

"Go now!" Sydona yelled. Avani and Devon stayed low, and Sydona's eyes felt as if her pupils had grown to take in any slight movements. Another perfect shot. Another Vulture down.

Her adrenaline pumped hard, and her confidence soared. A grin grew widely across her face. Lacey took a few shots, covering Devon. It was the first time she and Lacey had actually worked side by side, and they did it well. As they got in the swing of things, one of the Vultures somehow slipped from their reach. Sydona saw it happen but was unable to stop it. There was just one more guy they didn't originally see. The seventh one. Sydona and Lacey focused on the two men after Avani and Devon, and they both didn't hide themselves as much as they could have. A stray bullet buried itself into Lacey's chest, causing her to fly backward. Whipping her head around, Sydona saw blood quickly soaking her clothes, and she was rendered immobile on the forest floor.

A cry from Devon screeched through the trees. Avani held him back with all her might as he flailed his arms and legs. Sydona ducked down behind her fallen tree to tend to Lacey who could barely breathe. Willow, Jet and Knox immediately took out the last three guys. Once they fell to the ground, Avani let Devon go, and he raced over to Lacey.

Jet dropped his gun in shock and ran to her, his knees falling to the wet, leafy ground.

"Lace!" he cried. "You're gonna be okay, babe. I'll fix you."

Lacey didn't answer but just held both boys in her arms. Tears flowed down her face and onto blood-soaked pine needles. "I love you--Jet. --And Devon."

Devon laid himself on top of her, covering himself in her blood. She winced but didn't stop him. Jet caressed her hair with the pink streak, over and over again. His eyes grew wet and full, forcing tears to fall. He pushed back her bangs to kiss her on the forehead.

"Sydona," she said softly. "I'm sorry… for what I said. I trust you." She coughed and took Sydona's hand. "Take care of them for me, please. And… one more thing?"

Sydona leaned in.

"Kill that mother fucking doctor."

Sydona choked but then smiled. "Not before he suffers."

Lacey closed her eyes as if the answer pleased her immensely. A shaky hand touched Jet's cheek, and he kissed it gently. Devon buried his head in her neck and laid his hand on her chest. But soon, that chest stopped moving, and her kissed filled hand went limp.

"No! Mom! Wake up!" Devon cried out.

Sydona's chin trembled, and she stood up. Lacey didn't mean as much to Sydona as she did to the boys, but the fact she was seen as a mother to Devon destroyed her. He had lost two mothers now. Her hands shook with an overload of emotions. The forest stood eerily still and quiet. They lost another.

They lost the last one.

Chapter Seventeen

Jet held Lacey in both arms as they walked back to the road. Devon walked beside him, still sobbing and saying ”mom” over and over again. It was almost too much for Sydona to manage. Visions of her own mother and her death kept flashing in her head. Life wasn't fair, especially to this little boy who has had it worse off than Sydona. She lost one mother, which was more than she could bare, but he had lost two. Making Malik suffer was high on her list. He didn't deserve to be killed with one fell swoop. No, he needed to pay for everyone he ever hurt.

The sun dropped from the highest point in the sky, and shadows grew long. The group split into couples on their way back, walking slowly as they mourned the loss of Lacey.

Raoul took his usual spot on Sydona's shoulder. "Poor Lacey…"

"Yeah…" Sydona said and cleared her throat. "I hate the last thing she and I spoke about. She was just protecting Jet. She really loved him."

"She did. Still not sure how, but she did," Raoul replied.

"He's all Devon has now."

"Devon seems to like you, too. He did bite Knox for you. Got more guts than any of us."

She smirked. "He's a special kid."

Raoul made a noise of agreement. "What are we going to do with 'you know who'?"

Sydona sniffed and rolled her eyes. "I have no idea. I know what I want to do with her, but Avani wouldn't approve."

"I'm sure whatever any of us want to do to her, Avani wouldn't approve."

The truck and white road came into view, and her stomach dropped like a cement brick. Silas was in the front seat, but Natalia was not where they left her. Sydona sprinted to him like a bat out of hell.

"Where'd she go?!"

Silas shook his head. "I fucked up."

"What happened?" Knox added with nostrils flaring.

"She is… one smooth talking vixen."

"Dios mio, child… Did she talk herself out of the handcuffs?" Avani asked.

"No…" he said, then looked up with confusion and cocked his head to the side. "Is that--Lacey? What happened?"

"Vultures…" Jet growled.

"I'm so sorry…" Silas said and scooted out of the car.

"No, you don't need to get up." Jet stopped him. "I'll take care of her. Come on, Devon."

Silas stayed sitting with his feet over the edge of the seat, facing outwards Devon and Jet took Lacey back into the woods on the other side.

"We'll come with," Harold said as he grabbed a shovel.

Jet kept walking. He didn't have the energy to say no. Sydona could tell all he wanted to do was cry.

The group walked behind Jet as they entered the woods to say their goodbyes to Lacey. Sydona, Silas and Raoul stayed behind.

"Silas, how did she escape?" Sydona asked.

"She was talking to me about my family and kept asking questions. Like, really in-depth questions. Stuff I hadn't thought about in years. And somehow, during that time, she unlocked the damn cuffs and ran off…"

"Didn't you have a gun?" Raoul asked, just as confused as Sydona.

"Exactly. I should have checked to make sure there was ammo… I had never used this gun before. The weight felt fine to me, so I didn't bother to check. I'm such an idiot." He bounced his head off the back of the seat a few times, then rested it. "You guys should just go on without me."

"What? No, we would never do that," Sydona said softly and touched his arm. "Come on. Let's go down. Give our condolences."

Silas limped out of the truck, and Raoul sprinkled him with fairy dust. She took the keys and locked the door before helping Silas down the hill. The group didn't go far, and a few of them were already busy digging a hole in the ground for Lacey. Devon lay next to Lacey, while Avani was off gathering foliage for the grave.

Once they had made the hole big enough to put Lacey to rest, words were spoken. Knox admired her spunk and positive attitude on life. Avani knew how much she loved Jet and Devon, and it showed in everything she did. Willow said she always had a smile or a face of deathly seriousness. She fought for everything she had. Harold didn't know her as much but said he loved that he was able to meet her. Silas mentioned the fun night at the cabin everyone had together and how entertaining she was. Devon had no words as he was too busy crying. He did utter something that sounded like 'I'll miss you, mom". Raoul loved being in her presence as she always had positivity surrounding her and reminded him of a mother bear.

It was Sydona's turn. "Lacey… I didn't know you for a very long time, but from what I learned about you, I knew you were an amazing person. You were welcoming, warm, hilarious, your dance moves were out of this world… You will be greatly missed and cherished. Miss you, Lacey."

Jet was last to speak. The man of many words. "Lace--" he paused to choke on tears. Sydona never saw his face so red. His cheeks were fresh with tears glistening in the sunlight that peeked through the trees. The pure, unashamed feelings had Sydona swallowing her own tears. He was a person, after all, who had great feelings for a girl. A girl who would never stand by his side again. He was fragile and vulnerable. Seeing him that way let Sydona feel empathy for him. He had a great deal of loss in his life as well.

He continued. "--I know we weren't the most perfect couple. God knows we weren't. I never deserved you. Not a single day we were together. I'll never understand why you stuck around through all my shit. All you did was carry me while I constantly weighed you down. You're the strongest person I've ever known…" he paused to catch his breath. "After Devon lost his own mom, you stepped in to instantly fill that void in his life. I can't speak for him, but you did an amazing job. You kicked being a mom's ass. I don't think I'll be able to fill your shoes, but I'll do everything I can…" He looked down at Devon who was hugging his leg. "Anyway. I love you, Lacey. And I don't care if everyone standing around here hates me. As long as I have you in my heart, that's all I need."

He took one last long look at her grave decorated with white flowers and red berries and headed back up toward the road. Jet didn't look back. The group headed back up to the truck still sitting on the edge of the road.

"So, Nat got away, huh?" Knox said with a sigh.

"I'm so sorry, Mr. Knox… she's like a wizard," Silas said.

"She is. And please, never call me Mister Knox again. It's just… weird," he said with a smile.

"Yes, sir."

"Well, what's our next plan of action, y'all?" Willow spoke up.

"I wouldn't mind finding a place with a shower… or running water of some kind," said Sydona.

"Whoo-wee, girl! You smell worse than me," Harold joked and waved a hand in front his face.

It somehow made her giggle. "Thanks, Harold."

Knox pulled out the map to see where they were. After several minutes of deliberating, they figured out that they were in Colorado. Mountains lined the horizon. Both flying and driving would be difficult. Sydona had never seen the mountains up close before, but she knew it wouldn't be easy.

"We won't be able to fly from here on out. But this truck won't hold all of us," Knox said.

"Not without turning some heads," Harold commented.

"Those other Vultures had to get here somehow. Harold and me will look to see if they had a vehicle somewheres," Willow said and saluted Knox.

The two went off into the forest again, and they held hands on their way. It was still strange to see Willow like that and to see Harold being a decent person. Harold was a prime example of how people could change. She searched around for Jet, but he was nowhere in sight.

"You guys seen Jet anywhere?"

"I think he went back to the grave. Poor chico…" Avani said.

Even Avani was beginning to feel sad for him. Sydona went back down there with Raoul flying by her side. The leaves were somehow both wet and crunchy. There was no way to sneak up on Jet, but then again, she didn't really want to. She just wanted to be by his side. He was in a dangerously fragile position. His dark hair shone in the sunlight, and he tilted his head backward, then forward. Cries of sorrow made their way back to her ears, and she walked slower. Her heart crumbled at his vulnerable state. Jet was a metal barbed wire fence, an invisible forcefield, a castle with a hundred-foot moat. She wasn't sure why, but she needed to get through to him. He had a lot of pain, that was obvious. But now that Lacey was gone, he had no one left to talk to.

Her boot snapped a twig apart, and Jet pivoted his body.

"Who's there?" he asked. "Oh, Sydona. What do you want?"

"I'm here, too!" Raoul added with a sour tone.

Sydona walked normally and answered. "Just came to see her again."

Jet lowered his head and turned back to the grave.

Sydona stood a few feet away from him. Her heart pounded and throat throbbed. She wondered if Jet could hear it. He wiped his face on each side and took another drink. Sydona saw the flask from the corner of her eye. She had no plan on what to say to him, but she tried something.

"You mind if I have some?"

"No, you still owe me from last time," he replied without skipping a beat.

"Well, it's not like we're stopping at a store or anything for me to get you back. Just a sip."

He didn't look at her but held it out just barely. "Fine, whatever. Just a sip."

She grabbed it from him and put it in her back pocket.

"What are you doing?" he asked and finally looked her in the eye.

"You don't need this stuff. Trust me."

"Fuck you, give it back!"

"Let's just talk." Sydona stood her ground with a high chin.

"I don't want to talk. Just give it back!"

Sydona stepped back as Jet got closer with his hand out.

"I know it hurts, Jet. But alcohol is only temporary. It won't fix what's going on."

"It's not temporary if I constantly have it, so give it here."

"No."

Jet put his hand down and reached for his gun. He aimed it directly at her.

Her heart pounded even harder, but she didn't move.

Raoul whispered in her ear. "Uh, Syd. Maybe you should give it back now…"

"You willing to kill me to get this? That's what it means to you?"

Jet used both hands to steady his shaking. "Yes."

"I don't believe you…"

"I'll shoot you, Sydona. I swear I will." Jet hardened his face aside from more tears leaking out from his reddened auburn eyes. He wasn't angry. He was afraid.

"Your eyes are brown, Jet. I know you don't want to kill me."

Jet's hands shook like leaves. They began to crumble. He squeezed his almond eyes shut and dropped the gun. "Fuck."

He then took off running past Sydona. He went so fast she knew he wanted to fly away. Not on her watch.

She ran after him.

"Raoul, help me out."

"You got it, captain!"

Jet weaved in and out of the trees to find a clearing but then turned his head back and saw Sydona chasing after him. "Leave me alone!"

"No!"

Soon, he took off flying, and Sydona followed him up into the air. She soared as fast as she could, but Jet still kept a good distance between them. Wind stung her face and eyes as she flew roughly five-hundred feet in the air. Raoul worked vigorously to keep her afloat. With only one and not a whole group though, he didn't need to donate as much dust. She still felt bad and straightened herself out as much as she could to catch up to him. Her arms stuck to her body like magnets, and she pointed her toes.

"Jet! Stop running!" she yelled as loud as she could.

The wind carried his voice back to her. "Stop following me, then!"

"No! We need to talk!"

Sydona narrowed her eyes, hoping that would somehow make her go faster. "What would Lacey say to you right now?"

He didn't answer right away, but he slowed down slightly. "Don't bring her into this!"

Sydona used one leg to push herself further. She didn't know if it would work, but she thought pushing the air back could boost her forward more. It was either that or Jet slowed down because she caught hold of his foot.

"Get off!" he said as Sydona climbed up his leg.

"I'm not leaving, so you might as well land!"

Jet kicked his leg trying to get Sydona off him, but her grip was deadly tight. He went for the gun in his holster and fumbled. It fell five-hundred feet back to Earth.

"Damnit."

"Jet, you're not getting rid of me. Just land so we can talk!" she said as she climbed up farther, trying to freak him out enough to land.

Jet kicked his knee hard into Sydona's stomach. She winced with pain but balled her fist up and punched him in his jaw. It was hard enough to throw him off balance, and they began to fall. Raoul did his best to keep both of them dusted, but they continued to descend.

"You're gonna kill us!" Jet screamed as he tried to pry Sydona off more.

"If you just listen to me, we won't!" Sydona retorted.

She finally pushed herself off, and within seconds, they both fell into the lake below. Sydona plummeted like a missile far into the depths of the water. Her body instantly froze. She felt water leak into her lungs, and she wanted to cough. With nothing to push off from, she had to swim as fast as she could back to the surface. Once her face hit sunlight, she gasped for sweet oxygen. Her lungs retaliated, and she coughed, but the choppy waters kept putting water back in. With her energy quickly draining, she struggled to swim to land.

They both crawled onto the semi-sandy shore. Dead logs, branches, rocks and broken shells littered the beach, making it hard to lay down for a second to catch a breath. She managed to find a soft bit of sand to rest. From the corner of her eye, she saw Jet slink away from her. He was escaping again.

She jumped to her feet and quickly grabbed his foot. "Jet! Stop it! Stop flying away!"

"Leave me alone, Sydona," he said with a voice of defeat. But he still tried to kick her.

Sydona had enough. She mustered up all her strength, turned him over and sat on top of him.

"Arg, get off!" he grumbled and weakly squirmed around.

"Talk to me."

He moaned again and kept his eyes shut. "Just let me die…"

As Sydona sat on top of him, it felt almost as if he deflated. Raoul and Sydona exchanged a worried look. She knew he wasn't alright but had no clue he felt that depressed.

"Jet…"

"Let me fucking die!" he screamed then began to sob.

She was speechless. In his current condition, she was sure he wouldn't be running away, so she got off him and sat by his side. What was she supposed to say? She wasn't a therapist. But she did know how he might be feeling. Before she could say something, he continued.

"I can't be a father. I don't know how to take care of a kid. He doesn't even like me…"

"You're talking about Devon? Don't be silly; of course he likes you!" Sydona said confidently. She honestly wasn't sure though.

"He likes you more than me. You saw what he did to Knox to protect you."

"What? No. He would've done the same for you…"

"Lacey took care of him. I only watched him when she wasn't around. And even then, he has no reason to be under my care." His emotions were draining.

"What do you mean?" Sydona asked.

Jet took a deep breath and sat up to face the vast lake. He grabbed a twig and peeled the bark off little by little. "My best friend was the one who killed Devon's parents…"

"What?" Sydona said as she let out all the air in her lungs.

"What does that have to do with you?" Raoul asked.

"His wife is really sick. All the doctors he's talked to won't see them because she's a flier. So, he asked me for money, and I turned him down because I just don't have any. I wanted to help, but I couldn't. The day he came into that store and tried robbing it, I guess he was just that desperate. He got so nervous that he just shot them both. If he didn't see me, he might have killed more. Maybe even Devon... But..." he sighed again, reliving everything. "If I had just given him the money or something, none of it would've happened."

"You can't blame yourself for that. You didn't have the money," Sydona said softly.

"But I could've helped somehow! Called around more, sold shit, *something*. But instead I did absolutely nothing. Not only was I a crappy friend, I'll be a crappy dad."

Sydona timidly put her hand on his shoulder. "There may not be anything you can do about the past, but you can still change the future, Jet. You can't assume you'll be bad. You have time. And Devon *does* like you."

Jet hung his head low and drew in the sand with his stick. "I miss her so much..." He turned around and hugged Sydona. Taken off guard, she took a few seconds to picture what he was doing to her. He wrapped both arms around her wet clothes and squeezed. He was broken. She couldn't fix him, but she would be there for him while he put the pieces back together. Her arms gingerly touched him back. She let him hold her while she listened to the waves of the gray water crash against the barren shore. Catching her breath, she then felt his heart as his chest pressed against hers. If she listened hard enough, she thought she could hear it beat irregularly as if it had recently been shattered. Maybe it was all in her head. Maybe it wasn't.

They pulled apart, and Jet hid his face. "Sorry... "

Sydona smiled. "It's alright. You're not so bad, Jet."

"Ha. Thanks, I guess." He stood up and dusted the sand off his clothes.

"I'm glad you told me about that."

"Yeah," he sniffed. "Me too. Can I have my flask back now?"

Sydona furrowed her brows. "Uh, I thought we had a breakthrough here."

"Sure, but I'm still thirsty. And it's my flask. My dad gave that to me."

"Oh, um... Well, we flew for however long, then fell into a lake. I don't know where I lost it."

Jet rolled his eyes. "Are you kidding me right now?"

Sydona shrugged. Jet sighed heavily and walked away from the shore and into the woods.

"Where are you going?" Raoul asked.

"Back to the group. Where do you think?"

Sydona and Raoul grinned at one another. "I thought you said everyone hated you," said Sydona as she followed him.

"I did, but Devon's back there."

The three walked through the woods until they found another clearing. They quickly realized they had flown farther than they thought. It would take too long to get there on foot. Once they hit the air, it was simpler to navigate where they came from. The road helped lead them back as well. Five minutes later, they landed next to the truck and a van that Willow and Harold must've found.

"Why you two so wet?" Avani shrieked and laughed.

"Jet!" Devon called out and ran toward him with a big, gap-toothed smile.

"Hey, bud." Jet rubbed Devon's head.

"Yeah, why are you all wet?" Devon asked.

"Long story, Dev."

Sydona joined Knox who was busy searching through the other car. There wasn't much to find though. The SUV looked brand new, Mercedes class. There were no other weapons, tools, maps, nothing.

"Everything good?" Knox asked as he searched through the glovebox.

Sydona shrugged. "I guess. Jet was at a pretty low point. But he should be okay now…"

"Great." Knox slammed the glovebox door shut. "I know he just lost Lacey, and he might be going through something right now, but…" he lowered his voice, "I'm thinking we need to cut him loose. He's too unstable for this mission."

"You want to leave him behind?" Sydona said with narrowed eyes, a little irritated after everything she just did for him. "I don't think that's such a good idea, Knox."

"Are you questioning my tactics?" he asked, stepping out of the car.

Sydona stepped back. "No, but… you didn't see what I saw. He let everything out with me. He's going to be fine."

"I can't risk our lives with your assumptions, Sydona."

Her jaw tightened and hands fidgeted. "If you're so confident on him leaving, why are you bringing it up to me first, then? You must've wanted some common agreement."

Knox blinked a few times and looked away.

"I know his record; he's been an asshole. He's made that abundantly clear. But believe me when I say, he's been through a lot, too. He's dealing with it the only way he knows how. And he's not drinking anymore. I lost his only flask… I'll make sure he won't cause more problems."

"How? Are you going to be watching him twenty-four seven? I can't have my recruits doing that; that's not why you're here."

"I understand that but--"

"Sydona. Enough. What's done is done. Jet! Come here, please." Knox bellowed over her, and she flinched. The loudness of his tone never ceased to surprise her.

Both Jet and Devon made their way over to him.

"What's good?" Jet said, extremely nonchalant.

"Jet. You… have done a great service to the Sparrows, and we are very thankful for the commitment and sacrifices you have made thus far. However, I regret to inform you that this is the end of the road for you. Please surrender your weapons and return home promptly."

"What?!" his eyes turned to a burning emerald.

"Don't make this difficult," Knox said, keeping perfect composure.

"You're fucking kidding me right now! This is such bullshit, Knox!"

"I won't ask again, Jet. Surrender your weapons, now."

"No! You can't just kick me out like this! I have no fucking clue where we are. And don't I at least get to defend myself?!" Jet waved his arms around.

The rest of the group also gathered around as if the road was a courtroom, and they were the jury.

Sydona felt upset by this sudden decision and had to say something. "Knox, I agree. I mean, we should at least do a vote or something."

Knox turned only his head to speak to her. "Oh, we have. You were the last one I needed to talk to."

"What?" Sydona felt her eyes would be turning green, too. "What do you mean?"

"While you were away, I spoke to everyone else, and they, and myself, all agreed to let Jet go."

Raoul flew to the middle of the gathering circle. "I haven't voted!" he cried out with one hand on his side and the other in the air with a tiny balled fist. "And I think he should stay!"

"Alright, well, that's two votes against five. So it still wouldn't matter. Plus, no offense, Raoul, you're not really a Sparrow."

"You all voted to kick me out on my ass?" Jet asked and looked around the group. Not a single person looked him in the eye.

"Silas?" Sydona whispered.

He glanced up at her from the car seat, then avoided all eye contact. Shaking her head and licking her lips, she felt as if she might explode. She never thought she would be so emotionally involved in what happened to Jet. He was a jerk, but he was a jerk that had real problems. Sending him home was the worst thing they could do.

"Doesn't my vote count?" Devon asked below in a soft, innocent voice.

Knox broke his composure for the first time in five entire minutes. "Uh, sorry, little man. This is just for adults."

Devon's face changed like wildfire. "I'm *not* a little man, and I wanna fight!"

Knox looked around for support from his soldiers, but no one had any idea how to react to a ten-year-old wanting to join a rebellion group on the edge of a war. Sydona had to give it to him, he had spirit.

"Look, uh, Devon… I know you might be angry, but we can't let you join…" Knox said.

"Why not? 'Cause I'm too small or weak? I bit you, didn't I? I stopped you from killing Sydona. I *can* fight!"

Knox was speechless. Avani took over for him and bent down to level with Devon.

"Sweetie, look… even if we were to let you fight with us, *if*… It would have nothing to do with the decision we made for Jet."

Raoul stuck his tongue out and buzzed away. Jet rolled his eyes and paced back and forth like a hungry lion.

"No!" Devon spoke up, his voice seemingly a little lower than usual. "My mom said that we need to kill the doctor, and that's what I'm going to do! Isn't that why we're here?"

Avani smiled, though it was clear she was uncomfortable. "Sí, but…"

"Let me join! I want to fight with you! And Jet too! Please."

Avani stood up and faced Jet and the rest of the group. "Can you two wait for us over there, please?" She pointed to the other side of the vehicle while everyone gathered in a huddle. This *was* a jury.

"Don't tell me you're havin' second thoughts," Willow said.

"We can't set them on the road with no idea how to get home," Sydona interjected.

"He's as unpredictable as Natalia, Sydona. We can't keep him," Harold said.

"Do none of you believe in second chances?" Sydona barked.

"He's had several chances, hun," Silas said.

"Are we really considerin' a little ten-year-old boy joinin' us, though? I mean, he's just gonna get himself killed," Willow added.

"He wants to fight, though. I say let him fight," Silas said. Sydona bounced him a tiny smirk.

"It's too dangerous," Knox said.

"He don't seem bothered by much so far. How's that scar, by the way?" Harold asked, hiding a grin form Knox.

"Very funny…"

"How do we know he won't go off the deep end again?" Avani asked.

"We'll keep an eye on him," Raoul said with confidence.

"I've already told you--" Knox started.

"--We're volunteering, Knox. We want to. We know he can be helped. He just lost a girl he loved; give him a god damn break," said Sydona. She peeked out of the huddle and saw Jet messing around with Devon.

Harold pointed his finger. "If he picks a fight with me one more time or calls me a red--"

"I'll take full responsibility, okay?" Sydona said. "They need each other right now. And right now, they both want to be here. Together."

The jury finally concluded, and they all stared at Knox who took a deep sigh. "Alright then. It's decided then?"

Everyone nodded.

He stood up straight and called Jet and Devon over.

"Jet," he said louder than necessary, then sighed. "You can stay."

Jet smiled, balled up a fist and thrusted it out with joy.

"And Devon, this is only temporary… But welcome to the Sparrows."

"Yeah!" He high-fived Jet and jumped up and down.

Knox shouted over his excitement. "We will begin your training first thing... As soon as we find a place to do so. But be aware: it will not be easy, and I need your complete attention. We're in the middle of a war, and it's no time to be a child. Understood?"

Devon stood at attention with his hand in a salute. "Yes, sir!"

"Alright then. Onward!"

Chapter Eighteen

They all fit in the SUV and left the truck behind. That night, they stayed in a hotel in a small town. Mountains with white tops surrounded it, making it feel somewhat safe. While they waited for Willow and Harold to rent the rooms, Silas messed with the radio in the front seat. It was rare that a station actually came in clearly, but when one did, a familiar voice mulled over the static.

"...Thank you for having me." Malik's voice stung like a hornet in Sydona's ears.

"Dr. Malik, I must say, what you're doing is simply fascinating. Where did your idea originate to start these experiments?" the interviewer said in an annoyingly chipper tone.

"Well, Charles, I don't know if you know this, but my father actually started the idea way back in the day. Since he was a boy, he was just as fascinated as you are with these spectacular specimens. Unfortunately, despite years of dedication and experimentation, he passed away before his work was completed. I swore to him and my family that I would continue his work, and well... here we are."

"Fantastic. So, how close are you exactly? I mean do you think we could get this off the ground in a few years or by next Friday?" he chuckled.

Malik matched his laughter. "Actually, we are very close. We can look forward to getting the prototype out by as early as Christmas!"

Charles gasped. "No, you're kidding! That soon, huh? I can just imagine the kids flying about the snowy streets and having snowball fights from above the houses! How fun!"

"That's the hope!" Malik laughed. With every word that came from his mouth, Sydona wanted to gag.

"So, are we allowed to know how you will make the magic happen?"

"Oh, it's not magic, Charles. It's science. And we've been able to pack it all inside a small little pill, one tiny little morsel that you swallow. It gets absorbed into your blood stream and allows you to feel light as a feather. That's the hope anyway."

"Drugs, huh? I'm not sure how that would go over. Is it addictive?"

"Absolutely not! Yes, the feeling you experience while on it is like no other, but keep in mind, this will in no way make you invincible like some other pills on the market. It will simply grant you the ability to fly but does nothing to your mind or health. The best part of it all: it's practical and may actually help to save lives."

"Save lives, huh? How do you figure?"

"Imagine a common scenario where, say, you're stuck in a traffic jam, and all of a sudden your grandmother has a heart attack or some other severe trauma. But you're stuck in traffic. How can you help her? Well, instead of waiting for an ambulance that could take way too long, or a helicopter that would be much too tricky to maneuver, paramedics and even doctors could fly right to her and help her instantly. She could be helped within minutes, Charles.

"Interesting… You make a very valid point, John. It's also practical in other ways. If you need to attend a funeral or something across the country, you don't have to wait for a scheduled plane and spend hundreds of dollars. You could just leave on whim."

"Precisely! However, you can only carry so much on your person, so you must be a light traveler." He laughed.

Charles laughed with him. "Very true! So you're just missing one key element to complete these experiments, am I right?"

"Yes," he sighed. "Just one tiny little thing. But we are working on it! As soon as it turns up, you bet we'll be back, hard at work."

"Of course. And that one thing would be a woman named Sydona Wilder, correct? Have you heard anything of her whereabouts lately?"

Sydona wanted to punch the radio interviewer in the face so hard. Everyone's eyes radiated off her. All she could focus on were the dials on the radio and the waves of voices in the air.

"The last I heard, she was somewhere in Colorado, but you know how things can go."

Sydona had a flash of when she punched him in the teeth at Eagle Lake, and her heart leaped.

"So no one has turned her in yet, I'm assuming."

"Not to my knowledge. But if she were smart, she'd turn herself in."

"In a perfect world, right John?"

"Right!"

"But seriously folks, if you're listening out there, please be cautious if you do decide to apprehend this woman. She is dangerous and most likely with a group of other fliers. They aim to cause harm to anyone who interferes. Call the police if you know anything of her or her rebellion group called Sparrows. Dr. Malik has promised a great reward for anyone who turns her in."

"Absolutely! It will be well worth your time and effort!"

"It's been a pleasure speaking with you today, Dr. Malik. We hope to talk to you again soon!"

"Thank you, Charles. I look forward to it. God bless."

Sydona turned it off as soon as it ended.

"He is such a slimy punta," Avani said and shivered dramatically.

"He knows where we are," Knox said.

"Natalia must be his contact. Wish we knew where she went," Sydona said. From the corner of her eyes, she saw Silas drop his head.

Willow and Harold made their way back to the clown car. They had booked two rooms on the edge of property.

"Everything go okay?" Silas asked as they got inside. Willow turned the key in the ignition to take them to the other side.

"Yep, didn't suspect a thang." Harold winked and clicked his tongue.

Willow spoke from the driver's seat. "So, I was thinkin' me, Harold, Avani and Knox in one room and the rest of yas in the other? That work?"

The group nodded agreeably and walked to their rooms. Sydona, Silas, Jet and Devon ended up in the downstairs room with the rest in the room above them. It wasn't the fanciest hotel she had ever stayed in, but it did have a wonderful view of the Rocky Mountains. The midsummer sun set behind them but not before leaving pink and purple clouds that resembled a breathtaking painting. They had a small patio with a table and chair, but a large shrub blocked their view. She wanted to switch rooms, but seeing as the top room made it harder to escape, she stayed put.

Devon made his first priority jumping on both beds as much as possible. It was the simple things that brought joy to this kid's life. Even after everything that happened, he still felt happiness from jumping on something bouncy and watching television.

"Oh, man. This place does room service," Jet said as he looked over the hotel compendium. "That way we can sleep and eat without leaving the bed. Awesome…"

Silas looked over the menu with him as he lay back on the blue and white sheets and propped his leg up. Raoul stood on the giant wooden headboard to gander at all the food choices. It was like they were looking into a binder from heaven the way they drooled.

Sydona took the opportunity to finally shower. She washed as much mud out of her clothes as she could while in the shower. Stepping out of the tub and into the mist of her hot shower, she wiped the mirror down to examine herself. The darkness from the tea had completely washed out, and her hair was back to its natural golden color. It was still short enough to disguise her a little bit but not by much. Nicks and bruises covered her body from the most disgusting brawl she had ever been a part of. In the back of her head though, she still wondered what Knox had in mind for Natalia. She took a deep breath to absorb all the fresh moisture in the air and exhaled with a slight head rush. Nothing felt better than being clean.

She dressed into something more comfortable than her normal jeans. Maybe it would help her sleep that night. Leaving her clothes to dry in the bathroom, she left and watched all four guys staring at the television as if it had naked women on it. Unsure if her theory was true, she quickly turned to look, but thankfully, it was just a sitcom show. It was one of those shows where a creepy audience watched and laughed at the actors' lines as if it was the first time they heard a joke. She wondered if they ever got paid to act as well.

"Did you guys order food?" she asked the zombies on the bed.

"Yep. I ordered you fries and a garden salad," Silas replied.

"Aw, thank you. I don't care what Knox says about you. You're a good guy."

"What?" Silas turned all his attention to her.

Sydona laughed. "I'm heading outside for a bit. Anyone want to come with?"

Silas shook his head and rubbed his leg. Jet, Devon and Raoul barely responded as they mindlessly watched the show. Watching T.V. was something she never did and couldn't understand the appeal. But she guessed for them it was a taste of normalcy and couldn't fault them for getting sucked into the feeling. But for her, it was being outside in the crisp mountain air.

Sliding the glass door open, her bare feet touched the warm concrete, and she took in the beauty around her. The sun was gone now, and the stars shone even brighter, complimenting the moon who was not afraid of being in the spotlight. She didn't know if it was because they were in the mountains, but the night sky seemed to shine so much brighter. Bats fluttered in the quickly darkening sky, and the sounds of toads and crickets put her at ease.

She sat on the white metal chair and rubbed her wrist with the still prominent brown line circling it. She thought of Giovonna, home against her will. Sydona wondered if she heard the interview with the doctor and if it helped her at all in fixing the bracelets. The only positive of her going home was that she wouldn't in the crossfire, lucky to survive each day. For that, she was thankful.

Just then, she remembered Giovonna had written down her phone number, and Sydona quickly went back inside. She pulled out the torn piece of yellow notebook paper from her green tote. She sat in the chair next to the back door and picked up the phone.

"Hey," Silas called quietly, just over the television volume. "Who you calling?"

"Gia. See how she is."

"Come here," he tilted his head. His eyes were no longer on the television but completely focused on her.

"What?" Sydona asked.

"I want you to tell her something for me." He grinned.

She returned the smile. "You can't just tell me?"

"No… I have to whisper it. It's personal."

Sydona twisted her lips. "Sure you don't want to just talk to her, then?"

"Oh my god, Sydona, just come over here."

She turned pink and set the phone back down. Sashaying over to the bed without taking her eyes off his, she sat down next to him. Their shoulders pressed against each other.

"What did you want to tell her?" Sydona asked with butterflies going crazy down below.

Silas took his hand, turned her chin and pressed his lips against hers. Her eyes closed as she felt a surge of ecstasy. Leaning into him further, her hand found his side, and she pulled him in. He then quickly pulled away.

"I love you, too." His face was rosy but serious.

Her lips trembled as she watched his eyes take in every tiny feature of her face. Her cheeks were undoubtedly strawberry red, and she felt hot and cold at the same time. She studied every inch of his face as well. Hair slightly covered one eye and she absentmindedly pushed it back. His eyelids weren't perfectly symmetrical, and she had never noticed before. He had exactly seven freckles on his face and peach colored lips that hid his gorgeous smile. The man loved her. It wasn't just lust. It was pure, real love.

Her lips found his again before she started to cry. She focused her energy on being as close as possible to him. They pulled away, and Sydona tilted her head down to touch his forehead with hers. She wondered if he could hear her heart fluttering like a hummingbird's.

Lost in the moment, she finally spoke up. "Is that really what you want to tell Gia?"

Silas laughed through his nose. "Yep."

"Okay, but she might be a tad confused."

"She'll know what I mean." He winked.

Sydona shoved him playfully and bounced off the bed. Her head filled with air, and she picked up the weightless phone again and took it outside. As she sat on the chair, she floated on the lingering kiss and didn't care how uncomfortable the chair was anymore.

Staring at the numbers on the paper, she dialed Giovonna and waited for an answer. As she listened to the phone ring, she didn't think of the time difference. What time would it be there? And what if her parents answered?

"Hello?"

It sounded like a younger girl, so Sydona replied. "Hi, Gia."

"Oh my god, Syd? Is it really you?"

"It is! How are you?"

"It's so nice to hear your voice. Hang on… let me go to my room." Muffled sounds and crackles curdled in Sydona's ear as she waited for Giovonna to get situated. *"Okay, good now. I'm okay. How are you?"*

"I'm good. We're up in the mountains right now."

"Seriously? Oh man, you guys got far!"

Sydona smiled. She missed her so much. "Yeah, it's beautiful here."

"So jealous. My parents decided to start homeschooling me so they can keep an eye on me. Can you believe that?" she said with an increasing whisper.

"Oh wow. That really sucks…"

"But you'll be happy to know that I have made some progress with the… 'you know what's'. At least, I think so. It's hard to know without having something to test it on. God, I sound just like doctor douchebag."

"Yeah, and I mean, it's fine if you don't. I don't want you to be burdened with something like that. Since you're not here anymore." Sydona swallowed.

"No, it's fun. I like doing it. I feel like I'm still helping you guys even though I'm here…"

Sydona didn't know what to say. But Giovonna changed the subject for her. *"So, what else have you guys done? Come on, gimme details!"*

Sydona laughed. "Nothing much else. Just been driving and flying a lot."

"Flying? You? I don't believe it!" she gasped.

"Yep! It was strange, but it felt good."

"I bet! How's Devon? I kinda miss that kid.

"He's… full of surprises, I'll tell you that much."

Sydona stretched her legs and placed them on the table to get more comfortable. Looking past the curtains and through the glass door, she saw all four boys were still watching the television and hadn't moved an inch. As she leaned back in the chair more, she thought of the next thing she wanted to tell Giovonna: her new feelings for Silas. Before she could open her mouth, a whistling sound grazed her ear and something hit her head so hard she only felt the blunt pain for a second before things went black.

For just a second, before she fell unconscious, she faintly heard Giovonna say some words, but Sydona couldn't make out what they were. Who hit her? And why?

~~~~~

What felt like half a day later, Sydona opened her eyes but still only saw darkness. But she was moving. An engine revved below her, and her heart sped up instantly. Her mouth was covered in duct tape, preventing her from making a single sound. Bound by what felt like bed sheets, her hands and feet were completely useless. It was stuffy and smelled like carpet. Sweat dripped into her eyes and soaked her clothes. It must have been one-hundred degrees in that trunk.

Her eyes began to adjust to the darkness, and she tried to look around the trunk for anything she could use
~~~~~

to free herself. Wiggling around and breathing through what felt like a plastic bag, she was only able to see clothes, a bottle of some kind, a soccer ball and a tire pump. She didn't have her dagger. Worse, she was utterly alone. Someone was turning her in for their reward. She should have known better than to sit outside in the open, unarmed and shoeless. She hit her head against the floor of the trunk a few times to punish herself. This wasn't how things were supposed to go. The Sparrows were supposed to take over the doctor's mansion and kill him. She tried to let herself relax and prepare for what was ahead.

She never felt so vulnerable in her life. She didn't know who had captured her or where she would end up next. If it was a Vulture, she was sure she would be going straight to the doctor.

The air was getting tighter, and she needed more oxygen. Her lungs felt as if they were in the process of shrinking to the size of a prune. Licking her lips and curling them in toward her mouth, she wet them as much as possible to alleviate the stickiness of the tape. With each pull of the tape, micro hairs ripped from her pores. She worked quickly to moisten the tape and eventually got it off. It stayed stuck to the right side of her face, but at least she could breathe fully.

She took a minute to catch her breath and slow her heart. The one thing she knew was whoever captured her would not kill her. Her existence was too valuable. Scenarios of how to escape played in her mind. The car hadn't stopped in a long time, making her think they were on the highway. Escaping from a moving object at ninety miles an hour onto a concrete road with other cars fast approaching? Not a good first plan. She would wait until they stopped and find a possible latch to get out. Some cars had them equipped. Did people get trapped in trunks often? Taking another glance around, she saw no such lever, so that idea was a bust. Plan C: she could wait until whoever opened the trunk saw her, headbutt them and hope it would be hard enough to knock them unconscious so she could escape on foot. She was unable to fly away without Raoul, though. Plus, her feet and hands were still bound together. With each plan that fell apart, her heart pounded harder. All she could do was simply wait and watch it all unravel.

Another few hours passed, and Sydona eventually fell asleep. Once the car engine vibrated differently and slowed, her eyes opened wide. Her moment was coming. The vehicle made several turns, pushing her to either side and turning her body. Soon the car came to a complete stop, and the engine turned off.

The trunk opened, and the early morning sun scorched her retinas. Her eyes squeezed tightly, and she felt a huge wave of oven air blow over her. Once her eyes opened again, someone stood in the direct sunlight, casting a shadow over her face. With such extreme contrast, she was only able to make out the silhouette of her kidnapper but knew it was a woman.

"Welcome to Nevada, punta," she said.

All Sydona could do was scowl at her.

"You hungry?" she asked in a normal voice.

Sydona looked off to the side, not satisfying her with an answer.

"Suit yourself," she said and ripped the rest of the tape off Sydona's mouth. The after-effect burned her cheek, and she squirmed in disapproval. Natalia dug in her purse, pulled out a large roll of duct tape and put a fresh one back on her lips. "This place has some rad pie. Stopped here on the way to kill you guys. The raspberry is to die for." She giggled a high-pitched laugh.

Sydona mumbled curse words at her through the tape, but of course it was gibberish.

"What did you say to me?!" she backlashed. Natalia flipped open a small pocket knife and sliced Sydona on her right cheek bone. Sydona screamed out in agony, but it was unsatisfactory because of the tape. She could feel the warm blood instantly drip down her face, and her eyes watered uncontrollably.

"I'm gonna get some food; I'll be right back. Stay right here," she said seriously, then cracked herself up.

She slammed the trunk door shut to abandon Sydona as she writhed in pain. All she could focus on was her cut and the blood that poured from it like a faucet. With no way to tend to it or close it up, it could permanently scar her. She hated Natalia with every fiber in her being, and there was nothing she could do about it. It dawned on her that the main reason she normally got out of situations like this was because of Raoul. His tiny self and quick flying skills always got her out of a bind, so to speak. But she was alone and entirely out of ideas.

Chapter Nineteen

Natalia started the car up again and drove off down the highway. Her fresh wound throbbed as if it kept reopening itself, and blood dripped down her into her ear. She had nothing to do now but wait, and she grew tired. At least she knew where she was going now. The simple fact somehow calmed her, even if it meant she would be in the presence of the doctor.

Energy drained from her body. She managed to get the duct tape back off and craved the air like snow craved cold. Picturing snow was the wrong choice, and it was all she could think of. All the sweat leaking out of her pores left her feeling like a dried-up sponge on the kitchen sink. Saliva was the only way she could trick her mind into thinking she had water. The warm and bland taste left her even thirstier than before. She wished she hadn't turned down the offer for food, but she also wouldn't trust anything Natalia gave her.

Eventually, after what seemed like several more hours and a full bladder, the car acted differently again. The wound on her cheek had dulled and didn't bother her as much. Her bladder was the next concern. She was unsure why it was so full; she seemed to have expelled most of the liquid in her body already.

The car stopped a few times, and she heard voices including Natalia's. It then trundled on at a slow and steady pace. She rolled to the edge of the trunk as the car climbed what felt like a mountain. Smooth paved road soon dropped to a rocky road that made her vibrate so hard she had to clench her teeth together. The car crept slower and slower, then stopped.

Natalia slammed her car door shut and greeted someone nearby.

Sydona listened in closely. The voices were extremely muffled but close enough for her to hear full words. "Hey, Nat. Where the hell you been? You look like shit!"

"Fuck off, Jones. I been busy."

"You've been gone for like five days. I sure hope you were doing something out there."

"Oh yes. I have been doin' something. Wait till you see what I brought home."

Sydona's heart thumped harder. She was a prize. Disgusting.

Then a car door opened, but it wasn't hers. After a few seconds, Natalia spoke up.

"The best damn pie in Nevada. Got a blueberry one just for you."

"Is this from Henry's Bakery? Hell yeah! You're the best."

Sydona stuck her tongue out.

Natalia continued. "And I have another surpriiiise," she said in a sing-song, crazy tone.

The trunk flipped open once more, and light burst in but not as harsh as last time. It appeared as if they were in a garage, a very large one at that.

"Ta-da!" Natalia exclaimed and waved her arm over Sydona like a magic trick.

"Dude! You didn't! Ug, I'm so jealous right now."

"Fuck off, Jones," Sydona said with a dry throat.

"Oh! She's spunky! I like that!" he said while licking his lips.

His words and the perverted look in his eye sent a chill down her spine. A slimy, sweaty hand reached over and moved the hair sticking to Sydona's forehead, and he examined her with a tilted head. His fingernails scraped her skin, and she shivered to prevent him from touching her. A rat's nest kept together with a rubber band sat atop his head. A strand of it fell over his tanned, or dirty, face, and his bulging hazel eyes looked as oversized as his nose. Without warning, one of his boney fingers somehow found a way into her mouth and wiggled around. She couldn't figure out how, why or what possessed this man to shove his disgusting appendage into her mouth full of vengeful teeth. Overwhelmingly uncomfortable and appalled, Sydona bit down on Jones's index finger as hard as she could. Her teeth hit bone.

"Fuck!" He retracted with blood running down his hand like a river. "Bitch!"

Sydona felt there was no way to hold back a grin. Jones saw it and used his other hand to slap her across the face. Her teeth felt close to breaking from the shear force, and she tightened her jaw from the sting.

"Well, you shouldn't stick your fingers where they don't belong." Natalia shrugged. For once she seemed to be on Sydona's side, kind of. Natalia ripped off the rest of the duct tape again and untied her feet.

Jones sucked on his finger like a baby. "Where'd you get that car?"

"Stole it from the hotel I was stayin' at. Didn't plan on it, but you know, things came up," she said with a wink at Sydona.

"Is he in?" Natalia asked as they walked Sydona out of the garage and through a door leading inside a house.

Jones replied, "No, he's still in New York doing interviews and stuff. Been gone a few days. Should be back tomorrow, I think. God, this fucking hurts." He shook his hand.

All Sydona could do was smile as she looked at the ground. They were not going into a house like she thought. The door led down a large flight of stairs and to a narrow corridor.

"What was in New York?" Natalia wondered, talking normally again. Sometimes it felt as if it wasn't even the same woman next to her when she tried acting civil.

"Good Morning America."

"Good for him."

Their conversation ended. They kept walking her down a corridor that never seemed to end. The walls looked as if they were made of steel, and everything was brightly lit. Ivory and cotton were the only colors. She walked by several sections of walls that were see-through, like plastic. Flashes of the cabin at Eagle Lake came to mind. This was like the motherland. Malik had a look, and he stuck with it. None of the plastic clear walls had a single finger print either. She guessed he had a dozen or so maids that cleaned his entire house every day. Oh, to have endless amounts of money.

They arrived at an opened enclosure, though it was hard to tell because it looked invisible. Natalia undid the sheet bindings on her hands and pushed her inside, causing her to trip. She closed the door and entered in a code on the side of the prison that made the edge of the plastic walls glow a dull red. Locked. Jones had already walked away, but Natalia lingered behind to look at Sydona more. She pressed her hand against the plastic and stared at her with big sad eyes. Sydona stared back, unsure of what she was doing. Natalia fogged up the plastic as she let out a content sigh.

"This is like the best day of my life..." she said softly. Sydona could barely hear her but read her lips. She kissed the plastic while keeping her eyes locked on Sydona's, then waved and walked away.

Sydona looked after her and touched the hard plastic to observe the hallway and area outside of her prison. She saw nothing but glowing white and red. The cell adjacent from hers was vacant. It had a cot like hers and a small metal toilet.

She turned to see her own setup. She had a cot with a single blanket and pillow, a metal toilet like her invisible neighbor, a petite bookcase full of books and a rocking chair with another pillow. She sat down on the bed, touched her face with a shaky hand and winced. So much dried blood. Using the reflective toilet back, she attempted to look at the damage inflicted. It looked dreadful, and her face was completely covered in blood and swollen. One thing she was grateful for was at least she had a place to use the bathroom. There was even toilet paper. Once she relieved herself, she lay back on the cot and cried.

The floodgates opened. Her tears started as pure terror, then turned into sadness and depression, and finally into rage.

"Fuck! Fuuuucckkk!"

She clutched the rocking chair and smashed it against the wall with a growl from deep down. She ripped the pillows up until the room filled with more whiteness, beat her hands on the firm cot over and over again, pulled at her short hair and screamed until her throat physically hurt. Once her lungs went out, she went back to sobbing and crawled under the blanket.

She missed Raoul so much her heart had sharp pains that came and went. And Silas… she wasn't sure if she would ever see him again. Devon, Willow, Knox, everyone… never to be seen again because she was stupid and careless. She surrendered herself to the man who would use her like a lab rat. And now that she was there, the Sparrows would come after her in order to get her out, which meant more death. And there was no way to tell them to stop. She hoped they would rescue her, but she couldn't count on that. If she wanted out, or to do what she came there for, she had to do it herself.

Malik was coming back tomorrow, at least according to Jones. She would have to see his ugly face again. And then she would have to stab it, which she was more than okay with. Her stomach growled, and she clicked her tongue to the roof of her mouth. She was dehydrated. She became dizzier by the second, and her stomach felt as if it were curling up. If only the guys had ordered room service earlier, she would have lasted longer in her prison.

"Ug." Thinking of food only made the feeling worse.

The cell stood completely absent of sound, and it was already driving her mad. She never knew how much she loved noise. Time and sunlight didn't exist. She had no idea how long she waited down in the barren prison, but seconds felt like minutes and hours felt like years. Maybe it was because she was expecting Malik at any moment.

Unable to shut her eyes and sleep after what felt like hours of nothing, she decided to prepare. She grabbed a piece of the rocking chair and searched for something to sharpen it. At the base of the toilet, a screw stuck slightly out. It was just enough to grip. Sydona spun it out and revealed a screw about three inches long. In a rapid downward motion, she moved the twisted, jagged instrument against the wood to make a point.

The screw increasingly indented her finger. Her fingertips began to swell and bleed. Shreds of wood flew every which way. She wasn't sure what time it was or how long she cried for, but she didn't want to risk him catching her making the murder weapon. It had to be stealthy and quiet.

Once she fashioned the stake for the doctor, she sat crossed legged on the rug in the middle of the room with the dagger placed strategically behind her. Her eyes stared bleakly ahead, red and veiny.

She was ready.

She stayed in her ready position for a few more hours, and not one muscle moved. She knew as soon she let her guard down, he would show.

Her head jolted toward the first sound she had heard in hours. It was distant but clear. She gripped the stake tightly behind her while her other hand curled into a ball on her lap. She could hear her heart, but it sounded calm. Relaxed. Her gut told her it was her time. She didn't care if she was killed after stabbing the doctor. She had one chance, and it had to be in the heart. Somewhere he couldn't recover from.

The footsteps clacked louder. It sounded like four or five sets of steps. He brought guards. It was nothing she wasn't already expecting. Maybe even Natalia and Jones were with him to show off their winning prize. One pair of shoes was clearly louder than the others, and she knew it was those ugly reptile boots. As the time got closer, her heart sped up but not from fear. From excitement. Adrenaline flowed through her so hard she found it hard to sit still.

She stood up, smoothing out her clothes and letting her muscles get back to normal from sitting so long. She put the weapon in the waist of her pants and tucked her shirt over the back. It was sloppy, but standing as opposed to sitting when he arrived seemed much more practical.

The first and second guard walked into her line of vision behind the plastic prison. Her eyes darted to edge of all the white to see the doctor better. His boots clicked and clacked until he reached the door to her cell. His delicate right hand leaned on a mahogany wood cane topped with a golden eagle head. She eyed the leg she buried her dagger deep within. It wasn't enough to kill him, but it was enough to make him dependent. Maybe she could use it to her advantage. Their eyes instantly met. She felt her real eyes turn green with rage but knew they stayed blue. He couldn't read her anymore.

His head then turned sideways with confusion. His eyes narrowed, and he cleaned his glasses as he edged to the plastic surface.

"Why are her eyes blue?" he asked the two guards through the wall. They shook their heads and shrugged like two clueless gorillas.

Malik entered a code into the pad forcefully, and the red glow around the edges disappeared.

This was it.

Her right arm swung around behind her back to grip her weapon as he took a footstep inside her warzone. It seemed he had been so focused on her new eye color that he didn't notice the broken chair and feathers thrown all over the room.

Her heart tried breaking through her chest. It was now or never.

She flung the wooden spike out and positioned it toward the doctor's chest. Both hands gripped it as she used all her weight to push down and end everything. She used the yellow and purple silk pocket square of his suit as a target.

And as if Malik was already one step ahead of her, he quickly turned to the side, grabbed something from his pocket and jammed it into her side as she fell to the concrete floor. A ravage jolt of electricity pulsed through her body, causing her to spasm uncontrollably on the floor. Her hands and body were no longer able to do anything but feel the shocks singeing her insides.

After a minute, the pain slowly died away, but spats of it still made her jittery. The doctor bent over her and clicked his tongue, almost to say he was disappointed.

"Miss Wilder. What a brilliant display of foolishness you just performed. I must say, you look much different from our last meeting." He cocked his head again as if she were on a laboratory table and examined her like a cut open frog. "I wonder what your father would have to say about your behavior…"

The statement felt so random, and she shook her head to try to understand it. She then followed his eyes and soon focused on something else to her side. Adjusting her head and blinking the jitters from her vision, she saw a white-haired man to her left with a guard holding him.

Air escaped her lungs. Her own father, Ian, stood only a few feet from her, imprisoned once again. Tears welled up in her eyes. She wanted to scream, fight, kill. But her entire body was drained of all energy; there was nothing left.

The guards picked up her useless body, stole her weapon and put her back in her cell. Malik lingered in the doorway as he shook his head once more.

"Next time you think of hurting me, Miss Wilder, try thinking of how that might affect someone else." He grimaced and locked the door.

As she lay on the floor, all she could think of was the cabin in the woods full of life, friends and family. She'd give anything to be back in that chaos, back in the exact thing she thought she hated. Her dream came true; she was finally alone.

The End of Book Two

Acknowledgments

I've dedicated this page to everyone who has supported me greatly and I feel they need to be mentioned.

Sarah Jane Day

Yvonne Lozano

Heli Dundee

Heather Blaire

B. L. Moore

Zhana Johnson

Corry R. Heppler

Jensen Reed

Sam Hendrickson

M.J. Slate

More about the Author

Laura Mae is a Tucson, Arizona resident and lives with her sister, who helps take care of her four pets. This is Laura's second novel and already in process of writing the third. She's been writing for as long as she can remember and feels most comfortable in front of a computer, letting her imagination run wild.

If you are interested in following her, she is on Twitter and Instagram with the tag @lauramaeauthor.

She also hosts interviews with other indie authors and writers on her website: lauramaeauthor.com

Thank you for supporting indie authors!

Don't forget to review if you enjoyed this book!